Hurt You

BOOKS BY MARIE MYUNG-OK LEE

Hurt You

Marie Myung-Ok Lee

**BLACK
STONE**
PUBLISHING

Printed in the United States of America

First edition: 2023
ISBN 979-8-200-75809-8
Young Adult Fiction / Coming of Age

Version 1

Blackstone Publishing
31 Mistletoe Rd.
Ashland, OR 97520

www.BlackstonePublishing.com

"All the goodness and the heroisms will rise up again, then be cut down again and rise up. It isn't that the evil thing wins—it never will—but that it doesn't die."

—John Steinbeck

Prologue

March 23, 2019

SUNNYVALE, CA (AP NATIONAL) — A stranger attack inside a CostCut chain store Thursday caused chaos. A Sunnyvale High student managed to draw his gun and subdue his attacker, a man with a prior history of mental illness. Disability advocates clash with gun rights activists as the state legislature passed one of the broadest "Good Samaritan with a Gun" laws in the nation.

"This is the clearest case of freedom to self-defend and help others without worry of repercussion," said Mervin Taller, former state senator and now head of the Firearm Freedom Forum, a gun advocacy group. "This tragic example comes as if timed by God to show us exactly how 'Stand Your Ground' and 'Good Samaritan with a Gun' laws are supposed to work. It's not homicide, the child saved his own life."

Floyd Gunn of the state police union agrees. "Citizens need to be able to defend themselves—especially these days, as we can't always be there, everywhere. This brave young man kept the attacker, who was many times his size, under control so others could escape."

"Gun restrictors would just have the civilian populace be helpless in the face of these threats," added Taller. "That's why I left a secure seat in the state senate so I could devote myself fully to this issue."

- - - - - - - - - - - -

Georgia Kim wakes up the way she wakes up every day since the incident.

First, she emerges from the mists of sleep, thinks of her brother. Wonders if he slept okay. Worries briefly about SUDS.

Then realizes he is gone. Sudden Unexpected Death Syndrome—or any other way for him to die suddenly—is gone, too, because it's already happened.

The world dims. Feeling as if she has weights shackled to her limbs, she reaches over and taps her open laptop. She scans the news and the internet for stories, as if the right story—a national gun ban maybe—might bring Leo back to life. There's still the magnet sticker for "Leo's Lucky Rabbits Wallets" stuck to her laptop's cover. She will not remove it. She makes sure to get up a half hour earlier than the family so she can do this scan quickly, silently. Else, her mother will start worrying about her "burning out." Her mother doesn't know that fighting for Leo's legacy is what's keeping her alive.

The news makes it sound like Leo was a combination of Godzilla and King Kong. Sure, he could be rough, ungentle. She had once shown him a bumblebee napping in a flower. Fluffy, peaceful, adorable. And before she could do anything, he'd reached over, crushed the entire flower, bee and all, in his fist, then howled when he got stung. He might have even struck her, too. That's how he reacted to pain—it was confusing to him where it came from. His nerves were like a railroad that was all jumbled up. That was his condition. See, besides being her brother, he was also a human with a neurological condition that affected every cell of his body. This disease, this thing made him huge while also making him "developmentally delayed"—as if it was just a temporary matter of a train being late. Nope. That condition was also who he *was*. The bigness and the handicap of cognition. He could barely speak. But he also never lied. And he loved. He loved many things.

Georgia has gone on so many forums to type over and over (and over—with exclamation points!!!) that people with intellectual disabilities, even though often seen as scary by the public, are *much more likely* to be the *victims* of violent crime, much more likely to be *shot*. She keeps a file with links to the statistics at the ready on her desktop to fire off as needed.

And the shooter wasn't Leo's "victim" at all. Nor was he a stranger. He was someone Leo knew all too well.

One

GEORGIA KIM

Secret Diary
(if you are reading this—STOP!!!
This is an invasion of privacy!)

August 12

Umma and Appa, fighting. Again.

I used to be relieved once they had their daily fight. It was like some kind of pressure valve was released, and we were set for the rest of the day. There. It's done. But now, steam just keeps leaking, dripping sometimes, hissing, occasionally exploding when we least expect it. I have to get real: it's chronic, like those underground fires that are burning in Alaska because of climate change. I give Leo a look when I think a storm is brewing. He never looks back, because that's part of his disorder, the eye contact thing, but I wonder if he feels it, the bad air approaching. The daily bad air.

Obviously, I didn't know my parents before they were married, but I know from my aunt Clara that theirs was a whirl-wind romance, one with some Romeo and Juliet–type troubles (like Dad's family in Korea didn't want him marrying a Korean

American who could barely speak Korean) to overcome, two ex-
tremely good-looking young people. I want a time machine so I
can see this. Or, act as lawyer, judge, spy, family FBI investiga-
tor and demand they produce evidence for their union. Photos,
videos, courtroom sketches—I don't care. Not just for me, I want
to see them take in their first dates. Their first, fluttery kiss. The
love-blind light in their eyes. I want to see how each thought the
other could make them into a better person. I want to see them
with so much hope for their pairing that they stride hand in hand
into their future together, smiling. Wedding pictures don't count.
Anyone can fake their way through those.

I've never had a boyfriend, so I'm hardly the expert on why
people come together, no less decide to spend their lives together
forever. But I have zero doubt that they were once deliriously in
love. And likely still are (however, produce the evidence, please!).
And of course, they produced Leo and me.

* I want to know them when they were happy together.
* I also want to know that it wasn't Leo who changed everything.

I shut the book. A sparkly horse cover. I've been "off" horses since sixth grade, but my parents seem to think I just stay the same and don't get older. I can't help wondering if it's because Leo has never mentally gotten older since he was maybe three. I don't know. But I'm still thinking of my own line—"produced Leo and me"—and cringing. I don't even know how to talk about sex without blushing and metaphorically duck-ing my head into the sand, giggling like some middle schooler and not a rising junior. But I know that for most kids, picturing their parents having sex is the number one thing they do not want to think about. But I do. I want to know that they "made love" (also cringe, but a little better phrasing) and that Leo and I came out of that. Instead of Leo being the biggest barrier to our family happiness, the biggest obstacle to my success. When it's the opposite. Truly. Why can't they see that?

Oops, losing the thread here. I want to be a writer, maybe, but the diary is no longer a compendium of funny and interesting vignettes I could use in a novel someday. But to keep the pen moving (as one of my writing teachers recommended we do to keep the creative juices flowing), my diary ends up repeating words over and over in the pauses, kind of like Leo. *Why why why why why why? did we have to move?*

I know why we moved. Between my parents, their own refrain (with different tones): "Because of Leo."

That's a lot to put on Leo, who has never ever asked for any of these things. He hasn't asked for anything, because he can't really talk.

But I know he's sad. I'm not sure he knows exactly what's going on, but it's been a year since Aunt Clara's accident. Aunt Clara, the one other person who takes time to try to understand him. To let Leo be Leo even when it means he squawks like a bird when he's excited. Or when he calls me Nuna, older sister, and repeats "Nuna keep me safe, Nuna keep me safe"—Clara and I knew he wasn't being imperative but instead signaling that he felt safe and secure, at least in that moment. But Appa would sigh harassedly about Leo's "vocal stims" and how his behavior plan means we are absolutely not supposed to answer him. But I often do. I can tell he feels comforted when I say, "Yes, Leo, you are safe. Nuna won't let anything happen to you." Whether he understands the reassurance or it's just the reply he expects to hear, closing a kind of circle. See, the fact he can speak words makes Appa think, well, he should be able to talk and understand. But that's just not how it works in Leo world.

See, despite their good intentions, Umma is always too busy rushing to keep all the family stuff together—Leo's schooling, his therapies, his new clothes and shoes now that he's growing like the Hulk—to spend much time *seeing* him. She's the one everyone calls—the day program, the school—when there's a problem. Everyone waits for her to fix it. I get that she's doing the best she can on the special needs treadmill. I try to lie low and never add to her burden.

Appa also loves Leo (I know it!) but has turned most of his attention to me as if he's a car with its high beams on all the time—stuck on me as "college candidate." He's gone full tiger dad, applying himself as if *his* job is getting me into Harvard. Where I won't go unless, like, Leo moved to Cambridge with me. They don't think I'm serious. Who could say no to Harvard? Well, me. I'm as serious as hell.

Within this disconnect between all of us, every encounter of the mater and pater has the potential for fireworks and sparks (not the good kind, but the kind that leaves Umma quietly weeping in the thin-walled bathroom of the apartment, Appa walking around, his face a hardened cast). Don't they think about how this affects *us*?

My guess is that this move to Sunnyvale is a last-ditch attempt to reboot the family, our little self-contained operating system, glitches grown too frequent to ignore—the flickerings of if something isn't done, the whole thing's going to implode, that our motherboard is failing.

But I feel the need to point out that despite living in an "urban" area that was cramped—often smelly in the alley, yes there was crime—our whole apartment building was a family. Umma and Appa pride themselves on their self-sufficiency, maybe were a bit on the maniacal side of privacy, but there were a couple of times when, like, if they forgot something for Leo while waiting for the bus, if Mr. Goh the super was out watering the one gangly tree, they'd let him watch Leo for a second while they dashed back upstairs. Not everyone loved Leo, but everyone knew him. When he was in his phase of slipping out of the apartment, there would always be people retrieving him.

But living like sardines also means having some idea of what's going on with your neighbors, no matter how much you want to hide. There was always "I cooked too much!" food circulating between floors, especially when someone was sick or in need. And, like a family, there were fights over whether we could leave bikes and strollers in the hall (fire hazard) or if dogs needed to take the service elevator ("so insulting"— dog owners; but also, Leo is deathly afraid of dogs).

Like I said, we were a family. Now we're in a house and it's like we're living in outer space—soundless, airless.

I'm most surprised about Appa, an only child. He used to talk about how lonely he was growing up, especially as his mother died when he was five and his father had to travel for work and he was shuffled around relatives all over Korea—with varying degrees of welcome, including his uncle's wife muttering under her breath about the expense, his cousins cold-shouldering him entirely. It was lucky he had his friend Byun in middle school. Byun's family had an astonishing five siblings, which was good because that meant more hands on deck at the family's fried chicken place, King's, and showed Appa what a happy family could look like. With him in it.

"You and Leo are lucky—that is double what I had," he would chuckle. Sometimes, like waiting for the other shoe to drop, I'll wonder if he actually meant to have five kids like Byun's family. Byun married an Italian woman he met during a study abroad and moved to Italy. Their Christmas cards are wild—in the pictures, it seems like no family gathering has fewer than a hundred people in it, including all the nonnas and grandpas and zillions of kids and babies and pregnant ladies. I have heard Appa sometimes talk about Byun as "crazy" to Umma, how his family was so disappointed by what he did, especially as "first son," which I guess comes with all sorts of expectations in Korea. But Byun seems bursting with happiness in all the pictures. And it seems like his family, at least some of them, has come around. Is Appa maybe even a little jealous that his friend went and did something no one told him he could do? That people generally don't do? Like reaching for an unlikely happiness and just making it work.

I guess you could say the gift my brother gave me was learning early on that adults don't know much more than kids. They've been around longer and have the benefit of experience, but that's about it. So much depends on what you do with the experience. For instance, I grew up alongside my big brother. There hasn't been a time when I haven't known him. I know him better than anyone—including those harrumphing experts who spend five minutes with us and, one time, even told Umma to take Leo outside so he could hear what Appa was saying! From the very first expert, I saw they are faking it, parroting stuff from their books on genetics, on neurology, on behavior. They don't know much about what's going on with Leo, so they fake it and make it sound scientific.

Oppositional defiance disorder. Lack of mirror neurons. Emotional empathy deficit. Receptive language disorder. Must have a DNA deletion somewhere. An IQ so low it's almost negative. PGSU: possible genetic syndrome: unknown. Ideopathic (my favorite!). He's never going to get better from where he is.

That last one kills me. Who can predict anything about anyone's future, especially when they also keep saying he has an unknown syndrome? When I bring this bit of illogic up, Appa the science guy, the radiologist who literally works with black and white, doesn't acknowledge that I've poked a huge and gaping hole in their logic. He only says, "Well then, that's why you have to become a doctor."

It was through Google, when I was trying to find something about Korea for a school project, that I learned about the Sewol ferry disaster. Hundreds of schoolkids were going on a class trip and were giddy with excitement. What they didn't know was the ship was terribly overloaded with cargo. In the middle of the journey it started to capsize. The captain made an emergency announcement: the students needed to stay where they were so the adults could find them. This left the halls clear so that the captain, instead of going down with the ship as brave captains purportedly do, was able to be the first one off when the Korean coast guard appeared. He didn't even get his shoes wet, while, within the next half hour, the boat tipped over and water flooded the little rooms belowdecks where all the kids, patiently waiting for adults to come save them, died. The ones who didn't listen to the repeated announcements to stay put, the scrappy disobedient ones who went and saved themselves, lived.

I was especially haunted by the story of how one boy gave his best friend his life jacket because he couldn't swim and the friend lived but the selfless boy died. Why should such a wonderful soul be needlessly sacrificed on the altar of adult malfeasance?

Rightfully, the survivor kids have been shaming the adults, especially the captain, ever since. But, adults being adults, they protect each other. It's easy to dismiss kids as hysterical. Too young. But what else can we be if not young?

That's why no one asked Leo or me whether we should move. Or even what we thought about it. Even though they claim it was "for the children." Leo and I both have opinions—and they should count. Leo and I haven't even seen Sunnyvale!

My newest guess, discovered as I was researching the high school and right on its website:

#1 ranked US News & World Report!! For sending kids to four-year colleges.

It has to be why, at least partially, both Umma and Appa see this new place, this next year, as the on-ramp leading up to a break with Leo. The site actually had a list of students who got into Harvard and Yale and Princeton last year. And maybe I will be on that list, too. I'll go away to college and that will be that, they think, the start of Georgia Kim's own life. They don't understand who I am. That I am who I am because of my brother, and I don't know who I am without him. And that's truly okay with me. I am going to show them this year that we need to always be together. I don't care where I am— city, country, outer space—as long as I am with Leo. And I plan to stay by his side. Maybe they won't agree, but then it'll be up to Leo and me to save ourselves.

- - - - - - - - - - - -

WELCOME TO SUNNYVALE!

HOME OF THE FIGHTIN' BOMBERS

UNDEFEATED STATE CHAMPIONS

We take an exit off the highway filled with the usual road ragers and find ourselves suddenly . . . here. How to describe? Our City High journalism teacher Mr. Mack instilled in us the "vivid, original description," which also relies on "close, nonjudgmental observation" and "taking notes, notes, notes—you think you will remember details, but you won't." He gave us these skinny notebooks that fit in our shirt pockets and made us write down everything we saw for a week. He said it was better to write by hand. I cheated a few times and wrote into my phone and *then* copied it into the notebook. But he's right. I was surprised every time

I looked at it. I didn't remember seeing stuff with my own eyes, apparently a very selective camera.

Here's what I see as we drive in: new-looking houses doubled in size because of attached three-car garages and endless lawns, uniformly lush, each blade seemingly trimmed to a precise height by scissors. Mr. Goh had tried to maintain the strip of lawn in front of the apartment building but too many passersby let their dogs pee on it and it just looked like it was tie-dyed brown. So he put in fake grass, the same kind as on welcome mats. Here, the bright green grass looks fake but is real.

"These houses look like movie sets," I remark to Leo, who grunts. Each pristine, beautiful. No chipping paint or peeling window frames. But also no people in those windows or enjoying the green velvet lawns. Many houses have cars sitting in driveways in the middle of the day on a Tuesday. In one lone window I see movement—a dark-haired lady in T-shirt and jeans, vacuuming; her beater car says Happy Maids. Where is everyone?

Umma gets a text from the movers that they are stuck in traffic. Probably on the same highway we just got off of. The traffic was indeed horrific, hence the road ragers, whose honking and cutting off put us all in a mood.

"I thought they were supposed to be there already when we arrive." Appa is already sounding tense.

"They were," says Umma, as if it's obvious. "I notified the guards at the gatehouse to let them in." There's this trapdoor feeling I get, like simultaneously my guts are falling out and also I'm being punched in the stomach. Like things are out of control and there's this free-floating specter of blame, a big black blob that needs to attach to someone, and if you manage to get it attached to someone else, you win.

"It's not my fault," Umma says, with emphasis.

"I never said it was," says Appa, a little louder than is called for. See what I mean? I cross my fingers. I have nothing to do with this. Leo least of all. But the black blob whispers in my ear that this is all because of Leo.

The trapdoor is wide open. The blob slithers in; it punches me in the stomach from the inside, but at least it's not floating in the air anymore. "Leo," I say. "With all this grass—real grass—around, I bet there will be bunnies."

"Bun-yees!" he echoes. His happy tone reassures the people up front. Appa's jaw unclenches, slightly, a knot loosening.

"All right," he says. My father, even at his age, has bushy black hair, curly in front. He is a very handsome man. His moods can also pivot on a dime. "We have a tank full of gas, why not take a little tour of the town since we have the time?"

"That would be nice," Umma accedes, her tone softening as well. I pull the slim notebook out of my bag. Time to record my impressions of things—and read them back to Leo, later.

- - - - - - - - - - - -

If Sunnyvale is a wheel, the superstores (CostCut, SuperSavR, Home & Garden Warehouse, Mega Drugs & Sundry Emporium) are on the outer rim, the inner rim is the lawns and houses, the local streets are spokes that lead straight to the roundabout that circumnavigates the Founders Park. Each spoke carves out the different zones in town. I come upon a perfect description: the eight-slice pizza pie we used to get at Luigi's back in the city; the Founders Park is the huge garlic knot Luigi would place in the center, a delicious freebie (especially when it soaked up all the cheese and pepperoni grease) that kept the cardboard lid off the hot pizza.

Main Street and Founders Park Avenue create the pie slice for stores whose purpose seems like more set-dressing: penny candy store, old-timey pharmacy, Vineyard's Madras (weirdly: clothes, not wine), Fair Trade Caravan (ethnic gifts), Goldy's Golden (golden retriever–themed gifts and clothes). If you need actual things, say toothpaste or socks (both of which you could have gotten at Omar's, a.k.a. Deli 360, next door to our apartment building in the city), you have to drive a mile back to the CostCut, where you will also be forced to buy a dozen units of each.

Founders Park is bordered with flowers and contains a playground, a gazebo, and an artificial figure-eight-shaped lake. In the middle, a statue of the three so-called founders of the town of Sunnyvale (they all look like Mark Twain, while Sunnyvale hardly feels more than five minutes old). On the other side sits the pie slice with the post office, the public library, and a fire and police station that look, well, unused. The firemen are out front washing their handsome cherry-red engine as we pass.

Opposite that, Bomber Street creates the high school zone (Go, fightin' Bombers!). The high school is about the same number of students as my school in the city, but this building, instead of a lead trap, looks like a freaking castle set on a huge lawn with a track and stadium behind it. And beyond that, there's the vast expanse of a golf course, deep and green. I'm thinking about how Appa likes to play golf and wonder if he's happy to see it. I don't even know yet that the course belongs to the high school, for the sole use of the varsity golf team. There's a lot I don't know about this place. And you'd think I would have learned my lesson with Leo:

Surfaces can be misleading.

Two

T minus one day for school. Belatedly, we found out we have to get some things for class. An email last night labeled REMINDER and URGENT and PLEASE READ.

Mega Bulk Back To School General Supply Bundle Kit ~ 70 + items

1-5 items in duplicate for the FREE closet

You may keep this items in your locker

~ check with you individual teacher to see if you need any additional supplies~

(Um, for an impressive school, these are some pretty unimpressive typos and misspellings)

1 package #2 pencils TICONDEROGA ONLY
1-10 packages disinfectant wipes
1 package masks
1 waterproof backpack with kevlar insert and laptop sleeve

1 package highlighters

1 package markers

1 TI graphing calculator (check with individual teacher for
    exact model before purchasing this item)

1-3 USB flash drives

1 package looseleaf COLLEGE RULED loose leaf paper

laptop if not using school issued Chrome book

power cord for above

headphones or ear buds

After supervising the movers, unpacking, getting the house in order, feeding us, registering Leo and me for school, coordinating all of Leo's "pullouts" (where he literally gets pulled out of his special-needs class for more specialized therapy), and finding a new neurologist, endocrinologist, hematologist, and geneticist—all of whom need to also take our insurance—no surprise an earlier email slipped by unnoticed in the tidal wave of missives.

"At least they sent a reminder," Umma says. "We still have time to get the materials."

What kind of public school makes you *buy stuff*? And I thought this was the rich school district!

"Mostly stationery supplies," Umma says. "Probably to keep things standard."

"Oh, like so I should leave my diamond-crusted Louis Vuitton notebook at home and not show off, right?" I joke.

Umma smiles. Leo has been "good" the last couple of days. He has not reached back into the toilet to examine his feces. He hasn't broken or thrown anything. He seems to enjoy the yard, especially when I tell him there may be bunnies.

"We should go on an outing anyway," she says.

And—*say what?*—this trip sends us to the . . .

Korean shopping center!

Now, this is new! Back in the city, there was another Korean family in the neighborhood, the Parks, who owned the dry cleaner.

But they were just another nonwhite family, like the Alsaedis, who have owned Deli 360 long enough that everyone calls it Omar's—even though for the past few years it's not been Omar but Faisal, Omar's son, ringing up the Takis. Omar spends as much time as he can back in Yemen now.

Sunnyvale seems as white as the sandwich bread at the Panera outside the CostCut, but apparently, enough Koreans have settled here that, while there's no Koreatown, there is a Korean shopping strip. And we are just now pulling into it, almost fooled by its very un-Korean name: Pecan Plaza.

"Pecan Plaza," I say. "Where the nuts go."

"Very punny," Umma says.

"Vedy punny!" yells Leo.

In the far corner, I see rows and rows of Korean-language signage. There's something exciting and, well, exotic (is that the right word, for something that's already part of me?) about it.

She pulls out the email, which she has printed out.

From: CambridgeAcademy.k12.gov
To: Senior High Parents
Subj: Stationery requirements

"What's Cambridge Academy?" I say.

"Your high school."

"I'm not going to Sunnyvale Senior High?" My stomach clenches. Is this what they're doing since Leo is going to school for "free" now?

"No, it is," Umma says, to my relief. "But they voted over the summer to change the name."

"Cambridge Academy, is it?" I say. I try to say it in a plummy English accent, but it comes out more Sherlock Holmes. Or maybe Scottish. "We're supposed to buy all this ourselves, are we?" That one's definitely Lucky Charms Irish.

"That's what it says. The school board voted to change it." So this is the kind of stuff school boards here worry about, not like whether to get a DARE officer or a real police ("peace") officer as a hall monitor or not. But why the to-buy list, then?

In the city, I get it. The schools barely have the money to keep lead out of drinking fountains. One of the Alsaedi brothers said the city school was so poor back when they went that they put three grades together in the same classroom to save space. Almost ninety kids with only one teacher! However, with all that, Umma *never* had to buy us supplies. Shauntae and I shared the class graphing calculators in Algebra I and II, the numbers on the buttons fading already from so many sweaty fingers pressing them.

It's just occurring to me now that our stuff at City High wasn't free. My teachers paid. Every year, the supplies were mismatched. Some classes barely had anything except maybe those stubby truncated golf pencils that someone must have lifted by the handful from the public library. Did they pay out of their own salaries, their own time? One year, I somehow got a Moleskine notebook from the grammar teacher to whom I'd admitted that I secretly hoped to be a journalist. It's occurring to me now that I never said thank you to any of them.

- - - - - - - - - - - -

Pecan Plaza at first looks like your regular boring strip mall: dry cleaner, grocery store, haircut place, phone repair store. Anchored on one corner by a fake-brick Walgreens, on the other by a dog groomer (poodle specialist!). Umma drives as far away as she can from the groomer, respecting Leo's dogphobia (while Appa is big on "exposure" and Leo learning to "deal").

She parks in front of a store called Arirang Market, which looks to carry—could it be?—stationery supplies: notebooks, folders, fancy fountain pens, artist brushes, bulletin boards, gel pens arranged in the window by color tones like an artist's palette, as if they know me. I hope this is what Umma has in mind for stationery supplies and not Walgreens.

Next to Arirang is Bomb Haircuts, the English repeated in Korean in a cool, flowy font. Go fightin' bombers! That's the spirit. Leo and I stand on the sidewalk and look around as Umma tries to decipher the

parking meter. This is a little bit annoying—there certainly aren't parking meters at the CostCut or Home Depot parking lots. These all have
labels on the posts that say Curley & Sons.

The majority of the signs here are in Korean, which I cannot read.
It makes me feel deliciously off-balance, like I'm in another country
without having to leave home. Bomb Haircuts has the most English
on their signs.

"Look, Leo," I say. "This sign says All Dogs Require Leashes."

"Dog dog," he protests.

Ugh, I shouldn't have even said the word. It doesn't matter the size
of the dog, it's more the unpredictability. The hyper little dogs can be
the worst. But if they are on a leash they should be fine. "No, I mean,
Leo, you are safe here."

"You are safe," he says.

"And Nuna is here," I remind him. "I keep you safe. Always."

There's another sign, No Guns Allowed on Premises, which has a
bit of a Wild West feel to it. A few stores have this sign on their doors,
including Bomb Haircuts. I'll find out later that the local gun laws are
much laxer than where we lived, and establishments have to come out
and actually *say* they don't want guns. Otherwise, it'll be like the pub I
saw downtown that had the sign—don't know if they were trying to be
funny—Man Up: Guns Welcome.

Bomb Haircuts's windows are tinted, so I have to walk right up
to it and cup my hands around my eyes to see what's going on inside.

It's more brightly lit inside than you would think. Young dudes
occupy each of the three barber chairs. The cutters are all Asian,
middle-aged men.

Umma mutters, "Who installs a meter at a shopping center?" while
feeding it about a roll of quarters, then looks up to see me and pauses.
"You want a cut for your first day of school?"

My hair is famously unmanageable. Nice and thick, okay. But any
cut I get makes me look like the little Dutch boy on the paint cans. I
even dared getting it cut into a pixie cut in middle school and the jerk
boys said I looked like a hedgehog.

"I think this is a barber shop," I say.

"They have places like this in Korea. They're not quite barber shops, but they're not fancy beauty salons, either." She points to the sign in Korean, which I obviously can't read.

"Like a Korean Supercuts?"

"Better than that. You're always complaining about your hair," Umma reminds me, as if I need reminding. "Maybe this place will have more experience with your kind of hair texture."

I'm getting what she's saying. May the odds always be in my favor, here in the Asian hair-cutting place. "I could use a trim," I assent. When it reaches shoulder-length, not only does it resemble a broom at the ends but, as Appa says, "It emphasizes your chubby face." (I don't believe Appa means to be mean, he just isn't that good at description.)

Umma disappears into Bomb and reappears ten seconds later. "There's only one person ahead of you," Umma says.

And it's only twenty dollars, she says. Even Supercuts, with their legendarily bad haircuts, was more than that in the city. Umma has also just spied a huge Korean grocery store on the other end of the strip. "I can pop in there while you are getting your haircut, then we can get your stationery supplies at Arirang."

Bingo!

Umma hands me twenty-five dollars. "The lady said it's okay for your brother to sit in the waiting area."

Uh-oh. I assumed she'd be taking Leonardo with her. Shopping is one of his favorite activities. But of course, it's hard to do it with him underfoot; she'll try, say, to ask the butcher a question, and that's when Leonardo will start flapping and making noises like a seagull, so loud she can't even put in her order. Yesterday, we went to the CostCut. Umma and Appa could shop in relative peace only because I was there to enter-tain him and keep him from knocking over the two-story-tall pyramids of generic toilet paper.

Can I get my hair cut *and* mind Leonardo at the same time? Dare I eat a peach? I'm picturing having to leap up every few minutes to make sure Leonardo doesn't wander off, poke people, pee his pants, whatever, my haircut all jagged on the ends, left half done like the grocery carts we sometimes have to abandon midshopping.

"Okay, Georgia?"

I can see expressed in Umma's eyes how much she needs this. A few minutes to shop alone. I suppose a six-foot-tall seagull-noise-making Leonardo would be an even bigger spectacle at a Korean grocery than at a huge, anonymous supermarket. Such a small thing to do for my mom. I must do it. I brush aside my anxiety. Also, there's a clever stoplight-type fixture in the window.

YOUR WAIT TIME:

[Green] Less than 5 minutes

[Yellow] 5–10 minutes

[Red] More than 10 minutes—please come back later

We're in the green! They seem to prioritize being fast—one of the other signs in English says Have a Date? No Need to Wait.

Ha, I'll probably be done before she gets back. Maybe that means they'll skip the captive-audience hair-stylist chitchat that always includes, "Wow, I've never seen hair like yours!"

"We'll be fine," I assure her.

"I'll be back in a jiffy—ten, twenty minutes maximum."

"Let's go, buddy," I say to Leo, who shuffles behind me, each one of his steps carefully placed where my feet have just been. It takes him thirty seconds to walk through Bomb Haircuts' door.

Three

Inside, Bomb Haircuts looks like an aquarium married with a rustic stable. Each haircutter's station is fronted by a black wall on which is mounted a large mirror backlit with purple lights. The floor is so shiny and spotless you could eat off it, the way Umma somehow manages to keep our floors at home. One of the haircutters is sweeping up after his last customer, stooping to pick up the stray hairs his broom must have missed—they are serious about cleanliness.

It's walk-in only. You sit at a bench with your exact designation in line: one, two, three, four, five. Here's where the ranch part comes in: the bench is rough-hewn wood that still looks like half a tree. By the door, there's a large totem pole, a grinning head with Mickey Mouse ears at the top. I assume it's Korean. It's not straight, like totem poles, but retains the original bend in the tree. Not tying it all together is the crooning K-pop playing in the background.

A lady about Umma's age, but much heavier on the makeup, approaches.

"You can put your brother there," she says, pointing to number three.

"Okay. He should be fine," I chirp. It's important for me to project confidence, to set expectations. For me, for people who've never seen people "like" Leo before, and, heck yeah, for the universe—are you listening, or are you too distracted by all these people vision boarding or whatever? This is important! Keep Leo calm so I can get a haircut and Umma can get a fifteen-minute mental vacation. She's been working nonstop with the unpacking and then all the registering us for school, all of the therapies Leo needs. Appa is busy, too. He is so proud of the automatic garage door opener he installed himself.

And I do have a secret weapon: an NAD tablet. One thing Leo can do with reasonable accuracy is poke things with his finger. His NAD, nontalker assistive device, shows a grid of simple pictures that you just have to touch and it talks for you. It was invented for people who have traumatic brain injuries and can't talk but have enough motor control to hit a virtual button. *Water, please. I would like to go to bed. I need pain medication.*

One of the rare useful "interventions" that have been suggested by his army of therapists, but not exactly for the reason intended. Leo just loves tapping on one particular button.

Ihavetogotothebathroom. Ihavetogotothebathroom. Ihavetogotothebathroom.

When we first got this, we kept taking him to the bathroom, and he'd throw tantrums because he didn't need to go. I was the one who figured out he just likes that particular sound. The emotionless AI voice.

Ihavetogotothebathroom

I turn the volume way down, low, low but so he can still hear.

Ihavetogotothebathroom

Ihavetogotothebathroom

Maybe in Leospeak the voice is saying something else. Something much more profound. Something the rest of us are missing.

One of the haircutters approaches us. I hear a rush of Korean, through which my Korean name, Jiyoung, surfaces just for a second, like one of those fat goldfish that are stocked in the Founders Park pond, then submerges back into incomprehensibility.

He says it again, more sharply.

"Um, me?" I say, a bit timidly, half-raising my hand as if I'm in elementary school.

"Ill-ee-oh-say-oh," he says. At my look of incomprehension, his frown deepens. The lady Umma had talked to is now ensconced behind the register, staring at me. Because I'm a stranger? At my hearty midsection despite my slim-as-a-reed mom? At my frizzed-out haircut? Or at the way Korean words are bouncing off me?

Indeed, the man says something that I know is the rough equivalent of, "What? You don't speak Korean?" I've learned to discern those specific tones from when Koreans say that to Umma. She always turns red and says something that ends with, "Chalk, hey," that supposedly means that even though I don't speak Korean, I'm still a good girl and a good student. I *wanted* to learn Korean, I'd want to tell them. Back when I was little and it was a learning freebie for kids because they just absorb it. I tried, I really did. Umma turns red because she also doesn't speak Korean well. She was born and raised in Oberlin, Ohio, and learned Korean during one high school summer, which clearly wasn't enough.

"I don't speak Korean," I say. I feel a little ashamed each time, like my Korean card will be revoked.

"Oh, pardon me." The man switches to unaccented English like a magic trick. There's a slight Korean accent tickling the back of his words. He checks off my name. "So few non-Koreans come in here, I get in the habit."

Wait, is he saying *I'm* a non-Korean? Being greeted by a barrage of words you don't know can be kind of off-putting no matter if you are of that ethnicity, I'm thinking. But then I check myself. This is a Korean shopping center, it's this guy's business. Why can't he run it the way he wants to? And why should he worry if white people are uncomfortable (he shouldn't)?

I am so distracted by all my inner debate, I'm just noticing Leonardo squirming. I inspect his NAD. It's gone dark. Dead.

Dang!

"We'll have to recharge it," I murmur.

"Charge it!" he demands. "Charge it!"

There's another customer on the bench, and he turns to see where that odd voice is coming from. I get out my phone. Leo can play Angry Birds. Not "play" it so much, but after hours of guiding his finger until he could get the slingshot aspect of the game, he will happily rep on it (the medical word for his repetitive behaviors), pull back on the slingshot, and let it fly. He couldn't care less about targets or scoring. He can poke-slide like it's nobody's business. Of course, all the therapists say "screen time" is to be avoided, also things that encourage repping—but these confidently pronouncing professionals don't have to live with us. Ten minutes is all I need. I can hear, faintly, the bird screams from the game. Thank you, universe. I make my way over to station number three and sit in the chair.

"Your first time here, huh?" the man says, warmly now. "Welcome. I'm Mike." He flutters the protective cape like a matador. It settles around my shoulders perfectly. His station is labeled Mike Dongbang, Owner. I've never seen a Korean last name that was that long.

"When did you get your hair cut last?" Mr. Dongbang says. I can't imagine calling an adult by his first name.

"It's been a while," I admit.

"Hmphrph," he says, as if studying a puzzle. He lifts a handful of it and lets it go. It doesn't fall so much as attempt to fall. It fights gravity to the very end.

I glance over at my neighbors. The guy in the chair to my left is about my age and—wow!—actually reading a book instead of a phone. *Of Mice and Men*. He does not look impressed. Nor is he impressed with how amazing his hair is. Black and shaggy and a wave on top so dense it looks surfable. Asian guys often look like they have three times the hair a white person does, so when they get older, like Appa, while white people go bald, they just have a normal amount. To my right is a grizzled man in his fifties or sixties. (I can never tell with adults). He looks out of place in this youthful environment. The hem of his chinos is frayed, revealing white socks and navy-blue loafers that are puckered on top, a moccasin aspect that make them look like, well, an Asian knockoff of some kind of vintage American shoe. When finished, he thanks the haircutter a little excessively, bowing. An Asian thing, I guess. Instead of gathering his things, going to the counter to pay, and leaving, he turns the other way and disappears through the back of the store.

The pump-pump-pump of the barber's chair is reassuring, almost nostalgic. Most of the time I got my hair cut by Magaly, Mr. Goh's wife, sitting on one of our rickety kitchen chairs while she contorted her body sidewise to hack through my mess. She only knew one haircut—straight across—but it was reliable.

"What would you like me to do?"

"Trim it?" How can I tell him I secretly wish he'd just cut-cut-cut like Edward Scissorhands, hair flying everywhere, and then leave me with totally normal Korean hair. My best friend Shauntae once took a big-barreled curling iron and made mermaid waves, which looked very presentable—sexy even—for about ten minutes until the inner wildness and tensile strength of my hair took over and it resumed its topiary shape. "You could use a strand of your hair to tie up a boat, it's so thick," she'd said admiringly.

He fans it out with two hands. It falls into a vaguely pyramidal shape. "Ah, that's because it's so thick."

"What do you think I should do?"

"If we do an undershave, it will behave better."

My hair, the naughty toddler. Also, what's an undershave?

"There are several ways we can do it." He shows me some pictures of some Korean aunties with demure pageboys. Basically a better-behaving version of my Dutch boy. I don't see the shaving part.

He calls to the receptionist, who is now sitting at the counter, spearing cut-up fruit with a toothpick. She swivels in her chair and yells into the back, "Yunji-yah!"

From a doorway, a girl about my age with some major raccoon eyeliner and—whoa!—black lipstick comes out. That must be a normal look for her because the lady doesn't say anything or even glance up from her fruit. Now I notice how the girl's gorgeous, thick mane of hair spills past her shoulders. A vision of my dream hair, which I'm not going to get unless an undershave can cut your hair *longer*. She's carrying a book with Korean writing on it.

"Yunji, this is—Jiyoung?"

"Georgia," I say. No one uses my Korean name. "Like the peach."

"Georgia, this is Yunji."

"Hey." The girl isn't even looking at me. She's looking at her gelled black nails. She looks super bored.

"Yunji-yah—" He says a bunch of stuff in Korean to her.

Yunji suddenly grins like a pirate and dramatically swoops her head down, then raises it while turning to the side like some marvelous bird. A thick plume of hair flies up, revealing an almost bare scalp, close-shaved on the side. She looks like a warrior princess, especially with those raccoon eyes.

"It doesn't have to be that drastic," he says. "The more you shave, the more upkeep, too, of course."

"It's not that bad," Yunji says, looking at me. "I can go three weeks, maybe. If you got your own clippers you could probably do your own. But I'm here all the time, obvi, so—"

"Thank you," I say. "I really like your hair."

"No prob." She pauses to look at me a little longer. I'm wondering what she sees. With the cape on, I'm imagining I look like a wild-hair-headed volcano. "I've never seen you here."

"Our family just moved to Sunnyvale."

"Cool."

I point with my eyes at Leo, who is still swiping away. "That's my brother, Leonardo."

"Cool," she says again. "Well, enjoy your haircut." She goes back to where she came from, not a closed door, more like a darkened doorway, leading to where, I can't imagine. Narnia, maybe.

The handsome wavy-haired guy in the seat next to me gets up. His hair has been buzzed close at the sides, a smaller version of the shiny wave now sculpted at the top. He shakes off the hair debris like a dog with water, says something in Korean to the haircutter, and, instead of exiting, also disappears through the same darkened doorway the girl Yunji appeared from and the older guy also went into. Am I in a science fiction story?

"So, what do you think?" asks Mr. Dongbang.

"She's nice," I say.

"Of her hair," he laughs. "And that's my daughter."

Wow, I am thinking to myself. I've never met a Korean girl who has a hair stylist for a dad. I've actually never met anyone who had a hair stylist as a dad.

"Do you want to try that, or should I just trim following your current haircut?"

I ponder. Magaly's haircut, when it was fresh, was solid. She could cut straight like she had a level in her eyes. A trim would be fine, and faster, I think.

"A shave will be just as quick," Mr. Dongbang says, as if reading my mind. "I don't have to wet your hair. I razor the ends like Zorro."

Instead of putting Leo first and adjusting whatever I plan to do from there, I now have to make an actual decision! Just for me! It strikes me, I do need a new cut. If not a new *me*. The old me is shy, scared of . . . something. So self-conscious I have a prickling feeling on me almost all the time like people are watching me. Like when I get on a plane and the skinny person next to me carefully and deliberately puts down the armrest, like those train crossing things.

Ding! Ding! Ding! Fat person! I don't have to see his or her face to know. I know they don't like what they see. I'm a visual affront, my being Asian, my being fat. They look like they think I smell. I know they wish I'd disappear and fly to Mars.

That's the prickling feeling distilled to its essence. The only time I don't feel this is when I'm with Leo. As much as I hate the stares, the whispers, when I'm with him, I don't focus on myself, so, ironically, I stand up tall, my voice strong. It's like I have a cause. I'll defend him to the end, I am not the least bit self-conscious about that.

All right, then, how about a haircut to match *that*?

"I could do an undershave like Yunji's," Mr. Dongbang says.

"I'd love it, but my parents would flip out." I'm daring but not *that* daring.

"What I could do," he says, his arms folded, tapping a black comb on his cheek. "Is do a subtle shave at the nape just to get your hair to fall better, then a small undershave just on one side. That way you could gel it up for a more dramatic look, but day to day no one will know because it would be combed over."

As I hesitate, my mouth answers for me: "That sounds perfect."

Four

Mr. Dongbang uses huge banana clips to hold up my masses of hair, quickly shaves a swath at my nape with clippers, which immediately makes my head feel lighter. Then, with his comb, he draws a line across the right side of my skull, right above my ear. Next thing I know, the buzz of a hundred bees heading for my ear. Then a giant fold-out straight razor. *Zzzzt!* My scalp shivers. I feel more than see hanks of hair falling down. I feel air around my head like I haven't since . . . ever? I think of how in the humid summers in the city those underlayers took foreeeeever to dry, how they seemed permadamp with sweat whether I put it up in a pony or not.

"More?" he says. "I can make the shave line a little higher."

He swivels the chair so I can look at the huge backlit mirror.

I love it. *Love.* I don't look like me at all. I don't know who I look like, but it's not the old Georgia Kim. I wonder if Leonardo will have trouble identifying me. Leonardo has been known to see other girls with dark hair and call "Nuna!" to them in that plaintive way he does. I used to feel maybe I was interchangeable to him. But I have no idea how he sees things. Maybe he's so smart that he has classified things down to minute categories. See, I always thought nuna was Korean for "sister" but it's actually more precise than that, it's *brother's older sister*. It was Aunt Clara who told me that.

"But I'm younger," I'd said. Obvi.

Aunt Clara said she doesn't know where that came from, Umma or Appa.

But Appa is a native Korean speaker!

"Maybe it's because they thought *dongsaeng*, the word for younger sibling, would be harder for him to say," Aunt Clara had mused. "It is a little puzzling, though." According to her, there are words for every family member, including in-laws, that carefully fix each person's place by age and gender, like stars in a constellation.

I can't help wondering if with Leo's developmental delay happening when he was three and I was only a little more than a year old made my parents mentally designate me as the older one. That's very much how they still treat me now, like the older sister to a forever toddler—who's almost six feet tall and wears a size 12 shoe.

In the end, though, he likes saying *nuna*. Nu. Na. If he likes it, that's me. Umma, Appa, Nuna. That's the extent of the Korean in our family. For Leo, we just all call him Leo.

Mr. Dongbang has left barely an inch-long layer, the shorn hairs still cover my scalp like a carpet. My mind goes back to Umma and Appa. That's my line, my border. Be daring but not so daring it causes them any stress, because they already have too much of it. I tell him, "I'm good, it's perfect." Hair grows at what, one-sixteenth of an inch a month? If he shaves too much, it will take months, years to grow out, I don't want to risk it. I'm both admiring myself for my daring and wondering if I've gone too far already.

The receptionist looks up, pauses, a toothpick spear of fruit aloft, and says something in Korean.

"She said it looks good on you, that it harmonizes with your heart-shaped face."

Ha, I'm thinking. Appa's "chubby cheeks" is wrong, my face is *heart-shaped*. "Thank you," I say, but she doesn't respond.

Mr. Dongbang takes the long pieces on top and combs them to the opposite side, using a slick of gel to hold them in place. It's not even a quarter as severely shaved as Yunji's style and yet I look like some kind of Amazon warrior.

Nrrrrrghhhhhhhh—the clippers idle in the background. A little edgy for me. Umma and Appa would definitely not approve, I giggle to myself, if they could see, and I will make sure they do not. Mr. Dongbang sprays the upswept hair with a little water and shows me how to bring it back down by combing out the gel, smoothing the hair back over the shaved side. He's moved my middle part to the side. The hair merely falls on the shaved side more sleekly; the razored edges no longer immediately call to mind a broom. And, if you look closely at my right temple, you can see how it's shaved, a little reminder that I have a punk haircut, one that distracted parents will never notice.

I'm about to say "Wow," when I realize that the nrrrrrghhhhhhh-hhh sound that I thought was the idling clippers, which are actually switched off, is coming from Leo.

"Leo," I say. This sound sometimes comes before a seizure.

But more often before a tantrum.

In Bomb Haircuts' huge front window, I see a teen girl, blond hair glossy in the late morning sun. Skinny, tanned, wearing a tank top and short-shorts, laughing loudly and chattering to herself (must have those earbuds, or . . . maybe crazy) and walking a fluffy dog with a long, wheat-colored tail that has a poof at the end, like a pompom.

Oh no.

Even from across the room, I can see Leo's eyes bugging.

Nnnnnnrghhhhhhh!

"Leo, he's outside," I call from the barber's seat, avoiding the word d-o-g. But the air feels stretched tight, what's been set in motion is already in motion. "He can't get in, he can't hurt you."

"Hurt you!" Leonardo screams. The person sitting on the bench jerks his head up from his phone. The girl has paused, and with the worst possible timing, holds her little dog, as if it were a baby, up to the window.

Even though I'm still wearing a cape, I start for Leo, littering inky black hair shards in my wake. Leo's rocking and his nnnnrgggghhhs have turned into a scream.

I can't even see my phone; it is almost completely swallowed up by

Leo's baseball-mitt-sized hand. When he was little, people used to look at his large hands and say, "Oooh, with those big paws he's going to grow up to be huge." And they were right.

"It's okay, Leo," I say quietly. He needs a soft approach.

"HURT YOU!" he screams, bolting away from me, his arms windmilling.

There's a thud and a crash as the totem pole comes down, the top of it barely missing the window, its fall broken thankfully by the bench. Leo mashes his huge frame into a corner, he starts hitting himself on the forehead with the heel of his hand. I want to rush to him, but I know from experience that this will only make things worse. The tornado needs to pass.

I don't know what to do with myself but stand there. I have my own urge to hit myself in helplessness. The trapdoor opens, and my guts spill out all over the floor of Bomb Haircuts.

- - - - - - - - - - - -

"Is he okay?"

It's Mr. Dongbang. Instead of running to see the damage, he runs to us. The lady at the front is frozen in her seat, a piece of apple stuck to her toothpick en route to her mouth, her face an O of horror—one that inexplicably makes me angry, like Leonardo is somehow horrifying.

Would she be giving me that look if he broke his leg or went into diabetic shock?

"He's afraid of d-o-gs," I say. "Like, terrified. Even if the d-o-g is outside and he's inside."

"Ah, I see." The lady has now joined us. She gives Leo a wide berth but goes straight to the window, examining it for cracks. "He must have had a bad experience once. Was he bitten?"

"Oh, no," I say. "It's, um, part of his condition."

"Ah, his condition," Mr. Dongbang says, as if that explains everything, even though what Leo has is unexplainable.

Leonardo is red-faced, breathing heavily, but winding down.

Sometimes, a tantrum is actually a cure for the tantrum. It's like some kind of pressure has been released. A bomb's job, after all, is to explode. Gross example, but some pimples are like that. Leonardo is blinking, looking around as if wondering what bull just went through this china shop.

Now that the pressure has been released, we're good for the next ten minutes, half hour, maybe for the day.

I spot Umma walking down the sidewalk. She looks so happy and serene on the other side of the tinted windows I want to cry.

"Here, Leo," I say. "Give me my phone, okay? Umma's coming." My phone is still clutched in his giant hands, cartoonish not just because of their size, but because every one of his fingers is the same length, like how little baby hands look like stars.

I put my hand out, but don't expect what happens next.

No matter how many physical therapists work with Leo, he can't throw a ball. They put it in his hand, fold his fingers on it, help him practice the motion. They show him videos of kids throwing a ball. But he never throws. The ball just plops at his feet, like a lesson in Newtonian gravity.

Now, Leo hurls my phone like a pro baseball pitcher. It sails past me, just misses one of the purple-lit mirrors, hits the opposite wall, ricochets, and falls. Good thing I have an Indestructo case on it, with big rubber bumpers, for situations exactly like this. When I pick it up, I can hear a soft tinkling as tiny shards rain down on the floor. The screen has an actual hole, like a bullet hole, from which radiates an infinity of fractures.

"Does he need some water?" asks Mr. Dongbang.

"He's okay," I say. What I mean to say is that he is not physically injured. When he gets like this, nothing will help him. Giving him space and just keeping him from hurting himself or others—or property— is the only thing to do: minimize the destruction. "I'm so sorry about this." He doesn't reply but goes over to the totem pole to right it. I take the moment to grab my phone. It's still lit up, a good sign. I see people carry phones with cracked screens all the time. I shove it into my pocket.

The lady has brought us a mug of water, in which she's thoughtfully dunked a straw. The mug has a pink flower on it, a dreamy pastel design similar to the one on our rice cooker. I of course will not be handing that water to Leo, because I have 99.999 percent certainty he will throw it.

"Thank you, he's good. And I'm sorry," I say instead, handing her the entire wad of money Umma gave me to pay for the haircut to block her from giving Leo the water. I start an exaggerated, overacted walk toward the door. "Come on, Leo."

One aspect of his disorder is his tendency not just to echo speech, but to echo steps. He'll follow way too close behind, his step going into yours until he gives you a flat tire or bumps into your back. He did that to a lady once and she turned around, saw the hulking Leo, and started screaming for the police. But at least now, this tactic works: he follows me out. Step for step. I walk gingerly, lifting my feet extra high like a horse in mud, making sure he has footsteps he can follow.

Umma arrives, plastic bags that say Arirang Market hanging from both wrists.

"How was it?" she asks brightly.

She still doesn't know.

I'm so stressed I'm going to explode into a grenade of tears. But I stuff it back in, replace the pin. I smile and say chirpily, "It was great! Leo's fine!" while glancing back, waiting for someone from Bomb Haircuts to run out and demand we pay for damages for ruining their business or something.

Umma opens the bag and tells me she's so excited she found this kind of fish Appa likes (Tilefish? Filefish? It's written both ways on the package.). "But we need to get home so I can start defrosting it for dinner."

"Let's go, Leo," I say, hoping to get him into the safety and privacy of the car as quickly as possible before anything else can mar Umma's mood.

As Umma drives away, humming to herself, oblivious, I'm still glancing over my shoulder at the door of Bomb Haircuts. We both forget the whole reason we came here: my stationery supplies.

Five

Pulling up to "our" house is strange. It's been "our" house for weeks now. It still looks like a TV house, like I'm waiting to discover that the back of it is fake, a stage house for a cutesy family sitcom. It has a porch (with a swing!), an attached two-car garage (for our one car), and the newest marvel: a basement, an underground bunker to store stuff and where the washer and dryer are. Our apartment, like most city apartments, didn't have a washer and we had to use the grotty downstairs ones that took either quarters or (Mr. Goh found out to his chagrin) washers or certain foreign coins like Bolivian pesos. There were only three machines for almost fifty units in the building, and Leo's pee (and occasional poop) mistakes made laundry a daily chore. Too often when the machines downstairs, in what was also the creepy bike room, the bikes chained inside a cage like some Hannibal Lecter thing, were broken ("borken" as Mr. Goh spelled it on the hastily applied signs) from washing inappropriate things like heavy rugs, or occupied (probably some rug lady), Umma would have to lug the stuff to the laundromat between taking care of Leo.

It's suspiciously too easy, a house. The laundry, the new showers, storage. Something seems off. Missing. Then I realize it's the feeling. See, after being so cozy-claustrophobically ensconced in an apartment, this open air and order takes getting used to. Like there's too much space for the number of people we are. The extra space is loneliness. I feel like I spill out of myself here. It's disconcerting. For Leo, too. It spooked him so much he wouldn't even enter the house the day we got there, which I know annoyed Appa, because by the time he did finally take a step or two in, he was in the way of the movers, who'd of course just arrived, four hours late.

Leo's still not sold on it. He used to easily touch the ceiling in the railroady hall that entered the apartment. Now the ceilings are way above us, like we're in a cathedral. He goes from room to room furtively, creeping along the margins, trailing his fingers on the walls. He has still yet to set foot into the even more cavernous dining room. Appa has been too busy at work for us to have too many sit-down dinners, so it's not really a matter of contention (yet) that instead of using the beautiful dining room, I eat in the kitchen with Leo, at what's called the "breakfast bar" (the real estate lady proudly called it that, not us). In fact, Leonardo and I spend most of our time at the bar, me doing my homework, him playing with his tablet, pointedly not utilizing three-quarters of the house filled with lonely air. Including the outside. There's a basketball hoop uselessly installed in the driveway, making it feel like this is a house meant for a different family. At night we march off to our separate, spaced rooms. Umma and Appa have an "en suite" bathroom like an apartment within a house. In our city apartment, you always knew where everyone was at any time—hearing the voices, movement, the flushing of the one toilet we all shared, the shower that never got much water pressure, Appa's cartoonish snoring sometimes waking me at night. But still, yeah, I miss that.

I wish we would fill these spaces; people once naturally flowed into our lives, a river finding its level. Shouldn't the neighborhood kids be banging on the door, asking to use the basketball hoop? Shouldn't the parents be bringing over apple pies and tostones and wanting to hang out with Umma and Appa, bringing along their kids who are my age who'll explain to me what the school year will be like? Or even a young couple, bringing a chocolate-smeared toddler to run around from room to room would be fine. I think of how, in our building, someone always needed something—a cup of sugar, watching a child for half an hour, gossiping about other people in the building, neighbors stopping by to drop off goodies after they "cooked too much," Mr. Goh needing to unclog the toilet after another one of Leo's epic poops overwhelmed the elderly plumbing situation. Appa sometimes sighed over the "intrusions," but to me, that was *life*.

I find myself giggling about Mrs. Brekkie, who, after her husband died, rescued an adorable mutt that must have been half German shepherd because he was extremely smart and never gave anyone any trouble—he wouldn't even bother Arthur, their cat. But then Mrs. Brekkie started fostering from the same shelter and everyone worried she'd turned into a kind of dog/cat lady, especially when she brought this little French bulldog home who had the worst case of mange the veterinarian had ever seen. The dog was so miserable, and hairless, it hurt just to look at him. He also snapped at anyone who came within striking distance of his needle-sharp teeth.

But then, with enough love and patience—and maybe behavior coaching from Scout, the part German shepherd—Ernie, as the mange-plagued Frenchie was named, grew into a lovely, dapper dog who was so charming soon people were *begging* Mrs. Brekkie to adopt him, too. And she did. And she had so many people stopping by to say hello to the doggies she never had to worry about a stuck jar, a burned-out lightbulb.

It was stuff like that, even the fights in the laundry room over who got the dryer when two washing machines stopped at the same time, that gave the apartment complex a little village feel that was comforting.

Now we had space and central AC and heat, but no warmth. Appa bought this extra-large house hoping his parents in Korea would be convinced to move in with us.

See, one of the reasons we've never gone to Korea to visit them (besides the complication of Leo, of course) is because Appa coming to America as a young man basically deferred his two-year mandatory military service (they have a draft!). Because he stayed in America and never did it at all, he might be considered to have gone AWOL; it's possible he could even go to prison if he ever went back. Of course we don't want to risk that.

But that means Leo and I have grown up almost never seeing our paternal grandparents. I wonder, too, if Appa is thinking of his parents as a kind of replacement for Aunt Clara, who, since she was single and lived nearby, was always the one who was called when we needed a babysitter at the last minute.

However, the big house means plenty of places to read. It was definitely hard to settle into a story set in mystical Paradiseo when you're in an apartment as busy as Grand Central Station at all hours.

I'm looking at the house now and feeling more benevolent toward it, even a little hopeful. For the afternoon, Umma's home to look after Leo, I have a Terra, Gone novel I'm dying to dig into, and it's still summer, so no homework (besides Appa's weekly quizzes on SAT words). My mind is buzzing over the snacks I'll grab—I'll microwave rewarm the slightly melted and rehardened gluten-free brownies transported all the way from the city (yes, Omar's—don't ask me why, but they are better than the gluteny ones) and a blue polka-dotted can of Calpis Japanese milk soda, something Aunt Clara turned me on to (also yes, Omar's, the world bazaar deli)—before I sneak off.

Oh, wait. The stationery supplies! But Leo's already tumbling out of the car.

"Umma," I groan. "The school stuff. The list."

Umma's groan joins mine. She looks utterly exhausted. One trip to Pecan Plaza was a pleasant adventure. Going back would be a chore—even without knowing the disaster Leo left behind at one of the stores. But maybe it would be better to stay in motion. I need those supplies. Umma hasn't taken her seatbelt off.

I get a rank whiff of ammonia. I can't see a stain—Leo's pants are a dark navy—but I can smell it. Urine. Abort mission. I hustle him into the house, Umma unrolls about twenty sheets from the paper towel roll we keep in the car just for this.

In the house, I point Leo to the bathroom. "You need to go pee."

"Go pee," he echoes, still standing there. I have to guide him to the bathroom, pushing him gently on the back, steering him by a single elbow until he marches in the right direction. I shut the door to give him some privacy and strain to hear water dribbling into the toilet (or any kind of dribbling—I'll wipe it up later, that's my job). After an excruciating five minutes of no-drip silence, I open the door a crack. He's still standing where I left him, pants on. I see an outline of a stain around his crotch, a picture of an unidentified country of Leo.

Teen Leonardo approaching adulthood is weird. He has been delayed in everything, not just mentally, but physically. Like for instance, because of his seizure meds, his baby teeth never fell out. He has tiny, baby-corn teeth but then when he turned twelve, seemingly overnight the front fell out at once, pushed out by a Stonehenge slab, one front tooth and its neighbor fused into one giant tooth that sits in his mouth like a peg, half a Bugs Bunny bucktooth while a second, adult set grew (documented side effect) behind the baby-corn teeth. Luckily—I guess—he doesn't smile much, because the double row of teeth makes him look like a shark. Appa wants to get the baby teeth pulled but Umma wants to leave them alone. Given that this would be major oral surgery and Umma is the one who deals with all of his medical stuff, her word stands.

So there's the giant slouchy Leo with two rows of teeth. I think his voice has deepened, but when you spend every day with someone, you never witness it, it's just so subtle—it's the people who don't see him often who notice the change. He also didn't have adult-sized sex organs, until one day he just did. He'll run around naked as a jaybird, pay little attention to things like zipping his fly. Once, when the elastic (Umma lines all his pants with elastic to ensure they stay up even when he neglects to button or zip them) in the waistband of his pants stretched out, he had been with an aide who wasn't that attentive and let him walk around with his pants sagging past his underwear waistband. Another time he even had his fly unzipped, his penis peeking out like a shy little animal, having made its way through his boxers. Umma was shocked and, in her graceful way, called the aide on it, citing care and Leo's dignity, but all that girl said was, "It's the fashion"—she meant the sagging pants, not the penis. But what's worse, even after such a show of disrespect, Umma didn't fire her—good, even barely good-ish aides are hard to find, it seems, so you have to lower your standards a bit.

He's so innocent, who could take it the wrong way? But then I have to remind myself that someone who didn't know him would note his size, his burgeoning mustache, and just see a man with a you-know-what. I always wondered, was this going to be my first introduction to male anatomy? In a weird way I admire this about him: Why do we get so uptight over whether this or that piece of skin is covered or not? Men get to show their nipples, but women can't—I think it's actually illegal. So arbitrary. Given all the things Leo still needs to learn—he can't put a dab of toothpaste on his brush without squeezing out the whole tube, every single freaking time—do I want to use up learning time to *teach* him to be ashamed of his body? His lack of self-consciousness is delightful to me as a teen who is *all* self-consciousness. But I find myself hissing more and more, "Leo! Close your fly!" I don't want him to be known as the neighborhood flasher, either.

"Leo, take off your belt," I say through the door. "Pull down your pants. Then your underwear. Stand by the bowl and go pee."

I feel I may hear splashing in the bowl. My ear is pressed flat to the door; I look like a spy gleaning essential information that will keep the world from being blown up. When, in actuality, all it is is me trying to figure out if Leonardo is in the process of emptying his bladder or just standing there. Enuresis it's called when you urinate anywhere other than the appropriate place. When he emerges with his pants up but button unbuttoned, fly open, the stain seems larger. The toilet seat is also speckled with drops; his aim, as usual, is bad. I'm not even convinced he got any urine in the toilet. But it is not all in his pants, so that is a victory of sorts.

He nonchalantly shambles on by. I grab his arm.

"Take off your pants and undies, they're wet." I make a note to go out ASAP and do a final wipe of the car seat with a special enzymatic cleaner—Leonardo made one of our last cars unsalable because of his pee. Riding in our car, people kept subtly cracking the windows, asking us if we had cats. I'll have to do the laundry, too. There goes my reading time.

"No pee," he says, then repeats, "No pee no pee no pee." I have no idea what point he is trying to make, if any. I have him step out of his sopping undies and pants, I ball it all up and put it in the machine, adding a quarter-cup of the cloudy enzymatic cleaner to boost the detergent, press the button on the fancy washer, which answers with a cheery doodle-oo. I can hear the sizzle of whatever meat Umma is making for lunch, a warm smell of soy sauce. She tries to cook at home as much as possible, the sauce is always the same mixture of soy, honey, hot-pepper paste, and ginger. I don't complain at all because, though monotonous, it's delicious, especially when the meat gets crisped on the side, revealing a natural sweetness.

Umma gives Leonardo the tenderest pieces of meat, lets him eat all the rice he wants because Appa is not here to worry about Leo "becoming the fattest boy in school." It's true he's gaining weight but some of it's from the meds (Appa knows that), and also when the endless teachers and social workers want to know "what Leo likes," food is the only thing we can come up with. Food and bunnies are the only things that give him unequivocal pleasure.

Six

By the way, Leo was not always impaired/disabled/stricken, or however you want to describe it. Appa (and occasionally Umma) will recount how Leonardo could speak in full sentences when he was barely a year old, understood both Korean and English, seeming to live up to his namesake, Leonardo da Vinci (Appa came up with that). I was just a baby then, too, obvi, so I don't have any memories of a talking, interacting, bilingual Leo. I also didn't learn to read until I went to school, frustratingly normal.

I overheard Umma once on the phone, tearfully recounting to her friend how Leonardo used to love to go to the zoo and the botanical garden. That he was fascinated with the names of things like springbok, ibex, Crassulaceae, Aizoaceae—many of which she didn't know herself.

But as he came up to age two, the little boy in a strangely professorial voice who had astonished everyone by pointing to a yellow-diamond sign and stating, "Danger," started to have fewer and fewer words. Everyone was waiting for his vocabulary to really take off at this time, but it was slowing, stopping, then going backward, like a car pushed partway up a hill, then abandoned. As he talked less, his once animated little face started losing expression. Becoming "like a mask" Umma told the friend.

And that boy who rode atop Appa's shoulders or when he was sleepy allowed Umma to carry him like her baby koala, her baby sloth, was replaced by a Leonardo who kicked and scratched if you tried to hold him. Today, if you touch Leonardo even lightly, he quivers, like a horse when a fly lands on it.

His face changed in another way. When he screamed or cried (which was almost all the time, then, as Aunt Clara recalled), a muscle in his upper lip would rise up, like the tube of a wave, a strange flesh mustache that changed his sweet child's face into something else. Like he lost his natural child advantage of cuteness. He interacted less, stopped looking at people. He'd hit himself. His words dwindled to a few dozen random, not useful words ("corax," a raven) until only one remained.

"Umma," I'd asked her once. "What was his last word?"

"Rabbit," she said. "He started only echoing after that."

Rabbit. Of course. Leo is behind a veil that no one can penetrate, not even me. *Rabbit* is the word he says on his own, nonechoed. But he says it seemingly randomly, in places where it's unlikely there would be a rabbit, even a cartoon rendering. I wish I knew more things that he likes. But at least there is that. When he talks about rabbits, it means he is in a calm place. That rabbits belong in the same happy word family as nuna, in Leo-speak.

- - - - - - - - - - - -

Umma puts a drizzle of butter atop my rice, the way I like it, with a splash of soy sauce, *gangjang*. Appa is not here to casually insert into the conversation an article he read that said fat people do worse in life because of discrimination.

I know Appa cares about my future, but sometimes I just want a little butter on my rice and Umma gets that.

"My school supplies," I remind her.

"Oh, right," Umma says, a little flustered. "I'll text Appa and he'll get them—Pecan Plaza is on the way."

"Okay," I say. I don't voice any anxiety that he'll forget. Or not get all the details right: the pencils *have* to be Ticonderoga. I need a TI calculator, a specific model. And where does one buy a Kevlar insert for a backpack? Probably *not* at the Korean market.

All I want is to start this first day of school off right.

Seven

The Sunnyvale school district must be rich; the special-needs school bus is a sleek van, so new it shines. It comes earlier than my bus, so I am standing out in our front yard with Umma when it drives up, right to the door, so to speak. She is chewing on her lip. I know she wants to drive Leonardo to school, but we need to try it. School transportation is use it or lose it.

"I think this looks good," I say. In the city, we had to put a harness on him, one that zipped up the back and had a handle like he was a Labrador puppy or something. The smoky-smelling driver (we could smell the smoke even though we never entered the bus—not allowed) seemed mean and blared the horn angrily if we weren't waiting at the stop, even if he could see us scrambling out the door of the building. The crabby-looking bus monitor completely ignored Umma, at best greeted Leo with a frown and grabbed him by his harness handle even though he could walk and seat himself fine. She always looked angry when she clipped him to his seat, just as angry when she reversed the process on the way home. Shauntae told me that special-needs bus matrons didn't get any extra training, they were just there by the "luck" of the draw. Maybe that's why she was so mad-seeming. Not sure a bus full of rambunctious elementary school kids would be that much easier, though.

Who knows what people have going on in their lives? All I know is that Leo started coming home echoing "Simmer down!" and "Shut the f*** up!" Was it her voice? She never even grunted hello.

In our neighborhood, a mom whose nonverbal child with cerebral palsy had been coming home with oblong bruises on his arm, like someone had grabbed him, attached a spycam on her son's bag. Although they didn't get good pictures, from the audio it became clear the *driver* was leaving his seat and shoving and even punching the boy when he wouldn't sit still (he had cerebral palsy!) or made too much noise (again, CP! hence, the "Shut the f*** up!" report from Leo). At least it wasn't the monitor. But the parent was shocked to learn a few months later that the driver was supposedly still employed by the district—apparently the unions make firing difficult, plus the shortage of people willing to be a low-wage special-needs school bus driver, and, probably most importantly, the incident didn't make the news. If you can't get it on the news, it's like it didn't happen.

"Leonardo Kim, right?" says the monitor, a pleasant middle-aged white woman with a warm smile, a reflective vest.

"That's *right*," I say, looking at Leo, who echoes, as I'd hoped, "Right!"

The matron says her name is Carol, another good sign that she bothers to introduce herself. My eye's momentarily caught by her dangly earrings. Pretty daring if you ask me—lots of kids like Leo love to grab at hanging things—fan cords, fringe, you name it.

Umma still looks conflicted.

"Umma, let's just try it for one day and see." I know she's thinking about Simon, the boy with CP and his bruises. But Leo wants to grow up, too, risk his way into the world. Obviously he doesn't tell me this in words. But I feel it in my bones, like he doesn't want to just be "poor Leo," he wants to grow up and have his own messy complicated Leo life just like anyone else. First step: separation from mom.

"Eeeeee," says Leo. A happy *eeee*. Not quite "rabbit" calm, but a little excitement/anxiety is warranted here. I have butterflies doing backflips in my stomach right now every time I consider, ugh, it's the first day at a totally new school where I know no one. But back to Leo: at times, I can read a Leonardo mood like a sailor can look at the sky and then

predict tomorrow's weather. And this is one of those times. I know he'll
be okay on this bus. Or, at least okay for me to step away from trying
to control the scene.

"Rabbit," Leo says. And suddenly I realize what he's saying: *I am happy.*
I have that feeling I have when I think about rabbits. I'm calm for now.

Carol turns to Umma. "Would you like to take him on the bus?
Help him get settled?"

Umma is shocked. So am I. "I can?" she practically squeaks. All
the previous matrons and the bus drivers we had in the city acted like
their bus was their special kingdom. They'd even yell at us if they felt
we were too close to the door. One monitor, when I sprinted into the
bus when Leo started having a tantrum, literally screamed, "You can't
come in here!" I had gone up *one step* to grab Leo to, among other
things, protect *her.* "You're not allowed in the bus!" both she and then
the driver had screamed at me, even though (I am remembering now)
Leo started to struggle against her in a panic, clawing at her face, almost
pulled her earring out of her ear, and as she shielded her head from his
batting hands, an artificial fingernail flying off her hand like a beetle's
shell. I stood down and watched. Mr. Goh happened to be outside and
he helped Umma get Leo in the building while the disheveled monitor
turned to me. "A kid like that shouldn't be in public school." Like, we're
always wrong. No matter what we try to do.

"Of course you can go on!" Carol says now. "He's your child!"

"Georgia." Umma turns to me. "Do you want to help him?"

I reach out my hand to Leo. Then another instinct takes over and
I snatch it back. My brother is approaching college age. "Leo is my *big*
brother," I say. "All he needs is for you to walk on first so he can follow you."

Her eyebrows quirk up for a second. "He won't elope if I do that?"

To most people, *elope* means to run away to get married. For Leo,
it just means "to run away" in special-needs danger-speak, and Carol is
clearly worried about turning her back on him, not holding on to him.

Even though I don't always like the language, it makes me feel at least
like she's had more training than Mean Matron. I suppose it must be a
challenge having to deal with everything from kids in wheelchairs to the

kids like Leo. I like that she's being very responsible, worried about what might happen. The other lady (who'd never told us her name) treated all the kids the same: brusquely grabbing onto their harnesses, never looking any of them in the eye. Once, when Leo stumbled into her coming, instead of leaning in to right him, she jumped back, as if he were contaminated.

Leo follows Carol in okay, then swats at her as she bends to fasten his seat belt, but she doesn't pull back or cringe or anything. She just gets in there, takes a swat or two, gets out. The driver glances in his mirror, folds up the stop sign, and the van pulls out. It's completely empty except for Leo. It somehow still always feels like we're sending him away on a trip he may never return from. I don't know why, but even with "nice" Carol, it feels like that.

"Won't that be funny if he's chauffeured like this, the only kid, to school," I say just to fill up the air, lighten the tone. Umma only nods, heads inside, what's going on inside her head unknowable to me, as always.

- - - - - - - - - - - -

The first day of school in a new place is terrible, no matter how you slice it.

Normally, the night before school resumes in the fall is a flurry of texts with Shauntae—*Who do we want to see? What are you wearing? Do our classes match up at all? Algebra II is supposed to extra hard.*

Then, in the morning, another flurry. *Are you still wearing that? What are you really wearing? We're in high school now—Do you bring your lunch, or is that just for babies now?*

Shauntae and I ran as a unit, made even easier because we lived in the same building and could take the rickety, diesely bus together, and then in high school, the subway, where we would even get special subway passes that would let us ride for free during school hours. Shauntae and I knew all the same people—Magaly and Mr. Goh, the Alsaedis, and everyone. Half the time if Umma got hung up with something with Leo, she would dump me at the Windsors' apartment—Shauntae's family—without a second thought.

But now Shauntae has her own world, one where she's taking the subway by herself. Or, at least, without me. Her girlfriend, Arlena, a class below us, will be waiting on the sidewalk outside the building, subway pass in hand. Everything at City High will be familiar—sometimes good, sometimes bad—like the sandwiches at Omar's.

I'm sitting on the unfamiliar bus (regulation Bluebird, but newer and not diesel, and with seat belts) among unfamiliar kids whose eyes I can feel following me. The half dozen painfully preppy white boys with baseball hats on backward make me feel the most awkward and on guard. I want to play it cool, but I can feel, literally, the judgy gaze; it all has a weight, just like my extra pounds. My phone, still managing to light up despite the cracked screen, turns out to be functionally frozen—it's forever 1:21, the time it was when Leo hurled it. I still look down, as if checking for texts.

The bus has actual seat belts. It purrs rather than rumbles. I buckle in, lean my backpack (filled with cheap Walgreens notebooks) against the window as we pull up to stop number two: Herbert Hills. This is the part of town where the executives of the biotech drug firms in the industrial parks—PHarmRNA, NanoTech Industries, and SophY Genetics—live. That's why Herbert Hills is nicknamed the Capsule Corridor and probably why Sunnyvale seems like a newly constructed town, where the pharma corporation employees live. In fact Appa found out about Sunnyvale from a pharma rep, the people who try to sell drugs to doctors. The person moved to Sunnyvale right out of college to work at PHarmRNA, which explains the weird vibe of the town, a tourist town without tourists, like no one is actually *from* here.

In Herbert Hills, each house is set so far back from the street, many with high, angry-seeming fences and imposing-looking gates with the stone horses with the rings through their mouths, we can't even see if it's a shack or a mansion (a mansion, I'm assuming). I'm surprised any of these kids go to public school at all.

Aha: we pick up *two whole kids*. And they must be together, put on the bus by a lady decked out in mismatched Easter-egg pastels (jade green, pink, yellow), walking a puppyish golden dog with an adorable chrysanthemum face and whose fur looks permed. Almost everyone in the city wears black. Not just to look cool but also everything is, well, so grimy. The lady, fiddling with the leash (also a delicate pastel pink), suddenly looks right at me as I'm staring at her, and I'm startled.

In the city people seem to forget / not care they are being stared at.

Caught, I smile. She doesn't smile back, but continues to stare. The goofy dog prances and bounces around like it's on a trampoline or avoiding hot coals.

- - - - - - - - - - - -

Last week we had to come to Sunnyvale High / Cambridge Academy to register, so it's not exactly new to enter the building. But, should we say, entering it as an actual SH/CA student is startling to me. This school, though public, is not one beaten hard by decades of unruly students, eroded by time and graffiti and pollution. Everything here screams (silently) order and control. Everything is *new* new. Surfaces are glossy, untaggable. The trophy cases shine, the floor is waxed. And not flimsy new, like construction-dust-and-plywood new, it's odorless and shiny, like everything's been cast in gold. City High was marked inside and out. Graffiti on top of graffiti. Lockers dented into shapes of kids' heads. Scuffs on the floor. Lipstick on the mirrors. The sour ghost odor of barf covered inadequately by chemical-laden cleaning compounds.

Here, everything shines with a kind of benign intensity. Like if someone were shot, the blood could easily be wiped up and sanitized without a trace (and yes, active shooter drills will be held just like with fire drills; they will check to make sure we have our Kevlar backpack inserts, etc.).

Students are coming and going, and I'm just standing there like a fool, my mouth probably agape. A few impatient kids bump into me—I hope it's accidental. The larger attitude is indifference. I'm just an obstacle. Everyone has *important* things to do, people to see. A tall and short guy walk by, the shortish guy in a green-and-gold Cambridge Academy fleece vest bumps me, then frowns and growls, "Watch it, moron!" even though I haven't moved. He looks at me, does a double-take.

"Asian drivers, Asian *lady* drivers, worst combination." He snickers to his friend who snickers back.

It's going to be a long day, and it hasn't even started. Students are alphabetically split into different colored "cohorts" according to the primary color spectrum. I'm blue. At 8:20 the blues meet in the Martin Luther King Jr. Room. At 8:30 we have Block 1, then Block 2, then 3, and then we walk to some other room for Block 4, and then it's lunch.

It's too early to go to class (Block 1)—why does the bus get in so freaking early? Twenty minutes out of every day I'll have to fill up. Standing here doesn't seem like the best course of action. I decide to keep moving. I pretend I have somewhere to go, someone to see. I circumnavigate between the bathroom, drinking fountain (actually, a "hydration station" where you put your fancy water bottle to get your UV-sterilized water), trophy case. There are various rules and signs posted in the hall:

SHELTER IN PLACE —>

The arrow apparently points to a lockable panic room in case of an "active shooter" or "climate event."

Headphones:

Students may not wear headphones above their neck in the building; headphones must be visible and worn below a student's neck

How do you wear headphones below your neck? Around your waist? Not on your head? And honestly, do they think kids still wear wired headphones and not earbuds? I'm a dork but even *I* know that. I am strolling and laughing to myself like an insane person, my fingers itching to text these brilliant thoughts. Ugh, I miss Shauntae.

By my third pass, I still don't get the rules, but I have figured out that the bathroom actually isn't a bad place to linger; it appears not to be a place you might get jumped. No one's even smoking in it. Girls are arranging their makeup as they would in any high school bathroom. But no one's gauche enough to leave a lipstick kiss on the mirror. I think about how the janitors at City High got so angry one of them left a note *(Just FYI, I use same cloth wipe mirror as wipe toilet).*

There is also a huge library, hushed and unpopular as a museum devoted to an obscure subject. It is also, according to the big sign on the door:

POINT OF ASSEMBLY
EXTREME WEATHER REFUGE

Whatever that is.

It is also CELEBRATE READING WEEK!!! But I notice the date is from last year.

At Cambridge Academy, the real distribution of space—acreage—is devoted to sports. The gymnasium is the largest real estate in the school—the wood floor is so intricately laid and shellacked it's smooth as glass; in the center, beautiful lettering—BOMBERS—and an eagle, zooming for the kill, laid into the floor. Also, stadium seats, those electronic scorer things, natural light from dozens of skylights.

Off that, there's squash courts and a padded wrestling room, a fancy weight room just for varsity athletes. The football stadium / track is an expanse of Astroturfed green. There are separate fields for soccer, baseball, and field hockey (whatever that is), a golf course.

On the other side of this abundance of athletic fields is the Multi-modal Center, a.k.a. the Mod. That's where they do the pullouts for special ed. Umma is excited about this new therapeutic listening program they use that supposedly may help Leonardo talk—not just repeat the last three words someone's said. The kids wear headphones that have special frequencies piped in to stimulate the auditory nerve. It has also occurred to me that perhaps Leonardo has trouble communicating because he can't hear the way we do, and maybe repeating the last couple words he's heard is actually an ingenious way of communicating, of at least letting us know he has heard. No one's backed me up on that hypothesis though.

- - - - - - - - - - - -

When I was little, I didn't understand why Leonardo was constantly being bounced from different programs and schools. Private schools of course are more individualized, especially for the complex cases like Leo's that need not just educational but also speech and physical therapy. But oftentimes you can't prove you *need* private placement until you spectacularly fail at your public placement first. What a waste of precious time.

At least, in this, Leonardo seemed to have obliged. So for middle school, he got sent to the Adler School, a private school an hour outside of town that the city also had to provide a bus for. This is a super-fancy place that rich people send their special-needs kids to. It had padded, noise-controlled rooms (some that you could darken, to soothe the light-sensitive), music and art facilities, sensory gyms with swings and trampolines and wheelchair lifts the way Cambridge Academy has athletic fields and gym facilities. Each classroom had carefully modulated light, huge, cradley beanbag-type sensory chairs; part of the floor was even made of trampoline material so kids could bounce, if so inclined, while they learned.

You'd think this would be the answer to all our Leonardo problems. It had started off so great, with the teachers praising Leonardo (they could see his smartness!). We all kept hoping this would be it, a place that would understand him, help him learn to self-regulate his behaviors. Offer him a modified curriculum so he could learn at his pace and not be bored. Make our days a little more regular and predictable.

Indeed, for the first month, he returned home every day with little feedback—good or bad. No news is good news when it comes to Leo. The first parent meeting wouldn't be for three months; it was part of the protocol, they said. No feedback generally is good, that is, no urgent crises. And so we all held our breaths. He seemed calmer at home, we were sure of it.

The shocker came in June when the year-round special-needs school year ends/starts again.

In an email (an *email*!) the Adler School's director informed Umma and Appa that Leonardo would "not be welcome next year." I knew all this from overhearing a phone conversation, Umma sobbing to Appa, calling him at work at the hospital: "How can they just dump him like this? How will we find him a placement in two weeks, when everyone in the district office has already left for summer?"

So, moving to a suburb that supposedly has a good special-needs program in the public school was the way to go. Not dependent on Leo, just dependent on us buying a house in the district. They have to take him and can't kick him out . . . I think.

I'm wondering how Leo's ride to school was.

I check my watch. It's two minutes to class. Perfect.

Module 1

Instead of
    English
    Spanish
    Math
    Civics
    Social Studies

we have
    Great Books & Creative Writing
    Visual Arts
    Law & Society
    Wellness Studies
    etc.

And what the heck is "Wellness Studies"?

I soon find out it's what we would call "health" class.

I change classes (called "commuting" here), keeping my eye out for Leo, but I don't see him. I've been assigned a "newbie-buddy," a girl named Savannah who won't stop chattering ("Hi! You're Georgia? Well, I'm Savannah—we're like twins! Get it?") and I'm chafing, wanting to get out from under her so I can have my own unvarnished observations. She enjoys telling me about the minutiae of history and every little thing here ("and here's the hydration station where Jared Jones turned it on and it wouldn't turn off—*hilarious*!"). But at lunch, when I could most use a little insider help, she ditches.

Eight

The cafeteria is as big as the Grand Canyon. What is this, a taco bar?
A hydration and salad dressing *station*, as if we are, indeed, grown-up,
actual commuters?

Umma was so busy with all the stuff for Leonardo this morning, she
forgot to pack me a lunch—I normally pack my own, but look forward
to her first-day-of-school ones, where she usually makes a surprise, like
kimbap shaped into a smiley face with a curl of hollowed-out carrot, a
square of Spam for the nose. So I have no lunch. I head to the taco bar,
since tacos cure everything, and quickly gather up the contents of all
those fixings, including guacamole (expensive, real guacamole?) and a
watery salsa that I already know won't be spicy enough.

Is there a cash register to pay? Will I have enough money? Guacamole is expensive. A few kids push around me to the taco fixings,
muttering for me to get out of the way. I dumbly move away a few steps
only to find myself in various traffic jams: to the soft-serve machine, the
salad bar, the "hot" bar, the "beverage center." I'm staring in a bit of a
panic at what looks to me like an army of same-looking people—boys
with side-parted hair, polo shirts, cargo shorts, girls with shimmery
waterfalls of hair plunging down their backs, clothes with the same
Easter eggy colors—and feeling dizzy. I am in some teeny bopper's
dream of a high school with reflective waxed floors, a cafeteria that

tends more café than teria, there's none of that odor of mushy peas, of grade D meat.

There's a girl at my elbow, aiming her phone toward me like I'm a semi-interesting exhibit in the zoo. A ringtail. A lemur. (Ha, Leonardo once started screaming in meltdown at the zoo, and the lemurs answered, full-throated, back, in seemingly supportive yips and caws. I wonder what it was Leonardo had inadvertently said to them.)

She herself is an Instapix dream (or, what Shauntae would smirkingly call a CAWG: Conventionally Attractive White Girl): golden hair wound in careful curls, like ribbon candy wound around a pencil. And those Easter-egg clothes, which I see closer up are mismatching pastel plaids, are muted clashing complementary pastels, like the lady I saw from the bus. Instead of red and green, we have pink and honeydew melon. A soft blue and an orange of a barely lit flame. The chaos of baby colors almost looks like a visual joke, or: how ugly can a clothing company make their clothes and still gaslight you into buying them? She is a mermaid in plaid.

She suddenly takes her phone and aims it right at me, her lips mooshed together in a sexy smile/smirk—at me. Flattered (even though I'm not of that persuasion), I start to smile back. Then like a dorkus I realize her phone camera is flipped; she's selfie-ing with the lush greens and yellows of the salad bar behind her (including a basket of single-serve packets of some high-end *dijonnaise* ("authentic French taste!") for which I have to resist the cheapskate's urge to shove a few into my pocket). Another set of girls, in similarly matching pastels, wash up like a wave. Their heads magnetically move together like they're going to kiss, then at the last moment, tilt away. Something is whispered. They laugh, then move apart.

I finally figure out how to pay. In my fantasy the lunch lady also hands me a map of the lunchroom.

Here, the cool kids, stay away.

Here, the druggies, stay away.

Here, the artsy all-black-wearing group, check it out.

Here, the nerds, check it out.

Here be dragons, the male jock table.

I try to get the lay of the land, subtly, without looking like I am. Compared to City High, it's a sea of white kids. But wait—holy cats, over in the corner there's *a whole table* of dark-haired Asian kids. Of course there is. In fact, more than one. Archipelagos of Asians in a sea of white. I see that girl, from Bomb Haircuts, with the Amazonian hair and aggressive eyeliner, sitting with the biggest Asian group. She would be hard to miss. Right now she's holding court, gesticulating wildly, her hair swaying like a rooster's comb. People are laughing and holding their sides. Too much momentum in that group for me to try to butt in.

There are, however, no Black kids at all, except for one guy, conservatively dressed in a pastel polo and khakis. He's carefully spaced in between all the tables, a lone planet eating a sandwich, which is actually made with a baguette, while reading a book. High probability of being a member of my nerd tribe, maybe he's a Francophile on top of it—not that that would be me, but I do love languages. I steer my tray his way. When I jostle the bench a little while climbing in, he looks up—and to my relief, smiles.

"That's a banh mi," I blurt, looking at his baguette. Shauntae and I used to get those at Pho Sure after school. It's wrapped in striped takeaway wax paper.

He smiles again but returns to his book. Far from feeling rebuffed, I'm intrigued. He's reading a book called *Black Boy* and obviously wants to get back to it. I am happy just to sit here. No one else joins us.

— — — — — — — — — — — —

A few minutes later, Reader Guy puts the book down, slipping in a magnetic bookmark, then faces his sandwich, and me.

"Yes, that is a banh mi," he laughs. He has a slight lisp that whistles pleasantly.

"Where'd you get it? By the taco bar?"

"This isn't a real banh mi, it's my mom's version. These jalapeños from the farmers' market are the bomb." He salutes me with it. "The novelty wax paper is her joke. She's always complaining how she's a short order cook."

"She's Vietnamese?" I try not to squint too hard, looking at his eyes.

"Nah, amateur chef. Like, she could win one of those competitive cooking shows. See? She even slices the jalapeños on the diagonal." He breaks off an end. "Try?"

I'm not one to refuse food. The meat is well seasoned, tasty, there's something sweet, the jalapeños are fresh and green and set my mouth on fire.

"Is this from a summer reading list?" I ask, pointing to his book.

"This?" he says. "Richard Wright would be way too subversive for an English class. Nah, this is a pleasure read."

"We only get a half hour for lunch, and you spend half of it reading." I have an urge to hug him and scream, *Friend*! But, wisely, I don't.

He shrugs. "I have so much homework, it's hard to find the time otherwise."

"Reading is a dying art," I say. "These days people's brains are shrunk by video games—and they complain even those have too much plot to keep track of."

"Tell me about it. I don't even think teachers read that much. I'm Calvin, by the way—you're obviously new."

"You noticed?" I bug out my eyes, exaggerate surprise. "I'm Georgia."

I like his quiet self-possession. At first I wondered if he was using the book as a prop, to hide his awkwardness. But actually, no boy I know would camouflage awkwardness by *reading*. Also, he's not awkward. He's handsome and has the kind of lanky grace I associate with people who seem quiet but can go from zero to sixty if the situation requires. His eyes are kind.

Out of the corner of my eye, I spy a familiar form sitting at a table near the cafeteria entrance. I'm not an expert on disability laws, but over the years have picked up that schools must provide the "least restrictive" environment for kids, steering them toward "inclusion" rather than warehousing them out of sight, out of mind. However, every time I changed classes I raised myself up to full height and looked around; besides a kid on crutches (and it looks temporary), I didn't see Leo or anyone with a disability. Here, inclusion must mean lunch.

Lunch *is* important socialization time for Leo, so I scrunch down a little and feel a bit like a proud parent when I see him go up to the fancy hydration station and pour himself a cup of water, and without sticking his fingers in the flow and watching the drips fall in front of his face. He turns to walk back to the table, the only one also populated with adults—the special-needs paras—and two other students, a boy in a black full-body wheelchair that looks like a medieval torture device and a girl with Down syndrome, her beautiful blond hair carefully brushed and caught in a ribbon. They both look like kids while Leo looks like an adult. That he's balding a little already (probably something to do with his condition, mitochondria? or something?) makes the difference even starker.

The short guy in the green fleece who'd bumped into me in the hall gets up from the jock table and walks toward the water station, heading directly toward Leo as Leo starts walking back. I can see him staring, kind of sizing Leo up. The fleece vest says Cambridge Academy Varsity. However, as an athlete, whose job it is to move his body with precision, I'm a little surprised when he bumps into Leo.

"Watch where you're going, bro—" he says. Leonardo continues on, unperturbed.

"Hey I'm talking to YOU, Asian driver." Not that bad joke again. "You—Asian kid—you deaf?"

It suddenly becomes very quiet in the cafeteria.

When Leonardo started losing his words, he also stopped responding to his name, leading the developmental pediatrician to inform Umma and Appa he might have hearing impairment. They panicked and took him to audiologists and ENTs and other deaf specialists all over the state, crossing their fingers, praying he wasn't deaf. They envisioned a life of him standing on the train tracks not hearing the train. Of being in college and having to have someone take notes for him. Or not hearing birdsong, or their voices. Of me having to learn to sign.

But then one of the technicians wondered if Leo's not raising his hand when he heard a sound was more about not being able to follow directions.

Appa found a specialist who had a machine that could emit a puff of air into the ear canal to check hearing, no input required.

Puff.

Leo's ear drum quivered, as a hearing eardrum would. There was a setting for a sound they could use to stimulate the startle reflex.

He startled.

First they were glad.

He's not deaf.

But they didn't know yet what was to come. Umma and Appa didn't realize that all that time they should have been *hoping, praying* for deafness. Deaf people can still communicate. TV comes with closed captioning. They can still go to college. I would have learned to sign, no sweat.

I'm not even sure Leonardo knows his own name. About 50 percent of the time, he turns when I call it. But is he turning to his name or to my voice? Does it matter? Unless he knows the person, he will ignore them completely. He returns to his table, navigating his bulk so that he is sitting—quite primly for his size—next to his aide. The Cambridge Academy Varsity guy is still looking at him.

The blond girl who was Instapixing walks up behind the guy, covers his eyes.

"Curley Three Sticks!" she squeals.

Everyone's looking at her and of course noticing her beauty (she has the longest hair of anyone I've ever seen), and that is, I am guessing, fully what she intended, the Rapunzel look. I did not know a lot of girls, maybe any, like her at City High. A girl who looks like she walked out of a commercial for shampoo. I don't remember a single blond, no less white-blond, girl in our class. We all had hair that was shades of brown and black (and purple), our skin went from parchment to wet playground sand to more opaque shades of brown, red, black. The few white girls at City were the daughters of Russian and Ukrainian immigrants, with one or two who were kids of hippy social justice warriors /

gentrifiers, the kind always carrying signs for this or that protest, and when they lifted their signs, we all saw they didn't shave their armpit hair. But they'd always have the newest phone. These were the white kids whose parents didn't flee for the burbs, and they just became part of the vast moving crowd that was City High. They weren't "better" than anyone else nor were they picked on. They were just there. While here it seems like, despite that somewhat "diverse" population, each group is separated from each other as if by invisible borders, the clear plastic dividers in my notebook, and there is a hierarchy. I just haven't figured it out yet

The "curly three sticks" dude peels her hands from his eyes with exaggerated surprise, kisses her hand, then whispers to her. I can hear— or imagine I hear—him murmur to her, "Look at my buddy, Special Ed over there." She turns in Leo's direction, laughs. I wish life came with closed captioning. What exactly did they say? I swear he mouthed "Special Ed."

I want to ask Calvin about this kid, Curly Three Sticks. His hair is indeed curly. Little bronze ringlets. Who is he? Is he a bona fide bully? But Calvin is absorbed in his book again, reading as if I am not there. I've witnessed this whole drama, but I was looking for it. Everything's new to me. To Calvin, it was likely one of the thousands of dramas that go on at Cambridge Academy, business as usual in the cafeteria—which is probably why he prefers his books.

I am thinking about how no one knows me here. Calvin doesn't even know I'm connected to Leo.

Which means I get to write my own story.

But what would my story be without Leo?

Nine

After school, there are a few buses, of course, but more dominant are the lines of giant SUVs, reminding me, unaccountably, of the lines of tanks from that picture of Tiananmen Square in our history books: giant vehicles, little humans. And not just the passengers—the drivers are 100 percent moms, but moms whittled down to the bare essence of momness. If I were to make a mathematical equation, the size of the car would be inversely proportional to the size of the driver.

$$C_1D_1 = C_2D_2$$

There are some really tiny ladies in Sunnyvale. Some of them look skinny enough to fall between the subway grates back in the city. My mom is also small, but her smallness comes more from the bigness of other people.

But even with the helicopter/SUV moms, Sunnyvale school district provides two—yes, two!—bus *choices* every day for each student who must be transported: the normal bus or the late bus. The late bus is so kids can do after-school programs. Sports mostly, I suppose.

I immediately text that to Shauntae:

Living in the burbs means never having to
miss the bus. There's a second "late" bus.

> And probably another one after that.
> For people who are doing after school
> activities, or, if they're just late.

She replies:

> Not like in the big bad city, where there are
> no second chances.

Finishing it with a bunch of clown and kissy emoji to counterpoint her hard-boiled prose. I want to ask her how her day was, but I'll FaceCall with her later. Right now I'm waiting with Leonardo for walking therapy.

Monday through Thursday, Leonardo will do this therapy at some place in Sunnyvale's tiny downtown. It's not therapy to help him walk *per se*, it's something they do while he walks. It is supposed to help his sensory issues, but it also may help his gait at the same time. Appa tends to think these therapies are frivolous. But it may also help with Leo's need to practically step on people's heels while he walks, which would be a good thing. Plus, Umma points out, you need to use your eyes while walking, and maybe fixing this will help Leo to read. Umma certainly knows which buttons to press when it comes to Appa.

The perfect thing is that I can fetch Leonardo from the Multi-modal Center and wait with him for him to be taken to therapy by his aide. This therapy is somehow part of his official school program, not something Umma and Appa have to pay for out of pocket. Things really do work differently in the suburbs. I guess because there is money.

We're in front of an overhang that has another of those signs:
EXTREME WEATHER REFUGE
GATHERING POINT
Leonardo moves to sit on the bench, which looks like wood, but if you look at it closely, you see it's some kind of pressed plastic, probably weather- and whatever-is-the-next-pandemic-virus-resistant, I suppose. He plops straight down like a sack of cement; he has clearly had a long day. I imagine being him is like being a CEO of Leo's Systems, Inc. He

has to be places all the time, always on, always needing to be doing, thinking, answering, therapy-ing. If he wants to opt out, well, that's a behavior. When does *he* get to open a bag of Funyuns and veg and do nothing like an eighteen-year-old should?

Next thing I know, Yunji, that girl from the hair place, is walking toward us.

That eye makeup! Racoony black stripes but sharpening to dramatic daggers at the tip. I wonder if she applies at school, or if her parents approvingly let her go out the door like that. I don't think she was wearing it, or at least not like *that,* when we were at the haircutting place.

She looks like she will walk on by, but then stops. "Your hair turned out great," she says.

"Thanks," I say, a little stuttery, because to me she's like a celebrity. A celebrity who can pull off black lipstick and dagger-eyes.

I gesture to Leo. "Leo, this is Yunji. Yunji, my brother, Leo." I don't think she was there when all hell broke loose in the shop, but I'm sure his reputation precedes him.

"Hey, Leo," she says, deadpan enough that it doesn't hurt his ears. Lots of people think, "Disabled kid!" and immediately regress—"How are you, sweetHEART? What a nice TRUCK/HORSIE/TOY you have!"—to screechy baby talk that can immediately send him into a state of agitation. Leo, intently playing with the string on his hood, looks up at her. Or at least I *think* he's looking at her. She pauses a second as if to allow him to get used to her. "High five?"

High five is something Leonardo can do, although he doesn't know his own strength. He lifts his massive hand. I worry he's going to do it too hard, working for that crisp *splat!* sound. That stuff always splits me in two: of course I want to keep people safe, but I also want Leo to have a life. Including making his own mistakes.

He winds up pretty hard, and I tense.

Two beats before contact, he stops, jerkily joins his palm with hers. A technical high-five fail, but I'll take it.

"All right!" she says with quiet enthusiasm, drawing her hand back as if for a real high five. Leonardo turns back to playing with the string on his jacket's hood.

"Did you miss your bus?" she asks me. "Late bus isn't for another hour, maybe more."

"No, Leo's aide needs to pick him up for his after-school program." To not leave him out of the conversation, I lean forward into his line of sight. "Right, Leo? Your walking therapy."

"Walking therapy," he agrees.

Yunji joins us on the bench, which has a plaque honoring some rich donor. I've never heard of parents donating to a public school, other than, like, brownies and cookies. This place has the feel of a private school, with all the facilities, the private-schoolish name, the parents going in and out. (Today some mom brought in a bunch of expensive tropical plants and trees, saying she wanted to make sure the air quality inside the school was good, thus the huge corn plants and ferns with labels on them that say Approved by NASA.) There are also gold plaques everywhere, even on some of the classroom doors, including one of mine, like the room itself belongs to Vaughn B. Whippendoodle. Vaughn B. Whippendoodle (a name approximation, by me) obviously put a lot of money into that particular classroom. But then what does Vaughn B. Whippendoodle want in return? (Also, why the stationery supplies then? Vaughn B. Whippendoodle should be buying them!)

The last school bus pulls out, heading not in our direction but toward Herbert Hills. Except for Herbert Hills being richer, it doesn't make any sense that those students get dropped off first since where we live is basically on the way. But oftentimes, the simplest explanation is the best one.

I ask, "You don't take the bus?"

"Nah, I meet a couple of kids and we go back to my place for *hagwon*."

"Hawk-won?"

"Yeah, you know, Korean hagwon. My mom runs it as part of the business."

Korean words are all a delicious mystery to me, I pounce on them like I would bits of sea glass at the beach.

"I actually don't know Korean—I mean, besides a few words. Did you say hawk-won? Hog-one?"

"It's—"

Leonardo starts barking. "Wow . . . wow . . . wowww!" He scans my face slyly. He is either trying to join the conversation by vocalizing or he's bored and just wants to disrupt other people talking. He feels left out, I'd guess. The therapists call this "desiring negative attention," and we're supposed to ignore it so it loses its power. "Don't give him what he wants, and he'll stop."

"Wow . . . wow . . . wowwwwwwwwww!" His special trick is that instead of barking out, he barks *in*, on his inhale. Like a terribly asthmatic dog stuck in an accordion. It can be funny—for three seconds. I lost my humor about this years ago. This sound is on my top-three least favorite noises after, I guess, gunshots and nails on a chalkboard. It's less the noise than the occasion. See Leonardo knows it bugs me, and so when he deploys it, he is being mean—at least that's what it feels like. I of course try to ignore it, but he'll just do it more, and the more he does it, at some point there will be an explosion—me, for a change.

Easy for the experts to say, "Just ignore it." I try. I pretend I don't care. I pretend I don't hear it. But trust me, when someone's inhale-barking, it's unignorable. Appa once got so mad at Leo's barking when a relative from Korea was calling, he physically pushed Leonardo to his room, locked him in. Umma got mad about him manhandling Leo, and they had a fight.

"Wow . . . wowwwww . . . wowwww."

Yunji, perhaps taking my cue, talks over him, raises her voice: "Yeah, hagwon, like after-school school. You know, SAT prep and all that. I teach a Korean class for the little kids."

I want to hear more about this hawk-won, but most of her explanation has been swallowed up by Leo's barking. Also, out of the corner of my eye, I see that fleece-vest Three Sticks from lunch walking our way. His Rapunzel-hair girlfriend is a dozen yards behind him, rushing to catch up.

Leonardo, in perfect timing, adds a prehistoric bird-screech exhale to his barking—"Wowwww . . . wowwww . . . yeeeeeech!"—making everyone in a fifty-foot radius turn toward him, wondering what the heck that noise is, a cause and effect he seems to enjoy.

Three Sticks at a distance looks like a weird, humped animal with no neck. As he gets closer, I see giant padded headphones around his actual human neck, slung over one broad shoulder a golf bag as big as a city trash can, with Cambridge Academy emblazoned on it. In one hand he's carrying spiked saddle shoes, a black-and-white glove on the other hand, the left one.

The Rapunzel girl calls out, "Curley!" He turns and stops, practically in front of us. A button pinned on the bag winks in the sun—NRA Forever—kind of a bad taste thing, I'm thinking, considering all the school shootings that have happened lately.

"Hey, babe," he says.

She stops to stare at the Extreme Weather Refuge sign. Points, with a hand on her face. "What does that mean, 'extreme weather refugee'?"

"Oh my god, you are so *dumb*," he says, collapsing in laughter, rattling the clubs in his bag.

She pouts.

"Wow, wow, wowww!" Leo bark-inhales. "EEEeeeech!"

The guy, Curley must be his actual name, turns back, smirking. "Wow, wow, wowwwwww!" he barks back. Leo, excited, barks even more.

"Eeeech!" the guy then says, "I'm a monkey!" And makes ooh-ooh aah-aah noises, which Leonardo tries to imitate and, I'm glad to say, fails to.

"Say, 'I'm a monkey!'" he commands.

"Monkey!" says Leo. "Monkey!"

"You can't talk to him like that," I say, face blazing.

"I love the handicapped," he smirks. "I speaky their language." For a second—so briefly I'm not even sure it happened—he looks directly at me, squints, and puffs his cheeks out. Is he trolling me? My face is—contrasted with Yunji's delicate features—wide and chubby-cheeked. When I smile, my eyes practically disappear. Umma says there's a word in Korean, "charm pillows," for my kind of cheeks.

"Sounds like someone overdosed on their be-a-dick pills this morning." Yunji gets up from the bench. She stands right in his face. She's a head taller than he is; he steps back.

"Shut up, lesbo freak," he mutters.

Curley takes his girlfriend's hand, pulls her up to him. She's almost his exact height, which means Yunji is taller than a generic white girl. "Hey, you got keys, babe?" he purrs. "Let's bounce—tee time."

"Yeah," Rapunzel says. "You're damn lucky I keep a spare set in my purse." Leonardo starts barking again. As she hands Curley a set of keys attached to a BMW medallion, she looks over her shoulder at Leo with apprehension—like he might be one of those poisonous spiders that can jump out from behind a door—before climbing into the guy's gigantic black SUV, closing the door and emphatically auto-locking it.

There are, I'm thinking, some downsides to inclusion. When Leo went to a separate special-needs school there was some comfort in knowing he was among just kids with disabilities, in a place where everyone understood. His barking wasn't a big deal because half the other kids vocalized. Now, I'm suddenly seeing everyone else seeing Leo.

- - - - - - - - - - - -

Finally, Leo's aide shows up, walking from the direction of the Multi-modal Center. I want to say something to her about what just happened.

She's brisk, efficient. I'm a little annoyed when she looks past Leo and says, "I'm Ginger the para—is this Leonardo Kim?"

"It's really nice to meet you, *Ginger*," I hint, glancing over at Leo. She's not going to be a worthwhile ally, I'm guessing. There are people who work with special ed kids because they are called to, but too many just do it as a job. "Bye, *Leo*." I give him a hug, which he squirms out of. "I'm Leo," I whisper.

"I'm Leo!" he cries.

Ginger cracks a smile, looks at him for the first time. "Hi, Leo."

I give Leonardo another hug, which he pushes away, again. I don't care. It's important for me for every new therapist, teacher, sitter, whoever, to see that Leonardo is part of a family, the center of our family, and is loved.

Ginger scoops up his knapsack, tries to lead him away. Leonardo digs his heels in. Her eyes widen with uncertainty. I wonder if she's more used to those kids who wordlessly obey.

"You should walk in *front* of him," I tell her. "He won't run away."

He follows. Too closely, of course, which flusters her again, but she'll just have to get used to him, get to know him. A dozen steps out, he turns to glance back at me. "Nuna keep me safe," he says.

To Ginger, this probably just sounds like gibberish. It is indeed a "scripted" phrase, one Leo has come up with on his own or has heard someone else say, and now he repeats it incessantly.

"Come on, Leo," she says, clearly relieved he's on the move. She's in front and can't see my heart exploding: he looked back at me! He looked for *me*.

I can't wait to tell Umma and Appa about this. Leo knows on some level that I indeed will keep him safe. I love it. I check my watch. An hour plus change to the late bus. It's nice out. I could probably just sit here and do my homework.

I turn to Yunji. As always, Leonardo is on my mind. I also like that she smiled and waved to him as he left.

"Shouldn't we report that guy for his teasing Leo—and using a homophobic slur—to the principal?"

Yunji looks at me and laughs.

"What's so funny?" I ask.

"Nothing. Curley has a mean nickname for everyone, it's just the way things are here. He's a dick and there's nothing we can do about it."

"It's against the school anti-LGBTQ hate speech code, though," I say. "I read it on the website."

"Someone's done their homework." She rolls her eyes, clearly brushing me off. "By the way, I'm not a lesbian, I'm not even bi. I'm not even bi-curious. So don't get any ideas." She laughs lightly.

I'm more stuck on the Curley guy's dumb Asian driver comment, his smirk of superiority as he delivers those boring lines he's obviously used on other people. "What kind of person does that *and* makes fun of a kid with disabilities?" Newly fired up, I stand. "Let's go report him to the principal."

"Uh, no," she says.

"Why not?"

She turns. "You're new here. But do you know who owns all the businesses in Pecan Plaza, like, the buildings?"

"Didn't you just say that's your parents' business?"

She does her own bark. "Far from it. The Chois were the first to start a business in Sunnyvale. They opened the dry cleaner. That was fine; Sunnyvale needs a dry cleaner. But then when Koreans started coming out here from the city en masse, the white people fought to keep us out. Those dumb parking meters at Pecan Plaza charging customers to park! They made it hard to start a business and made it hard for our customers. The worst was banks wouldn't loan to Koreans. People had to use *kyae* money—"

"Kyae?"

"It's like a poker kitty, where everyone puts their money in and one person at a time takes it out. That's the unofficial Korean neighborhood loan association."

"Ah."

"But even still, the business properties in Sunnyvale are almost all owned by Curley & Sons, and they corralled all the Koreans into Pecan Plaza, keep us out of the picturesque downtown. Even when you have money, you have to suck up to them so they'll even deign to overcharge you rent. They are racist AF, but we have to stay in the lines so we don't get kicked out."

"That's awful," I blurt.

"Some Koreans like it that way—one-stop shopping. I think my parents' business, especially because my dad's so good, could compete outside of Pecan Plaza though—he and his team are great and they charge so little. Around here there's no barbershop, even. There's a single expensive old-lady salon, Christyanne's, and like a hundred of those places where you can get balayage highlights. That's not what people our age want or can afford. Actually, I *know* he could succeed elsewhere."

"So why don't you move?"

"We could." She shrugs. "Maybe after I graduate. Who knows if it'll be different anywhere else. My parents' turn in the kyae came up last year, so they used it to do some upgrades, including punching out the back for our hagwon."

I'm still thinking about Curley, though. "What he did was clearly against the honor code." Yunji rolls her eyes again and leaves without saying goodbye. She has big chains on her black ankle boots. They make a jangling noise like spurs as she heads to the student parking lot. I turn around and head back to the school. I might be new, but then let me be a breath of fresh air. Why should we let Curley be like some junior Mafia boss and run the school just because of who his dad is?

Ten

There are no kids in the office, and most of the staff is packing up to go home—half the lights are already out, like the life is leaking out of the school. Principal Gerard has gone already. I can see the assistant principal through the window in her door. When I say I'd like to talk to her, her secretary makes me wait. I sit there for ten, twenty minutes. Then I'm allowed in.

She shakes her head when she figures out I am talking about Curley. I have a sudden realization that the plaque in the computer lab is Curley's family. So is the Makers Room with the 3D printer and laser cutting presses, the video studios. They donated all those expensive things.

The assistant principal asks pointedly if I was a troublemaker at my last school. It's hard for me not to laugh in outrage and disbelief. An "excuse me?" slips out, which she takes as a challenge to her authority. She says she'll be keeping an eye on me. Through all this, I somehow miss the late bus home.

The secretary, Mrs. Alston, who has kind eyes, lets me use the school phone to call Umma.

"At least you're not like all the kids who are glued to their phone twenty-four seven," she says, handing me a cordless receiver that smells vaguely like hair.

"What's hawk-won?" I ask Umma. She doesn't ask why I missed the bus.

"I don't know," she says.

"It's Korean," I add. "At school, Yunji, this girl from the haircut place, said her mom runs a hawk-won there after school."

"Ah," says Umma. Here she says something that sounds like *hawk-won* but also doesn't sound that way at all: "*Hahg-wun.* Cram school."

"To cram for what?"

"SATs, good grades, college."

"Why would you need a special school for that?"

"In Korea, the college entrance exams are a bigger deal—there's one test, that's it. So people start studying really early; they get tutors and things."

"How do you know all this?"

"Appa." She pauses, as if trying to decide how much to tell me. "That's one of the reasons he left Korea to study here: the unreasonable pressure."

"Hah!" I let out an almost Leo-like bark at the idea of Appa fleeing academic pressure. He's the one so crazy-insistent on me going to Harvard or Yale even though he and Umma met at a small liberal arts school that's hardly the Ivy League. He keeps talking about how the economy is so uncertain for people my age, how going to an elite school is one of the few ways to distinguish myself to employers and to medical schools. Umma has always been, "pursue whatever makes you happy or a better person."

When you're a kid, you don't know at all which advice is best *for you*, and kind of have to guess. Shauntae, my brutally honest friend, said, "For better or worse, your dad *needs* you to succeed. Because of Leo."

"Maybe *for* Leo," I said. Would it matter, anyway? Like when someone becomes the president of the United States, do we care why they did it? For whom they did it?

Everyone says these are the most important years, that they set the stage for adulthood, so don't mess them up. But I won't know what it's like to be fifty until I am, well, fifty. See, we only go through this once, and who's to say?

- - - - - - - - - - - -

The walking therapist rents a block of time at a place called YogaTone, which has a giant stone Buddha out front and smells like incense inside. I hope the smell didn't bug Leo.

Ginger brings Leo out and tells us that indeed he did a good job in therapy today, i.e. no spitting, no peeing in his pants—apparently things he had done earlier in the day at school. Umma blanches at the school news, but I remind her it's just the first day, Leo is getting the lay of the land. It's all new, he's excited. I still wish Ginger would get a clue and talk *to* Leonardo and not about him like he's the Buddha statue or an obedience-school puppy. But, whatever this walking therapy is, even just getting in the car, Leo's joints seem less rigid; he's less robotic than the way he normally moves.

I buckle him in. Umma hands me his seizure meds, then a bottle of water, the top already cracked open. I was the one who taught him how to swallow pills, and I'm quite proud of it. He used to have crazy tantrums over taking his pills. Umma would crush the pills and mix them with water, Appa would often have to hold him in a bear hug as he cried, and Umma would tip the liquid in or use a syringe and squirt it in. Watching Leo cry and be force-fed the pill-water was almost unbearable to me. When they weren't looking, I dunked my clean finger in the water and put it to my tongue—ugh, it was terribly bitter. No wonder he hated taking those. I scoured the internet and found a social media post with the most interesting information: pills float. So the whole thing with people tossing back pills on TV was wrong. You needed to put the pill in your mouth, add water, put your head *forward*. That way the pill will float nicely into the back of your throat—all you have to do is swallow. Easy peasy. Umma didn't want me to put my hand in his mouth (he had recently bitten a dental assistant pretty badly), so I instead took his own hand and showed him how to push the pill into the back of his throat and use his other hand to tip his head forward. He has muscle memory now. When I put the pill in his mouth, he pushes it back just like I taught him. I pour a swallow of water into his mouth. He tips his head forward, the pill floats, like a twig on a river, right up into his throat.

But this is what makes me mad about adults. Even in the rush to help Leo, people seem to not stop to consider that he has his own feelings. Why wouldn't he?

Leo is bouncing in his seat. He gets a dark look for a split second, and the next thing I know, I see a hand, fingers out, in my peripheral vision, coming for my face. It makes a juicy sound on contact.

"Oww!" I can't help saying. I used to do tae kwon do when I was little and was pretty good at it; we did endless blocking drills to stop punches. But for some reason, every time, I sit there like a dummy when Leonardo hits me.

Umma steps on the brakes. We all pitch forward, then back. "Leo!" she says. "No hitting!"

"I got this, Umma," I say. He's just too excited. I know that. I have, occasionally, felt this too: just overwhelmed, even with love for something, like maybe a little kitten, and you just want to squish it. But you never would. But someone like Leo, well, none of us wants to admit it, he might.

I pull out his NAD tablet from his backpack. I pick ACTIVITIES. A bingo-like grid appears:

SEE A MOVIE	PLAY OUTSIDE
SEE A FRIEND	TAKE A BATH
SHOPPING	SWIMMING
VIDEO GAME	HELP
MOMMY	EAT

I enlarge the picture of the shopping cart and he immediately reaches for it, poking at it with his finger.

"Shopping . . . shopping . . . shopping . . ." says the computer voice. Umma, despite herself, laughs.

"All right," she says, putting the car into motion. "We could pick up some stuff for dinner."

- - - - - - - - - - - -

CostCut! Leo's Shangri-La.

Leonardo gets out, plants his two feet down on the asphalt of the parking lot, looks up at the familiar logo. He knows where he is.

Inside, Leonardo starts hopping in place, shaking his fingers like he has water droplets on them. In the city, people would often be startled by the sudden movements, but then realize they aren't in immediate bodily danger and do what city people do: keep going about their business. Here, people stare—and keep staring.

"What's wrong with him?" says a little boy.

"I don't know, but keep back," his mother whispers, but we can still hear it. "He may be mentally ill."

I hand Leonardo his NAD, hoping when they hear the computerized voice they'll realize Leo just needs a little support and understanding. But he leaves the NAD in my hand and starts making his barking noise, which makes mother and son swivel their heads around. The son looks terrified and clings to the mom. Why isn't the mom saying something to him, like, well, maybe this boy is a little different and that's okay?

I shoot the mom a death-ray stare, until she sees me, then looks away, ushering her son past in haste, turning his body away from us, as if trying to keep him from looking at a bloody crime scene.

"Some people should consider whether they are setting a good example for their children," I say, full-voiced. "That maybe someone has a *disability* and they need to do a little dance or vocalize in the CostCut aisle." Umma shoots me a look. They've always taught me, first and foremost, to be polite. But this protectiveness I have around Leo runs hot, right under the surface of my skin, so easily activated. The world is built as if only normal people exist—and that makes me furious. I feel that Umma and Appa go too far with the politeness sometimes, apologizing, practically in advance, as if Leo—his noises, his bulk, his wonky digestion that can cause farts, his inability to comprehend other people—is an inconvenience. Inconvenience to whom? A bunch of strangers? What about a world that is set up to be an inconvenience to *him*?

The CostCut is huge like an airplane hangar, piled high with any kind of stuff you might ever need: food, clothes, furniture, jewelry, craft supplies, sports stuff—there's even a gasoline station out back. As I understand it, each CostCut is absolutely identical. The deli section is always at the far end and to the left. The clothes are at three o'clock. Fine jewelry and video games in a center aisle. They all have the same red carts with the same logo, even the parking lots look the same. Sameness is great for Leo.

Umma doesn't actually have things she needs to buy right now. We're just "shopping" for Leo.

"We have a basement now, we can really do this up," I tell Umma, and point to a tower of toilet paper. "Leo, can you get us one?"

Leonardo beams. He walks over, grabs the package, sends it tumbling like a boulder into our extra-large cart. He's left the other part of the tower a little askew, like Chichén Itzá, which I straighten after we pass. Leo actually likes doing chores if they are simple and he knows what's expected of him.

By the refrigerator case, an aproned lady stands behind a griddle, handing out toothpicked samples of something called Camp Sausage.

Here, there's a bunch of Korean grannies jousting with their elbows, taking two or three at a time, despite the sign that says One Sample Per Customer Please. There's one tiny end piece left.

"Do you want some sausage? Go get it, Leo—that one's yours."

I cheer him on as, with catlike quickness, he beats a granny to that last sample. He takes it off the stick and opens his mouth wide like a cartoon cat about to drop a tail-caught mouse in. From this angle, I get a view of Leo's second row of teeth poking out of his soft palate, an untidy row of white stones. They are apparently caused by the very anti-seizure meds I just gave him and that he takes so trustingly. They look tender, bursting out of his gums.

So many of Leo's problems are problems from outer space: weird brain? Second row of teeth? Can't deal with certain sounds and smells? (What's the cure for that?)

Leonardo often hums while he chews, when he is eating something he likes. Sometimes, he makes up little tunes that sound something like *Mmmmyomyomyomyomnum num!* that are so cute. I take a quick video that I upload to Instapix.

L at his favorite activity!

I hope this doesn't sound like virtue signaling, but I make sure there's a Leo pic about every ten pics on my Instapix. I call him "L" for privacy and set all my posts to "friends and friends of friends." I notice Shauntae has "liked" all of my posts but "loved" the "L" ones.

Leonardo lets the toothpick drop to the ground.

"Leo," I say, sternly. "Don't litter." I point to a brown bag they are using as garbage next to the display. Leonardo amiably picks up the toothpick and puts it where I'm pointing.

"Do you want to go home now?" I ask him.

"Go home now," he says. Umma's and my shoulders relax at the same time.

Every so often, things are predictable and safe, even for a moment. Leonardo is happy, we know what he wants. He's calm and happy and in accord with the world. In those minutes I feel like I can relax the grip of my anxious mind. The trick we've learned is when he likes a place, he wants to stay too long, until he gets tired and cranky, so we need to cut it short while he is still having a good time, but not too soon—or too late.

This was a nice amount of time for an outing. He did some nice self-regulation so that we could make it into a success.

Umma and I happily lead the way to the exit. Then Leo just stops.

"Excuse me! I'd like to get by here!"

We happen to be in the middle of the aisle, just as a CostCut enthusiast / megashopper with one of those wide-load things that looks like a forklift pulls up behind us: pallet of outdoor furniture, propane tanks, an Egg grill. The pallet, much wider than a cart, makes it impossible to maneuver around Leo.

She makes huffy noises of impatience. White woman, I note.

"Let's move, Leo," I say. He doesn't seem to hear me. Sometimes he does stuff like this for no reason. Well, no reason we can discern.

"Did you give him his medicine?" Umma asks worriedly.

"Of course I did!" I say. "You saw me!"

"Excuse me," says the woman, openly angry now. If the pallet had a horn, she'd be honking it.

"Come on, Leo," I say, trying not to sound too desperate—why should *we* always have to scramble out of the way of other people? Sometimes Leo gets mesmerized by stuff, visually. Some people stop to smell the roses. Leo stops to gaze. Maybe the row of labels on the seemingly endless display of maraschino cherries is what's occupying him right now. He's staring at it like it's a work of art.

"Excuse me? Like, really?" She turns to another person who has inadvertently entered the aisle behind her, increasing the logjam. "Can you believe how rude? These foreigners."

"Yeah, immigrants," agrees the other person, white—I don't even have to look. I'm preoccupied with what to do next. How to get out of here in the least upsetting way possible.

I hate this chaos feeling. This trapdoor, stomach-punch, the iceberg of panic and fear and blame that we all three carry, and when something happens with Leo, pieces of it fly off like shrapnel. "Shut up, racist lady!" I say, gathering up all the cold shards in my heart and flinging them— at least safely away from us—at her.

We were *so close* to a successful afternoon.

Eleven

At breakfast, Umma tells me, "I will be picking up Leonardo in the afternoon to take him to Dr. Shah." It's impossible to know if what happened at the CostCut yesterday was just a quirky Leo thing or if he'd had an "absence" seizure. After I'd said that thing to the lady, coincidence or not, Leo started moving. He did not have a tantrum, even with all the upset vibes all around. I personally think Umma is overreacting.

We don't say anything to each other about our feelings, still raw. But honestly, "Did you give Leonardo his meds?" sounds to me a lot like, "You messed up and now he's having a seizure!" Even now when she says, "Dr. Shah will need to know, because if he didn't have his meds that's one thing, but if he's having seizures that break through the meds, that's something else."

"I would never lie about giving Leonardo his meds!" I protest. "Nor would I *ever* forget something that important!"

"I didn't say you did." Umma opens and shuts her eyes in a world-weary way that makes me sad—and also irritates me.

It was because of the impatient lady that I felt too rushed to do a check for strabismus on Leo's eyes to confirm if he was having a seizure. I suppose calling her a racist and then telling her, "Would you just wait a mother-fracking second?" was not the most helpful thing to do. But her "really?" just got to me. Like, she calls us foreigners and can't wait for a whole sixty seconds? And the other lady: "Immigrant"? We're all American-born!

The *Sunnyvale Tribune* had a story about how these ducks that live in the river wanted to get to the fountain in Founders Park. Someone driving by called the police, who stopped traffic in the main traffic circle, a huge line of smiling people sitting in their cars for an hour so the mommy duck could get a dozen ducklings across. What good people they are. What patience. But only for ducks!

In the most lightning-bolt-strike of fortune, the other person who had also become jammed in the aisle had been Mr. Dongbang. I was so distracted I only recognized him by his black Bomb Haircuts T-shirt. He offered to help the woman back up her pallet and exit via the other end of the aisle; he even pulled it around for her. In the weirdest way, there had been something so comforting about another Korean face. His eyes are kind and caring like Appa's. But also with something different. Like he had a calm appraisal of the situation. Nothing more, nothing less. No judgments—not on us, not on the impatient lady I'd just called a racist, not on Leonardo blocking the aisle. He just saw a knot in the flow and unknotted it. He didn't even stick around to say hi to us or anything. Maybe he didn't recognize us. No, actually, with Leo, he had to have known who we were.

"Appa will be at work, as usual, this afternoon. You can be okay being home by yourself?"

"Sure, Umma." I have neglected to remove the frost from my voice; I'm just not a big enough person. So on top of being mad at Umma, I'm a little mad at myself.

- - - - - - - - - - - -

At lunch I sit with Calvin again. I bring my own Terra, Gone series book, and after a little "hey how are you" chitchat, we both settle down to read and eat. We are occupying, geographically, the same table as yesterday. The table seems to be his, as if he's planted a flag on it. No one even glances at it as a possibility as they flow on to the other places. I can see why he likes this table. It is like being Switzerland: in the precisely unassigned airspace between the two large, almost dominant Asian groups, farthest away from the jocks and their fluttery girls. I will privately call this place CalTab. Calvin's Table: studiedly neutral, no need for a military.

But also, there are no other Black students in our entire grade, maybe even in the school. I wonder if that makes Calvin lonely, or if he notices.

I'm of course fascinated by Yunji Dongbang. I steal glances over my book. Today she's wearing ripped black fishnets with sleek black ankle boots that have a slash for the big toe, like those Japanese socks that allow you to wear flip-flops. In a black boot, it makes it look a little like she has cloven hooves, not feet. On most people, wearing a camel-toe boot would look weird. On her it looks great: edgy, ninja-like.

Adding to the fascination is the fact that her table, which I call in my mind the Size-Large Asian Table, has grown by one more: the handsome guy with the surfable-wave hair. His haircut still looks great; it's gleaming like it's been cast from glass.

Leonardo lumbers in, bringing up the rear of his small group: a student in the tall, black all-body wheelchair; the blond girl who wears pretty, paisley dresses; their respective aides.

With my bionic eyes, I measure the vector from Curley's table to Leo's, calculate the probability of a trajectory that will bring Leo in sight of him. I'm almost hoping he'll try something—*Special Ed!*—I want to see what the aides will do. I need to know they are on Leo's side.

It's the wave-haired guy who crosses Leo's line of vision. When he walks by to get to the hydration station, Leo's eyes light up—and he gets up, too. When Leonardo was little, he was always fascinated by conventionally attractive women. I remember going to some wedding for a classmate of Appa's and how big Leo's eyes were, just looking. We were, I think, like five and seven. But more recently he seems fascinated by male peers. I wonder if it's because his world is overwhelmingly feminine—me, Umma, his teachers, his aides, his therapists, a bunch of Gingers, Marys, Ashleys, and Mrs. So-and-Sos.

The guy is wearing a tank top, which is something Umma and Appa would definitely not let me wear to school if I were a guy. They wouldn't even let me wear shorts at City High—everyone wore shorts, especially in late spring when it got so hot and there was no air-conditioning, but Umma and Appa agreed it was disrespectful.

What would they think of this boy? A couple of the guys at the jock table hail him as he walks by. He has a certain something that I see that other people also see. Like, he knows how to *do* stuff, unlike the rest of us. Like the guy's already been tempered by the outside world and can face challenges. He can probably fix a car, MacGyver a clean-water drinking system, do his own taxes. If there were a zombie apocalypse, the jock table would be the first one I'd avoid—they might be number one in school, but they are for sure the most pampered, dumb, looks-good-but-useless-in-a-crisis group. This boy could kill zombies. He moves with a kind of self-possession. Then it hits me—here is pure evidence that he does not care what others think. As opposed to trying to be liked, or acting like he does not care what others think—which is just one of a thousand poses people try, to mask their mooshy vulnerable real selves. This is a true superpower.

Do I call him Tank Top Guy or Wave Hair Guy in my head?

Leo's up and following him the way he follows me. In fact, he gets too close and actually does give him a "flat tire." The guy whirls around, but his face does not look scared, only surprised. Most people when surprised look panicky for a split second, and when they see Leonardo looming behind them, their panic almost always increases. This guy, when he sees Leo, his face lights up into a smile.

"Hey, buddy!" he says. "How's it going?"

"How's it going?" Leonardo cries.

"Go ahead, bro." He lets Leonardo go first at the hydration station. Leonardo is delighted. I can see it in the bounce in his step as he returns to his table, practically skipping, leaving behind a trail of sloshed water. I'm about to leap up and wipe it so no one slips on the wet spot on the floor, but the guy is already there, kneeling and wiping. I watch a little enviously as he returns to the table, several cups of water in hand like a waiter, doling them out to his friends.

I'm now Georgia Kim, Private Investigator. From behind my book,

I continue to spy. The two Asian tables are very different. The smaller one is quiet, all boys.

The other one, the kids are as noisy and boisterous as the jock table, maybe even more so. I see the girls with the mermaid hair, whom I call the Mermettes, looking over from time to time shocked and a little annoyed that some other group, not theirs, is commanding attention. Normally only the dominant group, always white, got to do that. *Look at us! We're young! We're beautiful. We have all the fun.* All the other populations: band, female athletes, nerds, B-list popular kids, artsy kids, AV club, et al.—the leftovers know how to fold themselves more compactly, arrange themselves in relation. The popular kids will always be the popular kids—it was probably this way in ancient Egypt. And the rule has always been, have your fun, plebes, but keep it down, out of the way of the main attraction.

"I don't mean this in a mean way," Calvin says, smiling. "But why are you reading that? I mean, you're in honors English."

The Terra, Gone series has a trademarked neon-green cover. Terra is a sexy, raceless alien who battles evil forces. The plots are all predictable, the writing clunky. As Appa would say, "No redeeming value." I love them.

"Can you keep a nerd secret?"

"Of course!"

"I can't read these at home. My father thinks they are trash. I mean, they are kind of trash."

Calvin laughs. "So you need to smuggle books to read them at school. That's next level. My folks just moved here for better schools, and they figure I'll take care of the rest. You should let me borrow one and see if they notice, as a test."

"Wait," I say. "Why aren't *you* in Great Books with me?" Great Books is the honors class that leads up to taking AP English. Calvin is now reading *The Invisible Man* on his own. Way ahead of what we're reading: *The Legend of Sleepy Hollow*.

He shrugs. "Whoever are the powers that be didn't think I belonged there, obviously. My mom made a fuss, but then said we have to pick our battles."

"If it makes you feel better," I say, "we're reading *The Legend of Sleepy Hollow*."

"Washington Irving?" he says. "For real?"

I nod, sadly.

"Hawthorne, I could get. Melville for sure. Washington Irving, uh-uh."

"Good for Halloween, I guess." I had scanned the list for Great Books for titles by Asians and *Farewell to Manzanar* is the only one I could find—by Jeanne Houston, but, technically, her husband, James Houston, wrote it, "while I cried my story into the microphone of the tape recorder."

"Well," he says. "In regular English we're reading *Huck Finn*, although the teacher is making us do the voices."

"The voices?"

"You know, the N-word voices."

"Um, you mean the dialect voices. Of Jim."

"Exactly. And *I* get to read them." He looks at me like I should understand. And I do.

"I'm so sorry," I say. "You don't deserve that."

He smiles, wryly. "No one does."

- - - - - - - - - - - -

After school, I pull a Leonardo and just stand there, let the mass of bodies flow noisily around me. It's only now the school has any scent—sweat, expensive colognes, shampoo that comes in the flavor of gum, a really gross vape pen flavor (maple?), hormones. People growling at me to get out of the way makes me want to stand even more widely. I know Leo's not in the building, and I imagine that I feel his absence (or not). I say a little prayer that on his visit to Dr. Shah he won't get bored or irritable and that there won't be a screechy baby in the waiting room—another thing that, like dogs, almost always sets him off. I hope Umma remembered to pack his string stim toy and his tablet. Busy doctors and their forever-waiting rooms are other things not set up for Leos of the world.

What I'm thinking about mostly though is that Umma didn't ask me to come along. A few days earlier I heard her and Appa talking, as they do in the mornings, still in bed. I was going to the bathroom and could hear from behind their door.

"Let's remember this is such an important year for Georgia—these grades will make or break her college application."

Is this why? Less time with Leo means more time for my college applications?

As the crowd thins, I know I should hustle to make the bus. But my feet have turned to cement. I am literally standing in the hall the way Leonardo stood in CostCut yesterday. Sometimes, I feel like I know, in a small way, what Leo's sensory blackouts and seizures feel like, how the wires of his brain just fizz and short circuit. Right now, right here, the halls are so large, they feel like they are closing in from the top, like the way trees seem to form a cathedral on the road. Seconds ago it had been the slamming of locker doors, the voices, the irregular ringing of phones, ringtones foreign and not. The movement to and fro of people. The clip-clop of a secretary speed-walking by, constrained in a tight knee-length skirt. If I soften my eyes it all happens all at once: the roar, the colors, the movement, the maple vape smell. I don't mind it, actually. It's like being in a cocoon against chaos. I prefer this cocoon feeling to the more normal Georgia feeling of standing here worrying kids are thinking, *What's that new girl doing, just standing there?* or *How can an Asian girl be so chunky?*

- - - - - - - - - - - -

I've been waiting for the bus for almost half an hour when Yunji walks by. I'm so startled by her, that dramatic rooster-comb of hair, I blurt, "Hi."

"Hey," she says.

Then I add: "Where are you headed?"

"Where do you think?" she snorts. "Home. Where are you going?"

"Home as well." I'm thinking of what it will be like, that brightly lit but empty house, and something warm and sad blooms in me. Maybe I'll FaceCall with Shauntae. But she'll have marching band practice—City High improbably got a second audition for a TV show, *Battle of the (HS) Bands.*

"I think you kind of super missed the bus." Yunji cocks her head like she's not quite sure what to make of me.

I shrug.

"Where do you live?"

"Sycamore Estates."

"Ooooh, fancy," she says.

It seems of no relevance to mention we live in the absolute poorest part of Sycamore Estates. "You don't take the bus, do you?"

"I don't. I get a ride."

"Where do you live?"

She looks at me carefully. "In Sunnyvale, where else?"

Up close, her eyeliner is drawn on so thick that her eye looks like a drawing of an eye over her real eye, an Egyptian hieroglyph. What I thought was an armful of black bangles are actually hair elastics. She takes one off, then decides to take another, and corrals her thick hair into a giant top-knot, revealing, of course, in all its starkness, her shaved scalp, the dangly gold earring whose beads are, if you look closer, a bunch of gilded skulls strung together. "Where's your brother?"

"My mom is taking him to the neurologist—he may have had a seizure in CostCut yesterday."

"Oh, I'm sorry," she says. I wonder if her dad mentioned it to her or not.

"It's okay. He has a seizure disorder."

"Still, that must be tough," she says, and she sounds sincere. "He seems like a great kid."

"He is." I don't know why I predicted she'd say something like, "So what's it like to have a brother like *that*?" But then I remember the quiet can-do-ness of Mr. Dongbang.

"Your dad was there—he helped people steer around Leo."

"Not surprised. CostCut is his church."

"What do you mean?"

"Oh, just that he's there like all the time when he's not working. He doesn't even always buy stuff. I think he probably does it to get away from Umma and me and the shop and stuff."

I don't know how to take this.

"So how long have you lived in Sunnyvale?" I ask.

"Pretty much all my life."

"That's how you know everyone. At school."

She looks at me. "Have you been spying on me?"

"No. But I noticed your table at the cafeteria has maybe even more kids than the jock table."

She laughs. "Yeah. Asian power. A bunch of us grew up together. Like once Pecan Plaza became mostly Korean, the whole burb became like a beacon to other Koreans. Where *you* live has always been white, though."

"That's what it seems like," I say. "It's a little weird after growing up in the city. Like, none of our neighbors have come to say hi. One of them has already complained about Appa not mowing the lawn. 'But it's fall!' he said. 'The grass will die soon!'"

"Ah-ah, you just said 'Appa'—you do know some Korean," Yunji says, triumphantly. She's so nosy—and perceptive. "So what's it like growing up in the city?"

I tell her about our building, about Shauntae, about our grody high school that didn't really have any athletic facilities except for the basketball court with the wavy, warped floor.

"But that must have been so nice, not needing your parents to drive you everywhere."

"We did go everywhere by subway and bus," I say. "Starting in high school we get special passes and take the subway to school. After school we were supposed to go home, but the pass gives you one ride to anywhere."

"That is cool. I would probably just stay on the subway forever and ride it to wherever after school."

"Shauntae and I have done that," I said. "If I didn't have to watch

Leo, we'd go to the Indian neighborhood where they had the best snacks. Or if we didn't have enough money we'd go to the stop that had the sandwich place right on the platform, then we could just take the subway back for free."

"I can't imagine that kind of freedom. Honestly, why did you move here then?"

"Schools," I say. "Something different." I don't want to say the something different is Leo.

"What do you do after school? When Leo's not around?" she asks me.

"Same thing I did back home—" I correct myself. "I mean, back in the city: my homework." Most days, to tell the truth, Shauntae and I actually went straight home. We're both nerds. The biggest obstacle was avoiding some of the bullies who'd loiter by the subway station to shake us down—easy targets—for our lunch money or phones. What we learned to do was exit the station at a full run. This way, we could duck into Omar's until the coast was clear.

If Umma and Leo were out, first thing I'd spot was the Dutch cargo bike secured with a giant fabric-covered chain in front of the building, which would mean Aunt Clara was there. Sometimes she'd have a plate of cut-up fruit, or walnuts (brain food) to dip in honey, a tiny cocktail fork on the side so I could eat while studying.

While I studied, she did her bookkeeping on her laptop, which she docked with an extra-huge monitor that Umma and Appa had set up for her, like a workstation. She had to listen to music while she worked, she said, because what she did was so tedious. I would think music was distracting, but she said, no, the work she was doing was a lot like factory work, but on the computer. Also, what she played wasn't music but something she called binaural beats, which she said helped focus. To me it was just a pleasant white noise, like an arm of sound encircling my shoulders invisibly. Now it's going to be me and the huge, echoey house. Clean but sterile, devoid of life. I feel a lump growing in my throat, like those capsules you throw in water that burst into huge shapes.

"Hey!"

I jerk my head around. Yunji's staring at me, hands on her hips. "Well, do you want to come to hagwon?"

Again, that word. She adds: "The late bus won't be here for like another hour."

"What does hagwon actually mean?"

She peers at me more closely, like I'm in an exhibit of animals that look somewhat familiar but slightly strange—tapirs, capybaras, manatees. "It literally means 'academic place.' It's like the Breakfast Club—but for nerds. Good snacks."

"Let me call my mom," I tell Yunji, then remember I don't have a phone. It costs a lot of money to get a screen fixed, I learned recently. "Um, actually—"

"What's the number?" Yunji already has her phone out. It's a Samsung, the screen is also spiderwebbed and cracked, which fits with her punk aesthetic, I guess. She dials and hands the phone to me. I gingerly start to peck at the screen and look at my fingertip. She laughs.

"The cracks are fake—they're printed on the screen protection cover."

Umma picks up on the first ring, tells me, a bit tersely, Leonardo is going to see the doctor soon. I tell Umma about hagwon, but wonder if it's going to be easier for her if I just go home, do the predictable thing.

"This is the girl from Bomb Haircuts? Do you want to go?" Umma asks.

"Yes and yes," I say.

"All right. I have her number now, too. Appa or I will pick you up depending on who gets done first." It's harder to read emotions over the phone, but I think she actually sounds relieved. I will be doing a wholesome activity, not sitting by myself in the empty house. One less thing to worry about.

"Let's do this," I say, and Yunji grins. There's a dark-haired person making his way across the massive parking lot. Yunji waves.

It is the wave-haired guy. His name is Zeus. King of the gods. Of course it is. Even weirder, he takes out some keys and pops open the door of a Kia Sol.

"Georgia, what a pretty name," he says.

"How is it you have a license already?" I ask.

"Got held back a year," he says, grinning sunnily.

"Yeah, right," I say. "A real dummy."

Yunji shoots me a look. *What?* I telegraph back.

Zeus regards me. He opens and shuts his eyes, one deliberate blink. Other than that, his face is a polished blank. Over at the pickup waiting area, Calvin is getting into a Lexus SUV.

Twelve

Zeus pulls into Pecan Plaza, continues past the last store (dog groomer), and pulls around the back. I guess I never really considered stores had fronts and backs, though now that I thought about it, the term "storefront" made more sense. The backs are cabin-looking structures with drab and generic steel doors, each heavily reinforced further with roll-down gates, doors with huge padlocks. From the back, Bomb Haircuts is a long rectangular building, deceptively longer than it looks from the front. Arirang Market across the way has a similar elongated shape that ends in a loading dock.

For Bomb Haircuts, this space is a kind of bunkhouse, with daybeds and couches on one side, a counter on the other with a two-burner hot plate, a beat-up brass-colored pot, a rice cooker with pink flowers on it—I'm noticing the little cup that catches excess steam in the lid is streaked with mold, like too many people were using it and no one thought to clean it. Closest to the curtained doorway, where I'd seen Yunji pop out from, are shelves of hair supplies: shampoo, gallon pump bottles of Dippity-do, the sea-blue Barbasol. The striped multi-canisters of shaving cream I recognize from CostCut, so big they look like stage props.

In the center of the hagwon room is a long table with a dozen chairs on each side. The ends of the table are divided into carrels, like at a library or a language lab.

"That's for people who need isolation to concentrate, or to simulate reality when taking a practice test."

"*The Matrix* reboot: Korean study hall," says Zeus. Right now his hair, except for a really stubborn sprig, is covered by his backward Wu-Tang Clan baseball cap. He looks like he's just come from the beach, not school, and even smells faintly salty. He is even more handsome up close. I keep (subtly) looking for flaws in his symmetrical face; even his eyebrows look naturally like the kind women would spend hours fluffing and waxing and shaping.

Yunji mentioned that her dad made this addition himself, with some friends.

This is where Yunji's mom, a.k.a. Mrs. Dongbang, runs her hagwon. She is the receptionist who brought Leo the water. The hagwon seems to be for all ages. There are three little kids, elementary age, seated around a small table, doing an art project of some sort.

"That's Jae-Ho Choi and Jung-won Yi. The little girl on the end is Piper. She's adopted and her parents are hoping she'll learn some Korean, but mostly they use the hagwon like a daycare. The mom has some high-powered job and is always late picking her up."

"This is a Korean school but you don't learn Korean here?"

"I do a class for the littles once a week. But I'm hardly a professor. There's a Saturday Korean school at church—I've been going there for four years. You guys go to church, right?"

Now I'm staring back at Yunji. I don't know how to "read" her— the punkette outside, or her interest in church, the Korean language, the fact she *teaches* in a study hall?

Umma and Appa used to take Leonardo and me to the United Methodist, and as a family we even worked on a Thanksgiving project to serve dinner to the homeless. But we started going less and less as Leo's behaviors and seizures got to be a problem. I didn't miss it. Also, Aunt Clara is Buddhist—a rebellion against their parents being strict Christians, Umma told me—and I kind of got into her lighting incense and praying to the female Buddha, Gwan Yin, just as much as those images of Jesus nailed to the cross.

"Well, Korean church is like a big family." She spins a few of her rubber bracelets / hair ties and laughs softly. I'm just about to say that sounds nice when she goes on: "And that's not necessarily in a good way. All the aunties are so nosy, everyone needs to know everyone's SAT scores. And all our lives we've been like siblings, but all of a sudden our parents are all, 'date each other!'"

She's still waiting. Like what I say about church is going to mean something. "We haven't quite . . . chosen which church yet," I say. "But we would go to a Methodist church."

"Then come to ours, the Korean Methodist Church and Institute. The Koreans at the other one are snobs."

"There's two Korean churches? Two Methodist churches?"

"There used to be only Korean First Methodist, but ours split off."

"So there's like a First Methodist but also a Second Methodist?" I say.

Yunji laughs like I've said something really witty. "Something like that—Koreans can be really competitive. Even with church, they want to have the best."

I feel like I've kind of gotten my bearings when the back door opens, and Calvin walks in.

Calvin?

"Orthodontist's appointment," he announces. "But just a three-second tightening."

He has nice, straight teeth. That was something I'd noticed right off. I didn't know he even had braces. He will show me later that he has "reverse braces": a few clear wires in front, most of the work is done in the back (actually kind of like the stores in Pecan Plaza) which explains his slight lisp. I imagine they are expensive—how nice to not have to deal with a bunch of hardware.

"That's cool, Calvin," says Zeus.

My "Hi, Calvin," seems to come too late, off-beat. He heads off to one of the "isolation" desks.

I thought someone was going to come in and tutor us; this is a school, after all. But we sit and study. Yunji's burrowed into one of the beanbag chairs in the corner. Zeus is sitting at the table, spinning a pen on his thumb like a propeller. It's quiet. Even the three little kids color carefully, noiselessly inside the lines.

- - - - - - - - - - - -

It's just the first week of school. I think Appa thought this suburban school would be more challenging, more college-prep-y, but even though, say, the chemistry lab has all new equipment, there's a mini planetarium, the 3D printers, the classes all have fewer kids, the halls are bright instead of dank and depressing, there's no more academics than at City High. It's definitely not Hamilton Academy, the private school in the city where Umma and Appa were thinking of sending me. There, all the teachers have master's degrees, they teach their language classes (including Mandarin!) as immersion classes with no English. Every year they have at least one winner at the National Science Fair. In middle school, I'd taken their entrance exam and qualified for admission. Appa had actually half joked that he and Umma were grateful I was a good student on my own because it would be tough to swing the money for all of Leo's stuff *and* an expensive private school.

There's a certain feeling of an arms race in our family. Umma feels if Leo's behaviors can be controlled, if he can learn a skill, perhaps he can continue to live at home, maybe find a very, very simple job somewhere. He gets to go to school until he's twenty-one, but after that, everything just drops out: all the school-based therapies, the Individualized Education Plan, it just stops. His doctor told us that most kids like Leo, with "low cognitive functioning" and a tendency toward violence, will most likely end up in institutions.

"It's safer for everyone," he'd said. He was the doctor who was always bugging me to join a sibling support group. I went, once, and sat around with a bunch of kids, and it seemed like the counselor was trying to get us to say we hated our siblings, we hated our lives with such stress. A lot of the kids did. Not a few of them said their parents had gotten divorced over it. But the one girl who haunted me the most, Lisa, cried when she said one day her brother disappeared, like he'd been beamed up by aliens in the middle of the night. He'd been taken to an institution, and the family psychologist had told her parents it would be easiest for everyone if they pretended like he'd never existed.

"I never got to say goodbye," she'd said, over and over again. The other kids looked at her like she was overreacting. I wanted to console her, tell her she wasn't crazy for wanting to live with her brother, even if he was violent. But I had such a thick feeling in my throat, like a rubber stopper stuck in there, like I was afraid if it got pulled out I'd start crying and never stop, all my juices would drain out and I'd just collapse into an empty husk. So I just stared at her like the rest of the kids and kind of hated myself for it, for not at least giving her a small smile, a nod, some smidge of solidarity. Would that have been so tough?

"I like having him at home," I had said to Dr. PhD. He'd stared.

"Most siblings feel at least a touch of resentment, possibly at the stress of how they have to be perfect, as to not burden their parents."

"I'm definitely not perfect," I'd said.

"But are you being honest when you say you really *enjoy* having your brother around?"

The whole time the doctor was talking about institutions, Leonardo had been sitting on the examining table, swinging his legs like a little kid. But with giant wide feet pointing almost painfully downward, massive adultish calves, his socks with the heel part bunched on top despite how many times we've shown him how to put them on.

"Um, Dr. Levitsky," said Umma. "Could we not talk about him, in front of him, as if he's not here?"

"What would you have me do, banish him to the hall?" said the doctor, exasperated. "How's that going to work? I don't have enough nurses to look after him." After a pause, he said, "He is functioning at the bottom one percent of children in his age group. He'll never hold a job or be able to live independently. These state institutions can be, well, rough, so I would start doing research now, get him on some waiting lists—they can be years long. If you can pay, there will be a lot more options. But one year at these places, the good ones, runs six figures."

I was glad Appa wasn't there that day. I know he loves Leo, and

I've seen him secretly crying over him. But he's such a rule follower. If some scientific person tells him the protocol is X, he'll follow it. If Leo living in a "home" is the next stage, there he'll go. Umma and I think differently. We both feel that maybe Leonardo scores terribly on tests because he can't sit still, that, really, we don't know what's in there and it's our job to find out.

That's why Leonardo has walking therapy almost every day after school, private speech-therapy sessions on the weekends.

- - - - - - - - - - - -

Mrs. Dongbang comes in with a tray of fruit, a knife, a box of tooth-picks. It looks like the beginning of a science project.

"Want to help?" Yunji asks me.

"Sure."

Yunji takes a small paring knife and peels the pear-apple the same way Aunt Clara does, in one long gracefully spiraling peel. Aunt Clara, however, can peel so thinly there's not even the smallest bit of white fruit clinging to the peel. Yunji chops it in rough, rhomboidal chunks, not Aunt Clara's perfect little wings. She hands me a piece and I eat it. It's sweet like an apple, with the cool graininess of a pear.

Yunji uses her fingernails to puncture and peel a few tangerines, arranges the fruit on a tray to give to the little kids. Then she cuts up a fruit that looks like a squat, orange tomato but is hard as a rock.

"What is this?" I ask.

"Persimmon," she says, handing me a piece. It's crunchy, but not apple crunchy, and sweet as candy. "You've never had one?"

"Nope."

"Wow," she says, shaking her head.

"Where are the Choco Pies?" Zeus says. He sits down next to Yunji. Probably closer than is absolutely necessary, I observe. I don't think they are officially a couple, but there's something proprietary about the way Yunji acts around him, so I keep my silly crush to myself.

"This girl has never eaten a *gam*," she says.

"Fruit is way too healthy," Zeus laughs. He digs around in his knapsack and produces a familiar blaze-orange bag of Korean shrimp chips. Appa loves those; I, on the other hand, as a nonfan of fishy flavors in general, can't think of a more loathsome flavoring for a chip.

"You read about that kid in England, right?" says Yunji. "Who only ate Pringles and white bread for like three months and went blind?"

Zeus takes a pencil from a cup on the table and pops the bag.

"I eat Korean food eighty percent of the time," he says. "So I'm eating like five times the vegetables as your average American already."

He offers the contents around (I politely pass) then peers inside intently. "Don't worry, we left you a few," Yunji says.

"Mrrrphh—" His voice is muffled from inside the bag. "Trying to see if this is one of my uncle's bags."

"You're stealing his shrimp chips?"

"Nah, it's not like that. He makes the bags."

"Makes them?"

Zeus rips it open so that the bag splits down the center. "See how there's a thin layer of aluminum here, like foil? It's Mylar. Sprayed on."

"Wait, is this *that* uncle?"

"Yep, the unemployable one. The guy who trained as a nurse but couldn't stop smoking."

"Nurses can smoke," I say.

"Yeah, but he kept sneaking smokes in the hospital—they use oxygen there. All that training. He just couldn't stop."

"Good thing he didn't blow up any patients," Yunji says.

"That, too."

"He worked as a car salesman too, right?"

"That didn't last too long. He's not a people person. Potato chip bags are going to turn out to be his niche, I think."

Yunji looks bored. I'm kind of fascinated. Occasionally, Appa's friends from college would pass through the city. They would always be doctors or professors who went to Harvard or Yale. One was a freaking nuclear physicist. Appa would proudly introduce this or that friend and later say, "After family, education is the most important thing." But then what about the Dongbangs, with their haircutting salon? Or Zeus, the kid who was held back a year and has a driver's license already. I never noticed before that the inside of potato chip bags are lined with foil. Before I know it, I've said it out loud.

Zeus looks pleased at the interest. "It's kind of brilliant if you think about it. Mylar does all that and it's also really light."

"Mylar—what they make balloons out of?"

"Yep," he says. "Exactly. Light and airtight, doesn't degrade in the presence of oils. The thing is, sometimes the machines aren't aligned right and it's sprayed on crooked or they miss spots, and then they have to throw the whole sheet away. We have tons of this at home."

"What do you do with it?"

"When I was smaller, I made robot and Tin Man costumes. Now, not so much."

Yunji tells me later that Zeus's uncle doesn't own the factory or the company, but is just an employee. "He was the first son in the family, the golden boy. I guess the pressure was too much for him. His wife walked out on him, but he's so charming he always has women around. Except when the kyae money ran out."

Ah, kyae, the money-loaning club—I remember a Korean word!

"His uncle ran off with the whole thing, running away with people's life savings. Probably back to Korea. I think a few people tried to kill him, like with guns, when he came back."

"So what happened?"

"Well, Zeus's dad is really well regarded—Zeus is a PK—"

"PK?" I need a foreigner's dictionary.

"Haha, sorry: preacher's kid. Park Moksanim was able to talk everyone down and he promised every penny his brother makes will go into paying back the kyae.

"It'll probably take a century. But in the meantime, Zeus's dad was reassigned to some church back in Korea, so Zeus lives with that uncle. Good thing, too: Zeus is super neat and cleans to relieve stress, and his uncle is a total slob, like maggots-living-in-the-garbage slob, when he's between women."

Zeus, who's been silent during this summary of his life, proffers me the shrimp-chip bag again. The smell, slightly fishy, is gross, but to be accommodating, I take a chip. It tastes mostly like salt and fat. It's not that bad—some things can taste better than they smell.

"Yunji-yah," says Mrs. Dongbang, sticking her head into the hagwon. "Let in the twins, the door is locked."

"Yes, Umma," she says, but rolls her eyes to us and mouths *you're welcome*. She leads two middle school–age kids, a boy and a girl, to the table.

"Who's she?" says the boy, looking at me.

"What's it to you?" I say, kiddingly, but he looks stricken.

"That's Georgia Kim, my friend," Yunji says. I hearten to the word *friend*. "Put your stuff away and get some fruit."

"Our driver already stopped at Lemonade," says the girl, who sounds like the queen of England and has a bearing to match it. "I got to have anything I want so I got the supermax combo. With pomegranate lemonade."

"Fine, don't have a snack then. Do you have homework?" Yunji looks annoyed at these two, twins: Chandi and Pandi.

"Hah, their mom thinks they're getting Kumon-type tutoring," Yunji whispers to us when the kids are squared away at the opposite end of the room. "But that's her own fault. She's never asked to see a schedule or something. I write up daily notes, but on days when I run out of time, she doesn't seem to notice. So I've stopped altogether—all that work that was probably going into the garbage. Also, the twins are driven here by a fancy car service. She's never even set foot in the place—it could be a sex dungeon for all she knows!"

"Good thing they're so rich," Zeus says. "They pay full tuition for those two, which basically pays for the rest of us, ha ha."

"And Calvin's parents," Yunji whispers.

"Yeah, what's up with Calvin?" I want to know.

"His parents admire the Asian way of studying," Yunji says. "He even went to a Chinese charter school when he was little. I guess he speaks some Mandarin. He sits in when I do Korean lessons with the littles."

"Wow," I say, trying to wrap my head around a non-Korean trying to learn Korean. Then, because I feel a little bad that we're talking about him, suggest, "Should I go tell him snack's on?"

"Oh, he likes to study through snack," Yunji says.

"Has anyone ever asked him?" I ask.

"Sure. I'm sure." Yunji sounds bored.

Snack time at the big kids' table becomes, well, gossip time. Two more teens have walked in and joined us, snickering with the others. It feels a little wicked. Reality-TV-ish.

"So Curley's girlfriend—god! Did you see her today?"

". . . Thigh-high skirt, yeah."

"I heard she's gone all the way with Curley."

"Um, I heard Curley was offering up his glove . . . during gym."

"Gross!"

It's hard for me to keep track of who is saying what, the machine-gun volleys are going so quickly, between a bunch of people I've just met. Zeus mostly hangs back, engaged but with a slightly furrowed brow like he's listening to a foreign language.

There's a little residual poison in the air, like gunpowder. It reminds me of how when I ate peanuts, I'd get a glowy feeling inside and want more peanuts. I'd eat them even as the salt burned the corners of my mouth and made my lips itch. When I complained to my parents, Umma would say, "Then don't eat them." Appa would tease that I was so sensitive, sort of like they didn't believe me. It wasn't until one day my top lip bloomed to twice the size of the bottom one that Umma and Appa realized they hadn't paid enough attention and missed that I was allergic. Gossip is bad. But it also fires up something in me, like I have a tribe, a side to be on. It is, frankly, addictive.

Then the conversation takes a turn.

"So what's up with Leonardo, Georgia?" Yunji asks.

"What do you mean?" I ask, guardedly.

"Is he your only sibling?"

I nod. I thought she was going to just ask, "What's wrong with him?"

"I can't believe Curley called him 'Special Ed,'" she says.

"He said *what*?" says Zeus.

"Oh, you know Curley. He's not even that original—there was just a *Dumb and Dumber* movie with a character called Special Ed."

"Where is he now?" asks Zeus.

"He normally gets various therapies after school. But today he has a doctor's appointment."

Mrs. Dongbang comes in, asks Yunji to take over for her at the counter. At one point, she comes in and fetches a new bottle of Barbasol. Umma and Appa sometimes pay me to do chores, and I would get a whole ten bucks (!) a day catsitting when Mrs. Cadogan went back to Jamaica on vacation. But watching Yunji, she's doing real work. She's helping her parents run their business.

Thirteen

The beanbag chairs in the corner are comfortable and perfect for reading.

There's very little structure to hagwon, but I'm realizing I like it. I could easily do my homework, get a snack at home, but by myself it just seems sad. When Calvin, returning from the bathroom, sees me reading, he gives me a thumbs-up before continuing with his study. He has the concentration of a monk.

Zeus, who was lying on one of the daybeds and reading, comes to my corner and plops down.

"I need to sit up a little more. My body just immediately falls asleep in a bed." I glance at his book.

"You're still reading *Of Mice and Men*?" The book is barely a hundred pages, and with all that white space. I think I read it in an afternoon.

"I'm not a fast reader," he says, a bit mournfully. "You can tell something bad is going to happen. I'm reading it for Mrs. Kottke's class."

Mrs. Kottke teaches remedial reading.

"I still think you should get tested for dyslexia," Yunji remarks, returning. She immediately starts scrubbing the table, postsnack, finishing with a Clorox wipe.

"I don't have dyslexia," he says. "I just don't read fast. And it doesn't stick. I swear I can read a whole book and not remember what it's about."

"That sounds like dyslexia to me."

"I think dyslexia is more a thing like the letters look weird. I see the letters fine, I just read slow."

"Yeah, but remember Mrs. Crandall? Sixth grade? She's the one who was supposed to refer kids for testing and she kept saying, 'This is actually pretty good since English isn't your first language'—you were born here!"

"I can read," he says. "*Danger. Poison. Thin Ice. Hair must be contained before operating machine.* And that's good enough. I'm not planning to become a librarian."

"But wouldn't you like to be tested to at least know if you do or don't have it?"

"With what money, Yunj? Should I have my uncle steal another kyae?"

"I don't know." She throws up her hands. "I'm just trying to help."

"I know."

I was thinking of how just today I was told to gather my books in math class and go to a different classroom. I'd been placed in honors math. I don't understand why. I am okay at math, but nothing great. My English scores, on the other hand, are always at the top. There were no tests on anything, they just stuck me in honors math. The answer to why this happened appeared when I opened the door to the classroom: all the quiet, nerdy Asians from the other lunch table were in the class. A few white boys. I was the only girl. They probably had to make sure there was at least one girl in the class. I have no idea if Yunji is good in math or not, but I am wondering if her punk haircut and eye makeup were how the teachers made the decision to put the relatively mousy Asian girl in, and not her.

- - - - - - - - - - - -

Umma picks me up in our new car, a Hyundai Power Bongo minivan. Leonardo's riding way back in the third set of seats, either as a mere precaution while Umma's driving on her own or because he's been "rambunctious," as Aunt Clara would say. The way-way back is equipped with a special seatbelt he can't undo himself.

"Leo!" I say, climbing in the back with him. "How was your day? You got to go into the city!" Umma, when she had just received her learner's permit, had been in a fender bender. No one was hurt, but she found it traumatizing—she felt she had done everything right and yet someone still plowed into her—which made her hate to drive, especially into the city. Her overcoming her phobia is a huge act of love.

"Don't ask," Umma says tersely.

Does this mean he acted out or was it bad news about his seizures? In the front passenger seat, there's a bag from Gajok, the pharmacy in Pecan Plaza. I don't know if this is a refill, if we're trying a new drug, or if there's a new issue that needs to be addressed. I'll be the last to know, of course. Even if I ask, Umma and Appa don't tell me. Umma says she doesn't want to bother me with it. Appa says it'll take too long to explain.

Moments like these are about the only times I feel a clear purpose to my life. See, if I become a doctor, like Appa wants me to, maybe I could help Leonardo and kids like him. But by studying what, exactly? We don't know if his condition is genetic, infectious, maybe even the result of a traumatic brain injury no one saw him having. Or, what if it's a combination of things stacked up on one another? I'm realizing, for instance, "epilepsy" isn't an actual condition. It just means "he has seizures." So they throw meds at it. Surely we can do better than that. That's when I picture myself in a white coat with a stethoscope in one hand and a Beekman flask in the other.

And doesn't every little kid who wants to be a doctor start out saying they want to help people? It's too pat. There are many other ways of helping people. I still don't know if I'm saying I want to be a doctor or if Appa is saying it *through* me, and then, in some ways, it's *his* father's expectations coming through as well. What's funny, when I was nine, Appa bought me this clear toy called the Visible Man, which was a human form with all its organs (with a penis!). I left it on my desk, not terribly interested. But one day, I came in to find him staring at it—and sketching it. When he saw me, he quickly got up, almost as if he were ashamed. Or, perhaps, ashamed of enjoying himself so much.

I keep thinking of Appa and wondering how or if things would be different if he had just told his father he wanted to be a science illustrator and was by golly going to do it. Of course, there's not as clear a path to that, but someone has to step up and do it, so why not my appa? His father would be mad, but it couldn't last forever. Eventually, his father would pass on and Appa would have his own life to live. I have never seen Appa excitedly talking about X-rays, not even close to how his eyes lit up when we went to an exhibit of Vesalius and da Vinci anatomy drawings at City Museum. He rarely brings work up at all. We did go together for Bring Your Daughters to Work Day, and I was a little surprised and amazed at the radiology department—a bunch of people sitting in the dark looking at eerily glowing computer screens, like a colony of silent mole people.

"I like your ethnic solidarity, Umma," I say instead, still staring at the Gajok bag.

"It's very convenient to be able to get Korean groceries and other things all in one place. They even measure pills out and wrap them in sheets of paper, like they do in Korea."

"What does Gajok mean?"

"*Family*. Speaking of, your grandmother wanted to be a pharmacist. She went to the best pharmacy school in Korea."

"So what happened?"

"The war."

"So she never became a pharmacist?"

"She met your grandfather shortly after that and became a mother to me and Uncle Jaehyung and Aunt Clara."

"So she never became a pharmacist, ever?"

"No. During the war, she and a bunch of the students volunteered; they folded bandages and prepared medicines to be taken out into the field. But that was the only time she worked."

"Do you think she missed it?"

"Definitely," Umma says. "The head pharmacist at Gajok is a young woman. I'll have to take you there to see. I wish my mom were still around to see. She was always stressing I need to have my own career as well as children."

You don't have a career, I don't say. It hangs, like a heavy cobweb, between us. Almost as if on cue, Leonardo barks, "Wow . . . wowww-wwww . . . !"

Umma hates the inhale-bark as much as I do.

- - - - - - - - - - - -

Umma's mother died of cancer when Umma was only fourteen, Auntie Clara eight, and Uncle Jaehyung nineteen. At the funeral, there was a white lady who no one knew. It turned out Umma's father had a second family. His "American" family, he called it. The father had been the one all this time trying to make the family more white (as if that was possible!) complaining that the house smelled like kimchi, keeping everything Korean, including the language, out of the house. He made sure to buy one of those big cast-iron eagles to hang on the garage; the house's flag holder by the mailbox in the front always had a flag—an American one—impaled in it.

The siblings coped in different ways. Auntie Clara stayed single and became a Buddhist (apparently her father met his superfluous "wife" in church). Umma leaned into being Korean in college, where she met Appa. Uncle Jaehyung went on a Fulbright Fellowship to Korea during grad school, met a Korean woman, and never came back.

We see Uncle once or twice a year. He's a dean of a college and usually manages to come to the US for at least one conference a year. I call him "Uncle," but he treats us more like how I imagine he treats the students, not his own niece and nephew. I don't know if that's a Korean way, having lived there so long, or if that's just him.

Losing their mother and then finding out about their father's second family was too much. It was, Umma had recounted once, like a plate that's dropped on the floor, fractured, broken, maybe Krazy-glue-able. But then while it was still lying there, someone took a hammer to it and smashed it. Not fixable. Uncle has three kids. I wonder if the father, my grandfather, has seen any of them. Or if he knows about Leo.

For his part, Uncle ignores Leo. Not meanly, more like how some people don't know how to interact with babies because they can't talk. When Uncle visits, he'll say hi to Leo when he first gets here, and then that's it. Leonardo shat his pants once during a visit. I caught a glance of Uncle looking at Umma sponging out some of the stain in the carpet; he was gazing with disgust and something that looked almost like anger— at what, I can't imagine. What does he have to be angry about? He has three healthy—bilingual—kids and a great job. When he calls, I often tweak him: "Here, you should talk to Leonardo first," and I put the phone up to Leo's head and actually love it when he does the bird-screech.

- - - - - - - - - - - -

When I get home, I unpack the bag for Umma. There's Leo's usual seizure medication, wrapped in paper but with a normal pharmacy label on it.

One tablet twice a day.

There's a second packet, though, for Umma, with a long name like adenobitrobubutor-x, which I look up and find it's a generic version of an antidepressant. I don't look further, to give her her privacy, but I can't help wondering how long she's been on this. And is this something with the neurotransmitters in her brain, or is just having Leo, her life, depressing her?

I put both packets back in the bag as if I didn't unpack them, and leave it on the kitchen table. Umma finds it a few minutes later, sweeps it up, as if with relief.

Fourteen

The next morning, Leo gets up on time. He seems oddly calm. When he gets out of bed, his massive calves bulge as usual, but I notice his heels almost touch the ground; his earlier years of constant toe walking like a ballerina had left his Achilles tendons so shortened he'd needed surgery to cut them. He is walking, a little ducklike, but with his heels just slightly raised. Also, his toe walking makes him even taller than he is. Please please please, I'm thinking, let this walking therapy stick. No more surgeries, they sound so brutal.

Downstairs, I show Umma. Appa's already gone to the hospital.

"Wow," I say. "Maybe the walking therapy *is* also helping with his walking!"

"The walking therapist said that's one of his major alignment issues," Umma says. "And if he's not aligned, the cerebrospinal fluid can't flow freely and that can press on things and cause all sorts of other problems, including, possibly, the behavioral ones."

"What does Appa think of that?" I ask. He's generally not a fan of anything except drugs or surgery. He thinks Umma puts too much faith in alternative therapies, but Umma argues that doctors seem to have just given up on Leo. I keep thinking of the time when he was tearing everything in the house apart, howling; how he kicked out the window and cut his hand. When they brought him to the ER the doctors just

gave him a shot and he dropped, like they were shooting a tranquilizer
dart at a moose. That made me so mad. I was the one who found his
posture a little funny, hunched over like he was hiding something. I
learned later there's something called the Alvarado score, that you need
to fit certain criteria:

Pain in right lower abdomen

Loss of appetite

Nausea, vomiting

Pain that worsens when you cough

Low-grade fever

Flatulence

Appa thought he was farting on purpose to annoy us, part of his
pissy mood and bad behavior. But he was in pain. Umma took his
temperature, which, at 98.9 was hardly alarming. It wasn't until he
started vomiting uncontrollably and his fever blazed to over a hundred
that everyone stopped and considered there might be a medical event
going on. Leo was crying as they rushed him to surgery. Luckily, they
caught the appendix before it burst. That's always frightened me, about
any time Leo has a behavior—what is he trying to tell us?

It was amazing what a different boy he was after the appendectomy.
Happy again. Same after he had a cavity filled, alerting us by banging
his head on things. But after the Achilles operation to cut his tendons,
he had zero improvement in his mood. He gritted his teeth a lot and
seemed to be in pain. He limped with both legs. That was the one surgery
Umma had actually objected to, hoping there was a gentler alternative.

I'm more like Umma in this: we look to the tiny, easily missable
signs of Leo's happiness. If there's anything we can do to make him more
comfortable, more clear, and won't cause him pain, does not require
something like surgery, why not do it? Appa, though I love him, once
started talking about sending Leonardo away because he'd been doing
so badly at his special elementary school. It turned out his feet were in
shoes he'd outgrown; no one noticed until his big toe popped out of the
canvas, like a Halloween costume for a hobo. His ingrown toenails were
horrific. Appa seemed to subtly blame Umma for not keeping track of

Leo's growing feet. Umma seemed to feel guilty about that. But I bet Appa didn't know his shoe size. He rarely learned the name of Leo's aides "because they come and go so much." I know he's busy and has patients' names he has to remember, but I also get Umma.

"Leo, good morning," I say.

"Good morning," he agrees. He sits, less robotically, I swear.

"Are you sure you don't mind going to hagwon after Leonardo gets picked up?" Umma asks.

"No, I like it," I tell her. "Thanks for sending me."

"It's pretty reasonable money-wise," she says. "It seems she gives a slight discount for Yunji's friends."

"I eat my money's worth of snacks," I assure her. But even more, my ears are ringing at "Yunji's friends." I love having my group. Friends. Now I have a whole table to sit with.

I try to get Calvin to come with me. I don't want him to feel like I'm ditching him. He shakes his head. He truly does want to read during lunch.

"I'll catch you at hagwon then," I say, and he nods.

- - - - - - - - - - - -

Yunji and Zeus wait for me after school. I have Leonardo with me, and he of course is so excited to see them, he starts inhale-barking. We three stare at each other while Leonardo barks. In a Leonardo storm, the only thing you can do is wait for it to pass. It's futile for me to try to raise my voice to explain his vocal reps. I can only hope they understand. Leo's already caused property damage, had seizures in front of Yunji's dad, and we all three see him in school all day.

At one point, Leonardo grabs Zeus's hand. I reflexively step forward to gently pry them apart but then stop. Zeus smiles at Leonardo as if he doesn't seem to think there's anything weird about another boy holding his hand. In fact, they start swinging their joined hands. Leonardo giggles. Zeus leads him around in a little dance, turning and turning Leonardo in a circle. I don't think he could possibly know, but when

Leonardo was little, sometimes the only thing that would calm him down was putting him in a desk chair and just spinning it around. He would stop crying and raging, but the minute you stopped turning him, he'd start up again. So we'd have to spin him in shifts. I tried to make it playful—*whee!*—but I wasn't fooling anybody. Having to spin someone for hours upon hours was hard work.

"This is so amazing what you do for your brother," Yunji says after Leo's been picked up by Ginger.

"Um, thanks?" I say. People say stuff like this all the time, and I know they are being nice, so I don't know why I get so riled up, like the corner of my mouth always jerks to one side. I mean, yes, maybe I am a little proud of how I take care of my brother. On the other hand, that's what siblings do for each other. Who else would get praised for being a sibling—it's like they're saying Leonardo is a burden.

He ain't heavy, he's my brother.

That's a song I heard in some old movie.

"That's very nice of you to say," I add. At least she hasn't said it when Leo's standing right there—as if he's a piece of furniture. People do that a lot, and that's the worst.

"He's a great kid," says Zeus, opening the car door for me, in the back. Yunji of course sits shotgun. Zeus's car is so old you can see daylight through the pinprick holes in the patchy rust in the door. It makes you realize that a car is just a thin metal frame stretched over an engine and wheels, but what makes a car a car—an expensive Cadillac or a cheap Hyundai—is merely the shell they put over it. Given the messy way Zeus eats snacks, I would expect there to be wrappers strewn about, but it's neat as a pin.

I finally have some substantial homework to do at hagwon. In math and my honors English class. Umma and Appa are convinced education is always better in the suburbs, but I'm not sure. My math class isn't that hard; in Great Books it's things I've already read before. At City they had a pilot Spanish immersion program for middle school because, well, everyone speaks Spanish in the city. So on that front, I'm *muchos kilómetros* ahead of everyone.

In math class, Mr. Candy spent a good fifteen minutes taking our pictures for his Math Team Wall of Fame, including me. I told him I wasn't on the math team, and he grinned and said in that class everyone was on the team, that it was part of the class. It was a weird process, like a military draft. He put my picture next to a lank-haired white girl, Emilee. "To inspire other girls with a protractor and a dream," he said.

I can't even calculate in my head what two girls out of sixteen is percentagewise.

What he didn't address is that the class really is mostly Asian. The nerd boys from the other table, a few from ours, but no one goes to hagwon.

"Ah, Eugene and Ken and Dave went to church school with all of us," Yunji says dismissively. "Barely tolerated lunch buddies. Not hagwon crew."

"They're doofuses, Georgia," Zeus says.

"Doofusii," says Yunji.

"Doofus, I?" says Zeus.

"Plural of doofus."

"They mostly read comics and play Dungeons and Dragons. I mean, like they haven't changed since we were nine!"

"I play Dungeons and Dragons," I say.

"You do?"

"No, I'm joking. I don't even know what that is."

"Phew!" Zeus leans back, wipes his brow with an exaggerated motion. "You're Math Girl, so who knows?"

- - - - - - - - - - - -

At snack, Yunji wants to know more about where Leonardo goes after school. I tell her about his walking therapy, his short Achilles tendons, the cross-midline stuff he does that hopefully will help make new connections in his brain.

"It's so great he can get all these therapies through school," I say. But it sounds tinny, canned.

"So you moved here for the schools," says Yunji. "That makes sense. But it sounds like you liked living in the city—that's always been a dream of mine."

"We didn't just move here for the schools," I suddenly blurt, while thinking: *that's your dream?* "Leonardo got kicked out of his other school."

Yunji's eyes widen. "What happened?"

Ugh, do I really want to get into all this?

Zeus sees the alarm on my face. That I let a cat out of a bag with a torch tied to its tail, and maybe I want to stuff it back in now, before it runs around setting everything on fire.

"Yunji," he says, "there's a reason school stuff is confidential. You don't have to tell us, Georgia."

"Well, my parents don't want people to know about it. But it was on the news, so we can't totally keep it a secret."

Umma and Appa like to keep unpleasant things about Leo secret. Weakness in general seems bad (I think of how I fell off the monkey bars when I was nine, and I hid that I'd broken my elbow until the pain got to be unbearable). Or, it just seems that things that are not normal aren't "nice." When there's stuff about people hating immigrants on the news, Appa in particular doubles down on being the most normal American family we can be. But throughout that whole school debacle with Leo, with me, Shauntae, my best friend, had only the vaguest idea of what was going on. She certainly didn't think we were struggling at all, and, in fact, I could see in her eyes sometimes a kind of envy at the image that we were just happy and rich, a doctor's family.

She would ask about Leo, but rarely saw him since he was at the other school, so Leo wasn't a part of our friendship. Mostly, I glossed over so much, labored so mightily to shore up a facade that everything is great, because I never wanted to seem like I was complaining about him, and, if she didn't really know what was going on through all those years we've known each other, explaining now was going to be too hard. But denying what was really going on became a kind of lie.

Here, I've got a group of friends (fingers crossed) and Leonardo is going to be with me a lot. Why not give them a fuller picture? Why not stop pretending that he doesn't occasionally go berserk? Or that he pees in his pants? And, really, why not allow myself to vent a little bit about it?

"If you just don't tell anyone else, I think I'll actually feel better if you know Leo's whole story—and mine."

"Who we gonna tell?" laughs Yunji. "The Cambridge Academy Bugler? Put it on social?"

Zeus has been sitting back a little, quietly watchful. Like it's okay if I change my mind and don't talk about Leo. But he's also engaged and ready if I do.

"Hey, what's going on?" says Calvin, coming to the table. His eyes light up. "What are these? Pears? Apples?"

Everyone's kind of staring at Calvin in a way that he could take as exclusionary. Like he's barged up to us just as I'm about to reveal a secret.

"Um, okay if I hang out?" he says, tentatively reaching for a scrap of fruit.

"Of course," I say, making sure my voice is loud enough everyone at the table can hear. "You're part of the group."

I start over. "I'm telling you all—just you—about Leo's history, because you're my friends." I wait a split second, fearing someone is going to laugh in an I-beg-your-pardon disbelief—*friends*? But everyone's quiet. "I don't want people to have preconceptions about Leo, that he's violent or crazy or something. Let me start by saying, Leonardo would never deliberately hurt anyone."

"Yes, he's so sweet," says Yunji.

"Well, the thing is," I counter. "He *can* get violent." The trouble is, I don't know what to call this. Violence suggests intention. Maybe "aggressive"? But that sounds too much like—ugh—Curley.

"And it's not quite like he's spastic, like he flails around and accidentally hits you. He has what are called maladaptive behaviors. He's like a little kid. He can't control his emotions when he gets frustrated or mad. But being hit or bitten by an adult is dangerous. I'm saying this, too, because I don't want any of you getting hurt. He's pulled my hair and bitten me so many times I've lost count." I even have a scar of

a bite mark on my left boob—clearly teeth. Leonardo saw a dog and
started hugging me—but then his whole body got tense and he started
squeezing and also started biting whatever was in proximity—like my
big fat C-cup boob. I hope I'm never in an ER and have to explain that.
I decide to hold that and the dentist story in reserve—too shocking.
I don't want them to be afraid of Leo, so afraid they can't get to know
him a little first.

Now Calvin is staring at me intently. "Leo, he's the big kid in the
lunchroom, with all the other special-needs kids?"

I nod.

He pauses, thoughtfully. "Um, can I ask you something?"

"Of course," I say. "This is an AMA."

He pauses, again. "I'm not sure exactly how to put this, um, but do
you kind of purposefully ignore him?"

I suddenly remember scrunching into my chair. Ah! Does he think
I'm ashamed of Leo? I can see why he might think that.

"No," I say. "Leo is eighteen. Everyone treats him like he's eight. I
want to give him some space in high school." I don't really allow myself
to think it, but what if he were neurotypical? Would I totally ignore
him? Expect him to beat up people for me? Would I be insulting him
all the time like Shauntae and her brother do?

"So, back to your story," Yunji prompts.

"He was in a school that seemed good for him. But Leonardo has
behaviors," I explain. "We all call it 'repping.' It's a repetitive behavior.
Some therapists said we aren't supposed to let him rep, others say it's
good for him, like it calms him down or stimulates his brain or something. Who knows?"

Yunji shifts. "But what does that have to do with him getting kicked out?"

"I don't really know for sure. My parents don't tell me anything,
but I'm guessing he hit someone. Maybe he hit a teacher. They just said
the school waited until the last minute to say he couldn't come back the
next year. But by then it was too late to enroll him anywhere else, so
they hurried to find a good public program, and that was Sunnyvale."

"Do you think he likes it here?" Yunji asks.

"I don't think he dislikes it," I say. "And this new walking therapy seems to be helping him."

Zeus excuses himself, then returns with a bag of shrimp chips. His flip-flops slap rhythmically against the floor. I thought Mrs. Dongbang was going to yell at him for wearing shoes, but apparently he has "inside" flip-flops, carefully switching to the "outside" ones even if he was just running out for a minute. Mrs. Dongbang also keeps a stack of plastic slippers for people to wear, which struck me as slightly gross because, well, wearing other people's shoes. But the little kids often grabbed them and gleefully slip-slapped around the house in slippers way too big for them, and almost everyone wears socks when they wear the "public" slippers. I was learning a lot about Korean culture. At least Korean slipper culture.

"God of the gods and his shrimp chips," croons Yunji.

"Someone's gotta do it," he said. "By the way," he says to me, "you want to know what's the worst thing about being named Zeus?"

He doesn't even wait for someone to answer.

"As if being named Zeus by a pastor and his wife who are really into mythology wasn't bad enough, all the Koreans, especially the grannies, pronounce it *Zee-us*. At least I wasn't a girl—they would have named me Calliope." His eyes crinkle when he says this, partly because he's also shoving another handful of shrimp chips into his mouth. I tend toward dark-haired guys and have a secret love of bushy eyebrows. He has all that and dimples.

"I like your haircut," he'd said to me at the table. I know guys aren't supposed to comment on girls' appearance, but he said it in a noncreepy way, more like his way of welcoming me into the group.

"Thanks to Bomb Haircuts," I say.

The whole table starts laughing. "What's so funny?"

"It's *bohm*, the Korean word for spring," says Yunji, hiding her smile behind a fist.

"So why's it spelled 'bomb'?" I demand. "B-o-m-b?"

"Well, think about it," she says. "It rhymes with c-o-m-b. The Korean dude who named the place probably had his Korean-English dictionary out and thought it made perfect sense."

"Seriously, it does make sense," said Zeus. "If you spelled it b-o-m, the way it's spelled in Korean letters, it would actually be pronounced *bomb*. English is trash!"

"Hangul never changes, what you see is what you get," Calvin agrees. "It's super regular, like German."

Yunji goes to a closet and returns with a plastic place mat. It has a chart of Korean letters printed on it in a grid.

"Here," she says, putting the place mat in front of me. "One horizontal stick signals *ah*. Two, and you have *yah*. See, the next you have *uh* and then *yuh*."

And so forth. This grid actually works better than the one Aunt Clara and I used that mostly wanted to teach you the sounds and we got fixated on that and missed the underlying system. It reminds me of when we had to memorize the taxonomic classification of living things in biology.

"Korean letters have such a beautiful system," Yunji explains, with evident pride. "It was invented by a benevolent Korean king so 'the people' could have literacy, not just the scholars who knew Chinese characters, which is what they used at the time.

"King Sejong said he made it that way so that a reasonably intelligent person can learn it in an hour." She smirks.

"No pressure," Zeus says.

One hour. Here we go.

Fifteen

By five o'clock, I think I know the Korean alphabet!

At five thirty, I go outside of Bomb (i.e., 봄). I give myself a pop quiz, strolling up and down the stores that would still leave me in sight of Umma. Ah, the three Korean letters: ㄱ ㅣ and ㅁ: 김 actually spells out k-i-m. Dr. Kim, OD.

I'm surprised that after I've wandered up and down the strip twice, there's still no Umma. There are so many cars pulling in and out of the parking lot. This one, that one. Another one. None of them Umma's.

I call her. No answer. I call Appa, which I'm not supposed to do except in an emergency, and this is a low-grade emergency. His secretary puts me through. He answers but says he can't get away and he doesn't know where Umma is but that she must be with Leo. I go around the back, to check the hagwon, in case she's waiting there, but I'm not even sure she knows this back alley exists.

"You're still here?" It's Calvin, having popped out the back door.

A pearl-colored Lexus SUV glides up, directly in front of us. Inside is an African American lady in a suit.

"Hey, do you need a ride?" he asks.

"Well," I shrug helplessly. "It's possible my mom may have, um, mixed a few things up and forgotten me."

"Where do you live?"

"Sycamore Estates."

"No way—so do we. Hop in, text your folks that you have a ride."

"Okay," I say. Even if someone's on the way, they can turn around. I text and climb into the car, wondering, vaguely, why Calvin goes out the back. Why not get picked up at the front? He still eats lunch alone. I need to check in with him again. I mean, how kind of him to even think to *ask* if I need a ride.

"Ma, this is Georgia."

"Hi," I say sheepishly, my shoulders rising to my ears. In her mind, I'll probably forever be Georgia-whose-parents-forgot-to-pick-her-up. "Thank you for the ride, Mrs.—" The car is spotless and smells richly of leather. I've never been in a car with real leather seats; that is just not the Hyundai way (although I'm wondering if pee is harder to clean from leather than pleather).

"It's Ms. Charlie." She turns and smiles before she puts the car in gear. "Dr. Charlie works all right, too."

"Mom works at Sunnyvale Hospital all right," Calvin says. "But if someone comes running and says, 'Is there a doctor in the house?' don't look at her to do the CPR."

"I do know CPR," she says. "But Calvin is correct. I have a PhD in history as well as a law degree." It turns out Ms./Dr. Charlie is in the hospital's legal department.

"My father works at Sunnyvale Hospital, too. Dr. Kim," I say, in case she knows him.

"Dr. Kim . . . I have to say I know a number of Dr. Kims." Calvin cracks up in the background.

It's funny, Calvin sometimes makes fun of Korean things, like the Korean habit of slurping noodles, picking teeth with toothpicks like an archaeological excavation. He pointed out at hagwon that "Dongbang" could be a homonym for dong-bang, poop-room. It's kind of funny, but I also got this itchy feeling as he said it; like, it's okay if Yunji complains about her name or her dad's toothpick habit, but it's okay because it's hers. Maybe ours.

Or, it's funny how interchangeable we Kims are. But it kind of isn't.

"Dr. Kevin Kim," I say, shooting Calvin a look, mock-exasperated, but also with a dollop of real exasperated.

"My father was at City before that. We moved here fairly recently."

"So did we," Calvin says. "Move. Last June."

Ah, I didn't know: Calvin is also new. But I was so busy thinking of myself and my insecurities, it didn't occur to me there might be another new kid feeling, well, awkward and outside of things.

"Wait, so Calvin, how did you end up at the hagwon?"

"My mom." Calvin rolls his eyes. "She loves Korean study culture."

"Hello, don't forget how we found out about it, honey," she says, carefully checking both ways before pulling out of the lot. It's late, but I suppose you never know when there'll be a tractor trailer pulling into Arirang. From her warm tone, I can tell she and Calvin banter all the time. "Because of a certain K-pop fan."

"Yeah," says Calvin. "Besides studying Mandarin on the internet, I am a stan for K-pop."

"And a certain K-pop fan made me go to Korean book and music stores with him and I kind of couldn't miss the notice about the study hall in Bomb Haircuts."

"It's pronounced *bohm*, by the way," Calvin says, a little too pleased to correct his mom.

"Fine. *Bohm* Haircuts. I'm all for studying other languages and cultures, but not at the expense of sleep."

"It is a bit of a late-night vice," Calvin says, conspiratorially. "I watch a lot of K-pop videos and learn song lyrics—that's the fastest way to learn a language—I read a study on that. But Mom says the blue light will wreak havoc with my sleep."

"It already does," she says. "Did you do your math homework?"

"By the way, Georgia," Calvin says. "Nice picture in the Math Wall of Fame."

"Wall of fame?"

"In Mr. Candy's class."

"When did you see that?"

"Mom came to school to talk about that class and also Great Books.

She brought all my report cards and stuff, my PSATs. Mom talked PhD talk with Mr. Candy while I stared at all the Wall of Fame photos. I love how he stuck you and Emilee at the end, like the two girls are after-thoughts."

"I don't even know why I'm in the class," I say. "You have to admit, it is weird how it is just a mysterious process deciding who takes the class. Like there's no test or anything. I wonder if they just saw 'stranger with an Asian name, put her in the class.'"

"Exactly. That's how they've always done it, some secret decision by the teacher. Not anymore, though, if my mom can help it. I guess it's not kosher, like, not legal."

"By the way," I say, suddenly. "Why do you get picked up in the back of hagwon? It's so dark there."

Calvin's mom turns on the radio. A jazz station, the music is smooth as buttercream. Her head moves slightly to the music. I don't know if she's listening to us.

"Did someone tell you to go out the back? Like the Dongbangs?"

"I like the back," he says. "Anyway, if I were standing around in the front, people would probably accuse me of loitering."

I didn't really think of it that way. Damned if you do, damned if you don't.

– – – – – – – – – – – –

We pull up to the guard box of Sycamore Estates. They give you special sensors to stick on your windshield, and Dr. Charlie must have that because the gate lifts up so that she basically just glides in. The guard doesn't even look up. Would he know who was who without the sensors? What if Freddy Krueger stole a car? People say the city is big and anony-mous, but how funny is it that Calvin lives in Sycamore Estates as well, and I had no idea.

In our building in the city, we knew every single person in the forty apartments. If a stranger came through the door (which had a crappy lock), Mrs. Rosa would be there at her peephole, yelling through the thick steel door, "CAN I HELP YOU?" Our building was like family—a real family, crankiness and all, but always looking out for each other. This family also spread outward into the neighborhood.

We all knew the Alsaedis because at some point everyone needs a last-minute lightbulb or a quart of milk. I had a feeling Mr. Goh had a bulk deal with them for that purple, overpowering Fabuloso cleaner that he mopped the stairs with. The same people walked up and down the streets, their faces became familiar; you could end up saying hi to someone for years without knowing their name. Or maybe you'd finally meet them at the annual block party, quite a raucous affair. The police even shut down the streets. There was music and dancing, a basketball hoop set up, little kids gleefully scootering in the middle of the street, and so much food the airs on the block turned into an ambrosial mélange of spice scents, no one food achieving dominance.

Here in Sycamore Estates, they keep talking about how we're all in a "community," and yet the neighbors on our left side haven't even come out to say hello. The Brandts have warmed up a little bit, I think when they found out Appa was a doctor.

"Have you seen that huge, weird tower on the other side of the fence?" Calvin asks.

"No."

"Come to our house sometime and I'll show you. Actually, you can see it a little here." He points out the window.

In the dark, there is a tower, almost like a skyscraper, but cylindrical, maybe a dozen floors. It's wreathed in green lights, flying saucer–style, at the top. It's quite tall and strange for a suburban development that's otherwise just houses. I do remember seeing it before.

"I thought that was a cell phone tower!" I say. They have the lights to keep planes or birds or whatever from running into it.

"Nah, that's just the Gabilan Tower. The Tower of Power for the Curley clan."

Curley.

Today, Curley's girlfriend was haranguing one of her acolytes, who turned out to be Emilee, the girl who is actually in Mr. Candy's class with me, and Calvin. Curley's girlfriend needs to pass chemistry, something all the more advanced kids took last year, to graduate, and she was trying to get her friend to let her see her lab notes.

"I could tell Emilee wasn't into it," Calvin says. "So I just told Curley's girlfriend, why not actually try to learn it. Just copying the notes will teach her nothing about hydrogen reactions."

"And?"

"She told me to shut up, of course. And she kept on bullying Emilee to do her homework."

"Bullying her like how?"

"At first it was 'you promised!' with that crackly voice. Then it was kind of threateny, like Emilee would be such a loser without their group. And then it was a little gooey—and it got racist, too."

"Like what?"

"Like, 'Do you think it's fair that the Black kids get everything without being smart, that they get to have lower test scores than you but probably get into a better college, they get picked for jobs because of diversity. And the Asian nerds are just so boring and study and bust all the curves? So that normal white people get stuck, on both ends, at a disadvantage even when we didn't do anything? That's reverse discrimination!'"

"She did not say that!"

"She did. Going on and on about how this was their whole life!"

"So what happened?"

He sighs. "In the end, Emilee decided being popular was more important. It looked like she agreed to do the homework. Nothing to report. But . . ."

"But what?"

"Also, Curley's girlfriend told me to stop looking at her."

"What does that mean?"

"And I don't want to look at her skinny butt, either, believe me."

Calvin swallows. His throat practically convulses. "She said if I told anyone about this, about her trying to cheat, she was going to come up to me and then scream that I groped her."

"What?"

"Yep. Hashtag MeToo."

"Did Emilee say anything?"

"No. And I wouldn't count on any support from her. They're like the Mafia! Omertà and all that."

"Then what happened?"

"I didn't see a good ending for the situation. I'm just a nobody in this school. Less than nobody. Not to mention Mr. Candy and Mr. Gerard think my mom is this angry Black woman, even if all she did was point out where the school was coming pretty close to breaking the law. I'm just going to stay as far away from all of them as possible. I really just want to get through this year and get to college ASAP."

Poor Calvin looks so defeated, I don't even know what to say. "Ugh, well, the tower looks so weird and out of place," I say.

"I guess if you have Curley family money, you can do whatever the heck you want."

"Apparently."

We're quiet for the rest of the ride.

- - - - - - - - - - - -

At home, Umma is in the driveway, just getting Leonardo out of the van. He is following her, his abominable snowman posture a little better since the walking therapy (I'm sure of it!), but he's barking.

"Oh!" Umma says, seeing me debark from an unfamiliar vehicle. "Georgia! I'm so sorry!" She turns to Calvin's mom and waves frantically. "I'm Amanda Park-Kim—and thank you!"

Calvin's mom seems to understand intuitively that Umma can't stop to chitchat because she needs to keep an eye on Leo. She waves back and calls out, at the same time as Calvin, "Bye, Georgia!"

Then I hear Calvin's voice dopplering out the window, his hand waving, "Le-e-e-eo! Hiiiii! I'm Calvin!" Leonardo doesn't look back. But I do.

"New friend?" Umma says.

"Yes," I say.

Sixteen

On Friday, Umma says she'll pick both Leonardo and me up at school, so we don't have to take our buses home. For the past three days, she's apologized a million times about forgetting me. I tell her I don't care, and I honestly don't. In fact, I tell her, it was nice for me to get to know Calvin better.

"He is a nice boy," she agrees.

I guess I haven't seen him around because his mother drives him to school and, also, their house must be one of the more expensive ones, farther in from the gates than ours (but with the Gabilan Tower blinking over them).

"He's in all my honors classes," I tell her. He indeed showed up in my math class. I'm not sure Mr. Candy was the most welcoming. He started right away with some factorials and logarithms, having everyone answer when called on. I hate doing those in my head and feel a lot of pressure. Calvin hadn't even been there for the previous class where we learned this, and yet, when Mr. Candy's pointing finger landed on him, he answered it perfectly.

"He also reads during lunch," I say. "For fun."

"Then follow him and do what he does," Appa suggests. "He sounds impressive."

- - - - - - - - - - - -

At lunch, I fill up my water bottle, then take a minute to spy on Leo. He's at his usual table with the two other students, who I now know are Penny and Jack. He's not eating, though. He's scanning the room, almost 280 degrees, like an owl. I wonder if he's looking for me. I step back into the shadows.

At home he's been yelling "You do it!" for all sorts of things. It's my fault. When I was ripping up some lettuce for a salad, I saw him watching and asked, "Leo, you want to do it?" And his enthusiastic echo back was "You do it!" I hope his aides have figured out "You do it" in Leonardo-speak actually means "*I* want to do it."

Now, "You do it!" he says, wanting to

Button his own pants,

Brush his own teeth (I or Umma still have to floss for him),

Wipe his own butt.

I couldn't be happier about the last one. I don't know when this actually happened. I love him trying to be more independent.

He's happier, Ginger told me. He's walking better, and a funny thing has emerged: he has started skipping instead of walking behind her. Like, happy skipping. With his motor coordination problems, I'm surprised he can. Did someone teach him to, or did he just figure it out himself?

"He smiles as he does it," she said. "Like he really is happy."

I'll take it!

"I wonder if it's the walking therapy," I told Umma.

During the parents' meeting (Umma only; it was in the middle of the day), Ginger showed her a chart that showed he had only one behavior the whole week. One behavior! And that was peeing his pants. I remember at other schools, he often had more than a hundred aggressions a day. I kept thinking something had to be done. Kicking him out, that's what was done.

"You know, this one student I had," Ginger told me, "improved so much he was mainstreamed into a few classes."

"Which ones?"

"A civics class and woodshop class."

"Woodshop class," I'd said. "Like with the table saws and all that?"

"And all that," she'd confirmed. "His name was Jeremy. He was an absolute champ about taking directions and was so careful." In the therapist's office, she'd shown me a little coaster, a piece of a thick branch sliced crosswise, a design of a fish burned into it. *To Miss Ginger Richie, love Jeremy.*

"What's Jeremy doing now?"

"I don't know," she said. "But I did refer him to a vocational culinary program. He was very good with his hands; his being so meticulous made him good at following recipes."

Ugh, I just realized this whole time I hadn't included Leonardo in the conversation. But I tell myself it's okay, because something's been activated in my brain. Why are we always working from crisis to crisis instead of thinking how Leo himself could study, apply himself, thrive? That he could get better? Maybe not all the way (I'm realistic), but still have a life that's undeniably his.

I remember once Aunt Clara brought over a huge scrap of velvet, same cherry-black color of red velvet cake, that Leonardo was fascinated with. He particularly loved how he could run his fingers through it, leaving behind dark trails in the nap that he would then brush away.

Up. Down. Up. Down. In school they are using disruption and distraction, giving him fidget toys and things to try to redirect his habit of stroking: his finger, the NAD screen, random strings. A kid had some fringe on his jacket the other day and that was almost another Leo disaster. Of course, he has zero interest in the fidget toys, which are gears and propellers made out of metal. Metal! That's not what he likes.

"So you don't know what Jeremy is doing now?" I asked Ginger. "Wouldn't you be curious?"

"I have a lot of students. I'm happy when they graduate and I concentrate on the ones in school."

"But isn't there something . . . that they graduate to? Like a program?"

She looked at me. "No. When they hit twenty-one, they're done with school. The next step is up to the student or his guardian. Special ed kids get an extra two years. After that, it's real life."

Real life. What is that going to look like for Leo, once he won't have school to occupy his days? Marriage? Kids? I don't think so. A job? I actually can't see him doing that, either. Even something simple like bagging groceries. Or putting something in a bin at a factory. He wouldn't be able to concentrate for more than five minutes. He'd wander away. Who'd make sure he went to the toilet?

Also, why *should* he have to gravitate to that kind of job just because he is disabled? It reminds me, chillingly, of *Brave New World*, where at the babymaking factory, they put a drop of poison into the test tubes holding the embryos so the babies each came out a little intellectually disabled: the overlords wanted to create a whole class of people to work at menial jobs.

At one of those siblings meetings, they showed us a *60 Minutes* documentary about this guy who has cerebral palsy, a terribly twisted and useless body.

Everyone thought he was also severely mentally disabled because he couldn't speak. His birth parents abandoned him at the hospital. However, he had these foster parents who later adopted him. After a while, they could see he had a little bit of motor control in his right foot. He taught himself to pick up things with his foot, including crayons and pens. He learned to write. But even more importantly, created beautiful art. It almost looks like a joke, seeing a man (now) in a full-body wheelchair, his body bent like a tree that's been hit by light-ning, clutching a stem of a pastel in his bare foot. He taught himself how to make beautiful drawings of nature scenes—basically expressing his mind to the world.

In the discussion after, most of the kids felt this wasn't at all relevant to their situations. "My brother just sits there and drools." "My sister hits me whenever I walk by, and gives me this really evil look." But one other girl said basically what I was thinking but didn't know until she put it into words: "They don't have to be concert pianists. We just have to treat them with the same respect we'd treat anyone else."

It's kind of funny, I remember this girl so vividly. Her name was Susan Starr. What a great name. Her mom drove her all the way into the city for the groups. I had hoped to be friends with Susan Starr, but she didn't seem interested. The meetings were at the Boys and Girls Club down the street from our apartment. Her mom went out to check on their car at least sixteen times, like she was convinced it would either be stolen or just be a shell up on blocks the next time she looked for it. I don't know if Susan just didn't like me, or if her mom didn't like the city.

Ironically, Umma and Appa were sorting the mail and were surprised to find that in Sunnyvale their car insurance premiums actually went up. So money conscious, they called their broker right away, thinking it must have been a mistake.

"Insurance actually is more expensive here. It's less the theft problem," Appa reported, "and more problems with teens vandalizing and crashing cars. And also, everyone drives, so there's more accidents."

I hadn't thought of that. I thought of our neighbor Mrs. Sreenivasan, in her complicated saris, maneuvering herself with dignity onto the city bus that also lowered itself hydraulically with a whoooooosh to accommodate her. Or how Appa took the subway to work, me to school. I think if we hadn't needed the car for Leo, we might have been like most of the other people in the building and not had a car at all. Shauntae is planning not to even get a driver's license, which is the most city-kid thing ever. Apparently in Sunnyvale, driver's ed is a mandatory class. An actual class that we all have to take (except Zeus, I suppose) this spring, instead of going to the local driving school.

Leonardo, it occurs to me, is probably never going to learn to drive. How much will that affect his life? Does it have to?

- - - - - - - - - - - -

Umma and Appa have been arguing about Leo's future. Umma's always finding this or that therapy, Appa pitches in and accompanies her when he can (although most of this has fallen to me now), but he's often grumbling and skeptical, saying it's not practical to think Leonardo could improve too much at his age. I presume one thing they are united on is not putting Leonardo in a home, at least for now. But other than that, they don't know. Umma continues to search, Appa continues to veto and grumble—all these therapies are of course expensive—and wonders if it's practical to spend so much now when we need to save up for his future. But is it really Umma who is the impractical one? Appa also, weirdly, seems to think one day Leonardo will just snap out of it.

- - - - - - - - - - - -

"Yo, Georgia!" Yunji waves me down, and quite happily, I go over to their table.

Zeus is there, plus another Korean guy I recognize from my Great Books class—easy because he has hair that's slightly longer than Zeus's, spiky—and with pink tips. Hard to not notice pink tips.

"This is Oliver," says Zeus, putting his friend in a headlock. "He and I form the dumb Asian crew at the hagwon."

"Speak for yourself, Hyung," Oliver says, wiggling free. "I'm in Great Books with her—" He looks at me and nods in greeting.

Yunji looks pained. "Zeus, you are not dumb," she says.

Oliver wiggles free. "You're a genius, actually: these days it's the nonstereotypical blue-collar Asians who get into the Ivy League."

Zeus laughs with a *pffft!* "I'm not going to college, even community college. School is not my forte."

"Why not? You're using big words like for*tay*." This is Calvin, walking by.

His tray is loaded with salad and a book. A salad! He kills me.

"Calvin, please sit with us," I say, patting the place beside me. Yunji gives me a bit of a look, like I've overstepped her authority, but I ignore it.

Calvin seems to consider for a moment. Peaceful half hour reading, or sit with us? Using his tray like the prow of a ship, he nudges it onto the table as I scoot over to make room. My hip bumps Zeus's. Calvin is wearing a basketball jersey, like he was that first day I met him.

"Hi, all—I don't think we've met, yet," he says to Oliver. Calvin turns to shake his hand (what manners!). As he does so, I see the back of his jersey says LIN for Jeremy Lin.

"You're such an Asian-o-phile, Calvin!" I tease. He shrugs and grins. Then he looks up in shock. We all do.

The Girlfriend of Curley is approaching us. Last I saw her, she'd been at the salad bar, sprinkling Equal on a pile of carrot coins. Now she's heading over here with a half dozen of her Mermettes, all in blue-and-white miniskirts, sweaters with chevrons, a big felted *C* and *A* plastered on the front. They remain respectfully silent as she steps forward.

"Hey," she says. "Have you guys seen Curley?"

While her query in words is directed to us, her whole body, for whatever reason, is directed at Zeus. Also, what has she done to her hair? It's done up in a hundred little braids. Not cornrows exactly, more like EEG leads emanating from her scalp.

"I said, have you guys seen Curley?" She actually pushes her chest out at him. Unmissable. Her boobs are practically in his face. He is too gracious to move and acknowledge this space invasion.

I can see Yunji's hand flex—fist, relax, fist, relax—under the table. The rest of us are just staring, mouths agape.

"Hello? Anyone home?" She waves her manicured hand in front of Zeus's face.

Zeus finishes chewing, a bolus of kimbap travels down his throat. He frowns, upward, at her face, even though her boobs are like two eyes just staring at his level. "Are you perchance talking to me?"

"I might be."

"Why would any of us know anything about your boyfriend? Why don't you ask his idiot jock friends?"

I tense, expecting umbrage at "idiot jock friends." But she just laughs merrily. "You're a good judge of character, that's for sure," she says, her braids swaying gently.

With a *hmph*, Zeus goes back to his tray. One kimbap, two, peeling the disks off like he's making his way through a column of Oreos. The nori seaweed is black like chocolate.

The chorus of girls behind her watch, wide-eyed, as Zeus dares to ignore their queen.

Yunji smirks.

"Um," says Calvin. "Nice . . . hair?"

She turns and squints at him as if just noticing he's there.

"I'm Calvin," he says. So polite.

"I *know*." She smirks, swishes her head from side to side, making the braids fan out like a carnival ride. "Yeah, I got these—Kylie braids—done at Vroom! Hair Salon. Anyway, I'm looking for Curley. He's got a tournament today, you know."

Calvin looks back at us inquisitively. He doesn't realize this is all just as weird for us as it is for him.

"Maybe you could infer," Zeus says, demolishing the second column of kimbap. "That we haven't seen him? Or care to?"

She looks at him again. "Well, a person could be polite." Then her eyes find me. "Hey, you, you're the one with the brother, right?"

"I do have a brother, yes," I say.

"So what's his issue? Is he retarded?"

"We don't use that word," I mutter, staring at my hands. "No one uses that word anymore."

She laughs. Her voice tinkles, like breaking glass. "God, don't be such a precious little snowflake."

She's a good six inches taller than her attendants and looks a little bit like a mother duck leading her ducklings away.

"How can she even pretend she doesn't know the r-word is prejudicial?" Calvin says. "Not to mention the cultural appropriation."

"Cultural appropriation?" says Zeus.

"Taking things from other cultures for superficial use and abuse by the dominant culture without an understanding of the culture behind it. Like basically every white musician has done with Black music, starting with Elvis, but then we think of rock and roll as being white."

"Gotcha—like when that singer put the Indian bindi on her head and called it her 'mystical ESP dot,'" Zeus posits.

"Exactly," says Calvin. "When she does it, it's on the white body, so it's cool."

"But why can't she do that?" says Yunji. "She *is* saying Indian culture is cool. Isn't it *good* white people want to get out of their all-white boxes? Acknowledge there are other races and cultures instead of just theirs?"

They both have a point, I concede.

"But it's 'cool' because she's white. Do you remember the Oscar last year when that Indian actress wore one with that cool updated sari? The fashion police hosts *still* said something so stupid."

"What?" says Zeus.

"'She looks like she smells like curry,'" I finish. I remember that incident very well.

"Exactly. So with these Kylie braids that girl is playing safari and being all trendy but if *I* wore braids as a young Black person, I'd be immediately criminalized."

"You?" Yunji hoots. "You are *so* not ghetto."

"Um, that's racist," says Calvin.

"What's racist."

"Calling me ghetto."

"I just said you're *not* ghetto."

"But you're using ghetto in the context of me, a Black person."

"Oh em gee, are you saying anything about Black culture is off limits to anyone, *Asian* people, too?"

"I'm not saying it's 'off limits.' I'm saying Black culture *is* American culture."

"And Black people have borrowed from white people, too."

"Um, yes, because white culture is the normative culture.

"Are you saying, like, because Black people invented hip-hop, it should just be Black people doing it?"

"I'm not saying that at all," says Calvin, in his gentle voice. "I'm saying, however, that just sampling superficially from cultures without acknowledging the power differential is problematic."

"*You're* not culturally appropriating K-pop?"

"Maybe I am."

Ugh, this is too much at once. I'm good at studying but not that good at stuff outside that. Like, it took me forever to figure out what a "meme" was. Or half the stuff people are talking about on social media. Or these complicated political discussions. I see glimmers of truth on both sides but the minute I wade in, I can't see where I am. There's a lot of offense in the air right now and I kind of can't tell where (or if) it should be aimed. No one wants to offend Yunji, our leader. Calvin is undeniably smart, but no one here really knows him. *Is* he part of the group or is he just another paying customer?

"Anyway, back to the girlfriend of Curley and her cultural appropriation braids." Yunji pulls a metaphorical ripcord and the tension billows out from the conversation, at least for now. "All that money still can't buy culture and class. Can't she ever wear clothes that aren't cut to mid-thigh?"

"Well, to be fair, that's not on her, Yunj," Zeus says. "That's the cheerleader uniform."

"Yeah, but it's her decision to live her life only cheering on Curley or whatever."

"Curley Three Sticks," laughs Oliver, as if he doesn't want to be left out of the conversation.

"What does that even mean," I say. "Three sticks. Three sticks of what? Gum? Is that a golf term?"

"No, it's a fancy way to say 'the third.' You know, like Thurston Howell the Third," Oliver explains. "It's stupid."

"Did you see her and Curley have that fight yesterday after fifth period?" asks Calvin.

"I saw them arguing about something—who can miss that crackly voice?" says Yunji.

"What happened, Calvin?" I ask.

"I kind of feel bad for her," he says. "I guess Curley was mad that she wore heels to the photo shoot for Junior Royalty—whatever the heck that is—after he told her not to."

"Ha," says Yunji. "I guess it pisses him off when girls are taller than him. And, actually, pretty much everyone is taller than him."

"Apparently. He called her a c-word, in front of her friends," says Calvin. "And *his* friends, they all laughed and clapped."

"Ugh," I say.

"Ouch," Zeus agrees.

Yunji holds up her hand. "Curley is an insecure, racist dick. But she's not much better. She's, like, a female dick. I mean, who does this girl think she is? There is no way my dad would have made 'Kylie braids' for this girl, no matter what."

"You got that right," says Zeus. "And he's a guy who can do anything. Remember when that guy wanted Bart Simpson shaved into his head?"

"What happened?" I ask.

"He did it!" she says.

Zeus cracks up. "You can't ever forget something like that. Can't wait to see the Acolytes' hairdos tomorrow," he adds.

"You mean the girls who follow her around?" asks Calvin.

"Yep. They follow her around and do whatever she says to do, copy all her stuff. I think they've been like that since middle school. I call them the Acolytes."

Acolytes. Such a perfect word for the Mermettes. I can't help loving that Zeus and I were thinking on the same track, different nicknames. I don't have any particular feelings about Curley's girlfriend except for that general wistfulness about girls who are conventionally attractive, thin, pretty, blond. I wonder if she will be able to figure out how to harness her leadership power without being connected to some guy. Maybe she could become a politician or something. I feel a little bad that given her height and her hair color, no one even considers she might be smart or have other talents.

The boys at the jock table make their fingers into upside-down "OK" signs over their eyes and make beep-beep-beep sounds while yelling that with their special "glasses" on they can see through the girls' clothes. The Mermettes giggle and scream and cover various private parts, walking prettily knock-kneed out of the cafeteria. Only Curley's girlfriend remains erect, a slight smile on her lips.

Tomorrow, it's almost assured, the Acolytes will march in lockstep, sporting their own set of "Kylie braids," as each girl already has uniform hair of sufficient length as if grown via mandate. En masse they look like the sister wives of some cult, but we don't have to say this, we just have to look at each other, roll our eyes. Calvin does a perfect Kylie braid hair-flip imitation, and we start laughing like we're one, a combustion engine kicking over and roaring to life. We've fast become friends.

I've got a crew! The hagwon crew.

- - - - - - - - - - - -

Leonardo doesn't have any after-school therapies on Friday, so we're going straight home—on our separate buses.

My knee is burning. Today was Assembly, a program about what do to if there's a mass shooter in the school. Weirdly, in the slides in their presentation, the people with guns were black, the victims white and the occasional Asian, when we all know most (all?) school shooters are white. Ugh. Anyway, at Assembly we are supposed to sit with our homerooms, but for some reason, Curley, who is not in my homeroom, sat himself into the seat next to me.

In the dark, he put his hand on my knee. I was so surprised and repulsed I jumped to my feet, the kids around us laughed. "Georgia, did you see a mouse?" Curley said snidely, loudly.

"Sit down, you cow!" someone yelled. More laughter. But maybe my outsize reaction was good, for he didn't do it again. I was kind of daring him to, so I could sock him in the face and *also* claim it was an accident due to this hypothetical mouse. But no, the rest of the time he was looking with interest at the stage, like nothing happened, like learning how to duck and cover or tackle an active shooter (who the heck is going to do that?) is the most interesting thing in his life. It makes me feel a bit like I'm the crazy one, even though I know I'm not. I don't know what else to do, except file out with the class.

Seventeen

It's Saturday night, and we are taking the Dongbangs out for dinner. Even though Mrs. Dongbang always insists she just likes that Yunji has a "chalk-hay" friend—I guess that means "good influence"—Umma insists it would only be polite, if not expected, that we should treat them to a dinner, because Mrs. Dongbang has basically stopped charging us for hagwon and won't take any money when Umma offers it. She does accept the dinner offer, and Umma insists that they pick. I wonder if they'll pick La Vie En Rose, the French place, but—surprise!—we aren't even leaving Pecan Plaza. I am surprised they don't want to really go "out," but Yunji's always said they always feel best among Koreans. I know Umma always likes to know more about my friends, but I wonder if she is also lonely out here, in Sycamore Estates.

We pull into Pecan Plaza. It's like a little kingdom: food, stationery, dentist, pharmacy, dog grooming, coffee spot, haircuts. Except for the Subway, it's all Asian. And yet Curley's family owns this. Apparently they've owned this space all the way back from when it was just a barley field.

I'm about to unlatch Leo's seatbelt. It has a special safety buckle where you have to press two buttons at the same time to release it. Out of the corner of my eye, I see a moving yellow pelt, like a fluffy long animal, a lion dancer puppet. It's an optical illusion. It's Curley's girlfriend and maybe three Mermettes walking through the parking lot. Their hair is all the same shade of blond, and also ribbon-lank, so it looks like a bunch of hair just moving along. I'm wondering what the heck they are doing here, but then see them disappear into Aloee, a K-beauty store. White people are all over Korean beauty products.

"Love us like you love our fermented rice face wash," Yunji has quipped before. I'm not a cosmetics person, but one thing I have noticed is Korean stuff smells subtle, barely floral, while in contrast, American cosmetics and shampoos smell like air freshener.

I wait until the last blond head disappears behind the door. Appa is looking at me quizzically, standing outside. I pretend to fumble with the latch of Leo's belt.

I let him out when the coast is clear.

He sniffs the air like a horse, lets out a happy little *eeeee*. Appa's face is neutral, I detect a little jaw clench behind it. He often looks a little flustered and embarrassed when we are out with Leo, even if he is behaving perfectly. I wish Appa could relax and have fun. I don't know if he realizes how his tenseness affects all of us—and probably Leo, too.

The restaurant is called Koryo, which, we learned in hagwon, is a dynasty in Korea—in fact, it's where the name Korea comes from. Inside it's old-timey with wooden gourd dippers and braids of garlic, pictures of mountains. I know mountains are sacred to Koreans.

Umma walks in first, holding Leo's hand. I am actually hoping the people in the restaurant notice. I think sometimes, when I am out with him, from a distance people wonder, why is that handsome guy with that heavy girl? Until Leonardo starts barking or doing a finger-rep. But this tall teenager holding on to a middle-aged woman's hand broadcasts to the world that he is "special," and I want the world to be nice to him.

The Dongbangs are already there—not surprising since they just had to walk a few hundred feet—waiting for us at a long table with a pit in the center and what looks like a huge vacuum cleaner hose hanging above it.

The adults greet each other, *ooh* and *ah* some niceties. Leo, Yunji, and I hunker down at the end of the table and let the adults adult. I hand Leo his tablet and peruse the menu. Not that long ago, he used to have trouble eating, like chewing and swallowing in the wrong order, so badly sometimes he inhaled food into his lungs and had to go to the hospital. That made me appreciate what a complex mechanical process is it to bite, chew—your food and not your tongue—moisten with saliva, stop breathing for a split second, swallow in that split second, all in that precise order. Because everything is so hard for him, it helps me not take things for granted.

"Hm," I say, perusing the menu. Spicy beef soup. "Leo, you might like this spicy beef soup, Yuk Kae Jang"—I take a guess and pronounce "Yuk" as "Yuck," which is kind of a weird name for a soup. But then on International Day, in my elementary school in the city, this girl from India brought her favorite treat, barfi. We all laughed at that. But maybe I shouldn't have.

Yunji giggles. "It's *yook gae jang*, Georgia."

"Okay, yook gae jang."

"It's very spicy."

"He'll probably like it." Korean food is easy for Leo. He can have issues with temperature, texture. But he eats Korean food like a champ. Maybe because it's so spicy he can feel it better while he eats.

The waitress brings out bright pink, almost translucent slices of meat, which she cooks on the grill, turning them just before they begin to burn. The vacuum hose magically suctions all the smoke. I like the stainless steel chopsticks and spoons, which have a matching ginseng pattern on them. They are extra long, Korean style, to reach the little side dishes that glitter like jewels, to dip into the communal bubbling pot of soup or stew—today: a briny egg custard. We all dip our spoons in it. I blow on Leo's before giving it to him.

"Ew, don't you all catch each other's colds that way?" Shauntae had asked when she'd had dinner with us. At Shauntae's house, everything came separate, dished out by separate serving utensils, soda was carefully apportioned into glasses. The guest bathroom had a dispenser of Dixie cups by the sink, along with a stack of fancy paper hand towels that seemed too nice to be disposable.

I wanted to tell her that we didn't get sick, but that wasn't true. I remember once Appa brought a particularly bad cold home from the hospital, and we all got it: Umma, then me, then Leo. But I didn't want to stop doing that. I laughed at Shauntae when she painstakingly reversed her chopsticks to pick stuff out of the common bowls with the "clean end."

"Yes," said Umma. "In Korean culture, we share everything, even colds."

There's only one other family in the dining room. I'm sure Umma and Appa have picked this time—four thirty—by design. Going to dinner early means it's less likely we'll encounter crying babies, crashing dishes, anything that might trigger a Leonardo meltdown.

Leonardo uses chopsticks really well. It's something no one ever taught him. It is a little bit weird, as Appa tells me regularly, because Leonardo as a toddler did not have a "pincer grip," apparently a stage all babies go through. That was one of the first indications something might be wrong with him. That and the fact he didn't always "track" his parents with his eyes like babies do. I always wonder if it's some issue with his hand-eye coordination that makes it uncomfortable to write or draw. Most kids love to grab a crayon and scribble. Not Leo. You can't get him to hold a pencil to save his life. Even writing out *Leonardo*, he writes all the letters on top of each other so it just looks like a tangle of hair in the drain. My parents started me on "beginner's chopsticks," which they made by rubberbanding two chopsticks together, a rolled-up piece of paper making a hinge. I made one for Leonardo, but each time I wrapped his fingers around it, he just dropped it. But then he picked up normal chopsticks and, well, just started eating.

Another Leonardo mystery. At his last school, I insisted on going in for a parents' meeting, so I could show his team—his teacher, his physical therapist, his occupational therapist—how he can even pick up a marble with chopsticks. Leo's always been labeled as having "poor fine and gross motor skills." Well, then, what's this? Maybe he's so smart he's learned a back-end way to get around his brain and do this. At the very least, I want to show them there's probably way more going on with him than they think.

"A lot of adults can't manage chopsticks," I say. "Maybe if you treat him like he can learn, he'll try. Otherwise, no wonder he gets so frustrated!"

But when I say this to them, in front of the school's director, a man with a zillion degrees after his name—MAT, ABA, DPsych, PhD—who'd happened to be walking by and curious why all the therapists are in a room with a neurotypical child who is not a student there, he raises himself to his officious height and looks at me with pity. I'm a kid, a girl.

"I know you love your brother," he says, in that oozy, sugar-coaty way that I hate. "But something like that is what's called a 'splinter skill.'"

The therapists agree: "Even after repeated therapy, he can't even pick up a Cheerio," the PT says, and not to me, but to the director. It makes me feel wrong, and stupid, even though I'm pretty sure I'm neither. But I don't have a string of letters after my name. I was fifteen.

"A motor splinter skill is common," he drones. "Those kids who can't tie their shoes somehow manage a bunch of complex locks to elope. Common. Doesn't even rise to the level of savantism."

What makes me the maddest is when those guys with an alphabet soup of letters after their names charge Umma and Appa a ton of money (I can't help hearing them complain about it—"Two thousand dollars for a neuropsych evaluation?") to write things about Leonardo like:

"Minimally educable."

"Unable to live independently."

"Likely mentally retarded, but cannot get him to sit long enough to test."

"Violent, possibly psychotic."

"Concerns about the stress he may put on the family, especially the lone sibling. I have recommended peer counseling sessions, residential placement for the patient."

I hope to write back to them someday. Inform them Leonardo has learned to read, or has a job. Or maybe can speak non-echolalic talk, or type on the computer, maybe writing poetry.

I'd sign it

Sincerely,

Georgia Kim, F.U.C.K., Y.O.U.

For a moment, the heat in my soup, almost lava red, opaque with hot peppers, soothing strings of beef that are almost like pasta, matches the heat of my revenge fantasy. But even that begins to seem far away as our conversation fades and all you can hear is the clicking of the metal spoons scraping a rice bowl, the old-fashioned Korean music on the sound system, Appa's gaspy "*Aigu, massida*," which I know means "delicious!" Same way Leo hums when he likes his food, Appa always speaks in Korean and sounds like he's dreaming when he's eating Korean food.

Maybe it's a Korean thing, but like the adults, I don't like to talk while I eat. You need to wipe your mouth, concentrate, taste. With my family and the Dongbangs, including my new, maybe best, friend, we all sit in that cocooned silence, being with each other but also enjoying. The adults pass a plate of perfectly barbequed meat down to us. "Better than sex," Yunji whispers with a wink, as she places a piece that's charred on the edges—my favorite—on my plate. I am wishing I could live in a bubble like this forever.

- - - - - - - - - - - -

For a second course, Umma has also ordered some short ribs, *carby*, to share, also grilled. Now that I can read Korean a little bit, I see it on the menu, spelled k-a-l-b-i. The meat is so good, sweet and soy-saucy, I've inhaled those as well, along with two bowls of rice. I've eaten my delicious soup to the last drop. There are also dozens of little side dishes like spicy bean sprouts and an odd but really delicious apple and mayonnaise salad that comes in little bowls. The waitress refills the little dishes as we eat so I don't mind ravishing those as well. But as I look up, I see Mrs. Dongbang staring at me. It's an unguarded moment, maybe, but she doesn't seem to register that I'm looking at her looking at me—the way some people do whenever I eat or buy stuff at the grocery store.

Like, maybe if I stare at this fat person's ice cream choices, they won't eat it and I'll be doing them and the whole world a favor.

I hide my burp behind my hand.

- - - - - - - - - - - -

At the end, the waitress brings us something called chic-hay, which Yunji tells me is a kind of fermented rice tea, *sikhye*, which originated as a way to get out the rice burned on the bottom of the rice pan, fermented because they didn't have refrigeration back then. It's kind of like soaking the pan for dishes and drinking the dishwater, I'm thinking, and I'm half grossed out and half admiring of Korean thrift and ingenuity.

"This is a Korean delicacy," I tell Leo, handing him the cup when it's cooled down enough. "Sikhye."

"Shit-hay!" Leonardo shrieks, birdlike, loud enough that not only do the adults at our table look at us, but the other Korean family in the restaurant pauses, chopsticks and spoons in the air, to stare at us.

Mrs. Dongbang looks away, uncomfortably. So do Umma and Appa. A certain awkwardness settles on the table as we realize the whole restaurant is staring at us.

Mr. Dongbang glances at us with a slight, encouraging smile. He has an aspect that I also love about my grandparents, Umma's umma and appa. They seem like they are living in a slower time than the rest of us; they are content to just let things and people be, that things have a way of working themselves out. They also aren't like other people, always praising me for being "such a good sister" and "having *so* much patience" or even baby-talking me about it. Like I have to be encouraged into being kind to Leo. As if I deserve a medal just for tolerating being Leo's sister. Or for adapting to his handicaps. Halmoni and Halaboji expect me to be a sister to Leo—the love and fighting and everything that entails. Apparently, when I was little and Leonardo would grab something that was mine, like a treasured *dduk* rice cake, I'd squall and hit him. Halmoni/Grandma would tell me not to hit him, but she'd always make Leonardo give me my dduk back, too.

Fair was fair.

"That was good, wasn't it?" says Umma. The owner gives us the bill, which comes with orange slices and also Korean gum, which I know from experience will smell weirdly of flowers and lose its taste in maybe three chews. I nab an orange slice instead, make Leonardo laugh (I think!) when I put the peel over my teeth and smile.

Appa takes the bill, but Mr. Dongbang reaches for it at the same time.

"It's our treat," Appa confirms. But they play tug of war with the little plastic tray. For a flash of a second, I see them both as teens. Then Appa puts his card in the little pleather holder, as any adult would, and they return to their normal selves.

"Leo, you seem like you are walking quite gracefully," Mr. Dongbang says to him as we make our way to the door. Umma, coming up behind them, smiles and tells him a little bit about the walking therapy.

"Wonderful, Leo," he says. "You must be working hard at it to have made such progress." I think I see the corners of Leo's mouth lift anti-gravitationally. Leonardo doesn't smile in the conventional way. When they tried to teach him "smile" in therapy, he just grimaced and bared his teeth, so he looked like this emoji: 😬

Appa and Mr. Dongbang both take toothpicks from the little stand by the door, insert them in their mouths, and walk out like country hicks. Mr. Dongbang pauses to carefully pick something out of his teeth, from behind a hand.

I'm about to follow them outside when I reflexively look back for Leonardo, my shadow, but he's not there. He's back a dozen feet, frozen in place.

Oh no.

Umma is also back there, leaving a gap of a good three feet away from Leo, almost like she's expecting he might literally explode.

From the front I can see: it's subtle, but you can see a quiet fluttering behind his eyelids, nystagmus. He's having a seizure.

Just our luck, the other family has finished up, and is bringing up the rear. We're all stuck in a bottleneck near the door.

"Excuse," says the woman, starting to inch on by. Leonardo doesn't move. He can't. All we can do is wait for the seizure to end. "Excuse."

Umma says something to the family—mom, dad, young daughter and son—and the lady frowns like she doesn't quite believe her.

"Moment. Just please wait," Appa says. His perfect, American English always gets a little off kilter when he's stressed. "My son, he's sick. He has a neurological condition."

"*Aigu*," the woman sighs dramatically. To her, Leonardo is just rude, stymieing her exit. To us, he's having a seizure and shouldn't be moved until it passes.

The restaurant owner, a hard-looking Korean lady maybe around Umma's age, comes over. "Why is he just standing there?"

"That is my son, he is sick, he's having a seizure," says Appa.

She frowns like she's worried he's going to make a mess or something. And actually, Leo does sometimes throw up or pee on himself after a seizure.

"He shouldn't be moved until it stops," Appa says. "I'm a doctor."

"*Ohmunah*—" The instant respect the word "doctor" garners among Koreans saves the day. The restaurant owner busily moves a few tables with a terrible *screech!* so the family can get through. The family whispers among themselves as they pass, looking at Leonardo over their shoulders. I know they're talking about him and this makes me mad, but there are more important things we have to think about.

When he's released from his seizure, he just starts moving again, like a stop-action movie. His mouth is a little slack, a bit of drool leaking out of the corner. He looks sleepy.

"This new medication isn't working," Appa says, almost to himself.

"It's only been a week," Umma says tensely. "Dr. Shah said it might take a while to build up."

Appa pauses. "I told you I didn't think that neurologist is any good."

"So now this is *his* fault?"

They actually glare at each other. I get a feeling in the pit of my stomach.

"Georgia—" Mrs. Dongbang touches my arm. She and Mr. Dongbang and Yunji are moving unobtrusively away. "I think you have a lot to deal with right now—please call us if we can do anything."

"I will," I say.

Yunji waves at me, not smiling, avoiding my eyes.

Eighteen

At home, Umma and Appa argue. About what to do next, which neurologist to bring him to, whether they should bring Leo to the ER right now. I sneak a peek at Leo, who's been sleeping since we got home. Apparently, seizures are hard on your brain, so your brain self-protectively puts the body to sleep so it can repair. Yes, I hope it repairs. Poor Leo.

I slip into his room and bend over him like a mama bird looking at her babies.

He sniffs and changes position, and I relax a little. His breath smells funky, but I think it's mostly from dry mouth. He hasn't had anything to drink for hours since he's been passed out, because he could aspirate fluid if he threw up.

SUDS, Sudden Unexplained Death Syndrome, is something we all worry about. It's most dangerous at night because at night people who may have this unidentifiable disorder can choke or accidentally suffocate themselves with a pillow, or, sometimes for no discernible reason, they just die. No one can say for sure who has SUDS but anyone who has had a seizure supposedly has a high chance of having it. Umma wonders if it's just a seizure that happens at night. That's her theory, and that's why she hasn't had a full night's sleep in forever; she goes in at least once a night. Tonight, Umma asks me to help program her phone so it can go off every hour. She's going to try to stay up, but she's afraid she'll fall asleep. What I didn't know is that as a little baby, Leo had had what's called a febrile seizure, one caused by a high fever. Apparently it looks scary but is fairly normal, at least that's what Appa says. But she's sure that's when Leo's problems started, not all at once, but gradually. But Umma also remembers that febrile seizure as a before and an after, and she is sure that everything that's "wrong" with Leo has to do with seizures. But a lot of the doctors think Leo just has epilepsy *on top* of everything else. Who knows? Who is right when Leo has an undefinable disorder?

A few minutes after I leave, she goes into Leo's room. I can hear her voice; she reads to Leo at night. For the last month it's been *Harry Potter*. Why not have an escape to a little magic, to danger that exists only in a book?

Sometime after midnight, I have to use the bathroom. It's near Leo's room, so I creep soundlessly to it, bump around a little in the dark so I don't have to turn on the light. I already know where everything is well enough, including the toilet paper holder, directly to my side. I think about how this is what blind people have to do all the time. As I sit down, pajama pants down, the door, which I've shut extra softly, slips from its latch and in the dark silently swings a quarter of the way open.

Footsteps. Appa's.

I stiffen. I should get up to close the door or else he might think no one's in here. On the other hand, he doesn't use this bathroom. Getting up with my jammie pants at half mast seems the worst of both worlds. I stay sitting, quietly. Maybe Appa, too, is worried about Leo?

"You know, it's really not going to make a difference."

"What do you mean?"

"You know what I'm talking about: SUDS. Amanda, this isn't necessary. You'll only burn yourself out. He has no more of a chance of having a huge seizure now than he did yesterday. They don't come in clusters."

"We don't know that for sure," is all she says.

"If it happens, it happens."

"You know what?"

I cringe inwardly. I've never heard Umma use a tone like this before. "*What?*"

Or Appa. A normal, irritated voice but also with an undertone, faint, but like the far-off scream of a train whistle on a collision course to . . . something. And: *what*? That word he thinks is so rude and awful.

"I think SUDS would be extremely convenient for you. Painless, quick, done."

"What are you saying? Leo's my son."

"You said that once, jokingly. Not about SUDS, but about that time when Leonardo almost got hit by the car. When he ran into the street."

"I would *never* say something like that."

"You did."

"What did I say?" It sounds more like a challenge than a question. "Exactly? Since you have such good memory."

"You said maybe it would have actually been a blessing, that he was clearly suffering, and we couldn't help him."

"I would not wish anything like that on my own child."

"You said it."

"I think you're the one who is projecting on me."

"Right."

It's quiet.

"Do we have to do this?" Appa says. His voice is softer. "Ripping each other apart? We were having such a hard time with him then—remember?" Appa's voice is softer. "The screaming and hitting and destruction from day to night? And his running away everywhere?"

- - - - - - - - - - - -

Of course, I wasn't born, or was just a baby, during Leo's early years. But I did see one incident of his running away. It was caught on a video of a church picnic.

Gingham tablecloths on a wooden picnic table, pinned down by bowls of potato salad, platters of hot dogs. Happy chatter. Kids running around. In the corner, if you know what to look for, though, you see Leo, about three or four. It kind of looks like playing, but he is straining against Appa, who is holding him by his wrist. He's squirming and crying and snapping at his hand like a turtle, desperately trying to get away. It seems Appa is grabbing him too hard or maybe even kidnapping him—if you didn't know what was going on. At one point, to get away from Leo's trying to bite and kick him, he pulls his hand up higher. Leo's arm goes up with it, he's hanging from Appa's hand, flopping and spinning around like a yo-yo tangled at the end of its string. Umma says something to Appa, and he lets go with an exaggerated shrug, but then Leonardo takes off running. He looks like he's running blindly, like one would from gunfire or an explosion. Umma quickly runs up to him and catches him, more gently, kneeling and holding him by the hand, but then he immediately lunges forward and headbutts her in the jaw, like a mini MMA fighter. Umma falls backward in slow motion, like a felled tree.

It's like he needs to get free. From something. But then once he is, he just runs and runs, pursued by something invisible, to some kind of relief that exists nowhere. He doesn't look like, say, a lion suddenly running free in the savanna. He looks like he's trying to outrun himself and his pain.

That's what Umma told me once, after we'd survived another "Hurricane Leo." He'd started picking at some new silicone weatherproofing the landlord had stuck in our windows. It was a tacky, gummy substance, almost like Play-Doh, squished in the cracks. Leonardo would scrape it out with a finger and start eating it. Appa wasn't there. When Umma tried to stop him, he started clawing at her face. I stepped in and he punched me, quite mightily as he was ten and I was only eight. But we managed to corner him, coaxing him to drop the wad he still had, twiddling between his thumb and forefinger.

"Leo," I pleaded. "You can't eat that. It's not food." Then his face twisted into a mask of rage and he lunged—not as us, but at the nearest window, which shattered. I suppose if he were an adult he might have gone through the window. But instead he jerked his head back in.

All these glittery diamonds on the floor! He stopped screaming and stared, transfixed. Then bent down as if to sit down to play with them. He seemed, for a second, happy. Distracted. We both panicked, getting him away from the broken glass. Umma combed through his hair, searching for shards and cuts. It was a miracle: even though he was covered with bits of glass, besides a superficial cut on his forehead, no lacerations (although this wouldn't be the first time we'd show up at the ER with a bloody Leonardo when Appa was working).

In order to clean up, we remanded Leonardo to his room, put one of his chewy toys in his mouth like popping a pacifier in a baby's. When we returned, he was gnawing on it contentedly, his smile making him look like he was chewing on a cigar. I remember Umma crumpling, sinking to the floor, embracing her knees and crying. I didn't have a name to what she—and I—were feeling. But later I learned it: Despair.

- - - - - - - - - - - -

With Leonardo sleeping in his bed, Appa heading out, Umma probably crying in her room, despair comes again.

Like, will our family ever be able to relax and just be a normal family again? A family that has dinner together, complains about creamed spinach? And even gets bored and irritated with each other for being so predictable. Like if they forced us to go to Disneyland or something and we siblings hated it the whole time—that would be the biggest miracle of our lives. Actually, someone did nominate our family to the Make a Wish Foundation, and wouldn't you know it, they gifted us with a trip to . . . Disneyland! All expenses paid, with an aide as well. Of course, we couldn't take it. Just the thought of Leonardo on a plane gives us all the shivers.

Appa walks by, and I'm sitting on the toilet, still. I wait and wait until I hear Umma sigh and get up and go into their bedroom. I don't flush, and slink back to bed, but not without checking on Leo first. I don't have to go in, I can hear him snoring.

I snuggle back into bed. I'm more comfortable than I have a right to be. But bed is often where my most uncomfortable thoughts come in. I think of how, in the city, we had people coming over all the time but, except for Aunt Clara, no one spending a good amount of time in the house. With Leo throwing things or pooping in his pants or barking or when he had his strange rep where he'd yell "milk or dark chocolate?" over and over again, our apartment was never fully clean and uncluttered. Never in order. It just seemed too much. People meant well, but it would be the awkward silence while Leo would do something and Appa or Umma would have to run after him. Sometimes, we'd have to be careful he wouldn't attack the guests. Even with Shauntae, I'd opt to go to her apartment. Her mother came down once and after only five minutes in our apartment was saying to Umma, "How do you do it? Honestly, I don't think I could do what you do." She was offering her help and sympathy, but it kind of sounds like, "Wow, how do you manage the horror show that is your life?"

So then we basically stopped letting people in so they wouldn't see any of this. Even Aunt Clara, sometimes. Like, why not keep all that shame in the house? Being ashamed of how out of control everything was only added to our stress.

But did it help? Did we feel any better?

I think it just made me feel lonely (I admit to myself for the first time). If I felt that way, how did Appa feel? Or, Umma? I used to jokingly call her Woman Worrier, after my favorite Maxine Hong Kingston book. But that really was her full-time job. When things were out of control, she was the one who was called, she was the one everyone looked to fix stuff. When we felt queasy about something the doctors or therapists were suggesting, she was the one who had to figure it all out, even though she didn't know anything more than the rest of us.

Like when the dentist lost the tip of his finger because of Leo. Of course the possibility was there. Leo was biting and pinching people so much when he was twelve, his teachers wore martial arts gear. Umma didn't and sometimes had blue finger marks on her arm. The thing she had conceded was stopping giving him his vitamins. She'd been happy to find a liquid vitamin with EFAs that tasted good enough Leo would open his mouth and let her pipe it in with a dropper. But one day he closed his front teeth over the glass part. Umma tried to withdraw the dropper but it was stuck, that's how hard he was biting. He looked like a snapping turtle. We were so lucky that a corner of his front tooth, not the dropper, gave way (adding to the tooth mess that is his mouth). Umma took him to the dentist to check on the chip, and even though the man used some kind of plastic bridge to keep Leo's mouth open, when he was removing it, Leo lunged and did the same thing to the man's finger—it was just the tip, but I remember the normally gentle-seeming man shouting, "Jesus Christ!" the hygienist screaming, and the dental tools going flying, the dentist cradling his gloved hand and running out of there.

After that, no one would work with Leo unless he was sedated. A trip just to get his teeth cleaned was basically surgery that had to be done in the hospital.

Umma also fretted about the anesthesia interfering with his seizure meds. Not to mention sedation requires needles, so Leo basically would be traumatized regardless.

Leo's lucky he's only had one procedure with the sedation, a quick filling, and cleaning (that they do as long as the anesthesia lasts). What made me sad: it was an ambush, a bunch of burly guys grabbing him and holding him down to get his sedation IV started. I'd seen this before with his Achilles surgeries. Leonardo would cry and spit and kick; they'd get the IV started or jam the mask on his face . . . and then he'd suddenly conk out. Appa insisted they had to do it in the hospital because, apparently it's rare, but people can stop breathing or have other problems during sedation.

When he woke up from the dental sedation, he was vomiting, disoriented. He looked terrified but no one could get near him. How were we supposed to know what level of pain he was in? Normally doctors ask you to rate it on a scale of one to ten. Leo can't even count to ten on command. I had the trapdoor feeling the entire time even though this was considered one of the bigger "successes" with him.

No one likes being grabbed, disoriented, and then having stuff done to them.

What else to do but despair?

Halmoni came to stay for a few days to add an extra hand. She cooked and cleaned, took care of me. I loved how the house (and, faintly, her) smelled like ginger. When she cooked she stirred everything with her hands, even stuff with hot pepper in it. She'd laughingly claim it tasted better. She also made dduk, laboriously created pounded rice balls that are soft and chewy. If Leo has a favorite food, it would be that (of a similar texture to that weatherproofing stuff, now that I think of it). But it involved her mashing sticky white rice into a paste with a kind of wooden mortar and pestle. Generally, she made it only once a year at Lunar New Year. And for Leonardo after his dental surgery.

I desperately also loved the squishy feel of the pounded rice. However, I wasn't a baby anymore. I didn't keep a single one for myself, I wanted them all for Leo. I can't remember how old I was; all I remember was that Umma and Appa were praying nightly that Leonardo wasn't going to need his wisdom teeth removed.

Nineteen

"Leo?"

The next morning, he's sitting at the kitchen table staring despondently into seemingly nothing. I check his eyes to make sure there's no nystagmus. Nope. He's just sad, or has a headache . . . or . . .

His breakfast has stopped steaming and is lying there, cooling, cold. Maybe he's just depressed he has seizures, like any teen would be.

Then I remember the bag in my knapsack.

Last night, as we were getting Leo into the car, Yunji had run over and handed me a paper bag. I would feel it was filled with spheres, but surprisingly heavy.

It was full of dduk! Some granny had made some for their family to celebrate some big Korean holiday called Chuseok (*chew-sock*).

They've dried out a little overnight, but are still soft. The granny has wrapped them in a zillion layers of saran wrap. I take out one to give to him. I put it in the center of a fancy plate, like it's at an expensive restaurant. But he, puzzlingly, refuses. "Nnnnnnah!" he says loudly. I look worriedly at Umma.

"Is this from the seizure?" I say.

"Nnnnnah!" His mouth is a cavern.

And for the first time, I notice Leonardo has mustache hairs. Some baby fine, a few spiky black hairs. Maybe it's to my discredit that I don't think of him, really, as a guy, like Zeus. But as an eternal little kid. He's not little. He has a mustache.

"Nnnahhhhhh!"

"Dduk, Leo, dduk!" I say. I hand it to him one more time and he pushes it back, a bit roughly.

Umma and I look at each other, at the same time.

"Does your stomach hurt?" I ask. "Do you feel sick?"

"Nnnahhhhhh!"

"You know what?" says Umma. "He's saying *nuna*. Remember how he spelled it that time?"

"Do you really think so? Appa thinks it's just a coincidence." But he shoves the dduk toward me, and says "Nnnahhhhhh!" again, seemingly with intention.

"For me, your nuna?" I say, making my eyes extra wide. Leonardo doesn't gesture yes or no, something the smallest kids do. This was one of the first things, besides the fact he didn't point or pick up Cheerios (the pincer grip!), apparently, that alerted my parents that something was wrong. But as I say this, something lights up, a "yes." I can see it, flickering in his eyes.

"Your nuna," he echoes.

Umma and I look at each other holding our breaths. Did that really happen? Did he really just try to spontaneously call me, Nuna?

"Oh, thank you, Leo," I say and take a bite. The chewy outer layer gives way to something soft and sweet. Halmoni kept hers plain, or sometimes molded the pliable rice dough around pieces of fruit or a whole strawberry. Umma said that wasn't traditionally Korean, but it was delicious.

This one is delicious, too. I wait. No upset. No pinching. He's onto the next thing already, repping away. I take another bite. The chewy rice giving way to the silky texture of whatever this soft kidney-bean-colored stuff is.

"It's his favorite food," I whisper. Her eyes are watering, too.

"I know," she whispers back.

A good big brother taking care of his sister, that's what he is.

I rewrap it all. I bet if I zap it in the microwave for three seconds I can soften it up for him, later.

- - - - - - - - - - - -

Monday at lunch, I'm showing off to the table that I actually don't live in the Dark Ages. I have a phone and now it is finally fixed. I have a crackle screen protector like Yunji's—it came free with the screen repair from I Fix at Pecan Plaza, a store so small and narrow you practically have to go in sideways; it's just one (Korean) guy at a counter with a bunch of tools.

Ding! First thing I get is a text from Umma.

> Crown fell out need to see dentist

> Pls be home for L. Thank you, see you when I
> get home. Appa working.

Of course, I text back, with a zillion heart and flexed muscle emoji.

"Uh, I can't go to hagwon today," I say. "My mom needs me to watch Leonardo, she has an emergency dentist thing."

"Aw," says Zeus. "Hope it isn't too serious."

"Her crown fell out." Umma has soft teeth and is always having problems with them. So many that when I was growing up and heard the Jack and Jill rhyme—Jack fell down and broke his crown—I always thought it was about teeth.

"Ouch, harsh," says Zeus empathetically, but his teeth look perfect.

I am pondering. "I guess I should take the normal bus home so I can be there when he gets home," I say.

"They won't let you ride the bus with him?"

"No," I say. "Only people who are registered to be on any bus can be on it. It must be a liability thing."

Even though yes, duh, it would make sense to let me ride home with Leo. With a slight stab of anxiety, I realize I need to hope my bus even gets there before his. Because we perambulate around Herbert Hills first, to accommodate those precious children, I'm not 100 percent sure that's going to be the case.

"Hey," says Yunji. "Why not bring him to hagwon?"

"To hagwon?" I say—echolalically. Thinking: but what about the carnage of Leonardo in Bomb Haircuts? Also, the seizures. Her parents would be horrified, I'd think.

"Look, I do so much work at Bomb, my mom lets me bring anyone I want to hagwon. You don't have to pay for Leo, for real."

"Are you sure?" I'm wondering if she has sudden-onset amnesia. The totem pole. The angry faces blooming behind Leo at Koryo. He did, also, as he almost always does during a seizure, wet his pants.

"Of course! We'd love Leo." This girl seems sincere.

I don't want to get too greedy, but: "Um, but how will we get there?"

"I got you," says Zeus. "And Leo."

"Actually, I'd love it," I say. And I'm touched.

"Looks like he's got a girlfriend," says Zeus.

Penny and Leonardo are sitting together. Penny is talking to him, and Leonardo, as Leonardo does, is staring off into space. In the background, Jack, in his futuristic-looking wheelchair, is gazing at both of them. His mouth is open and his head is lolling a bit because he has "low tone," which means he has trouble controlling his neck muscles, which are also weak. But also the human head is disproportionately heavy. His slack mouth is turned up at the corners in what I recognize as a smile.

Leonardo has started repping with his fingers, not making eye contact. But I think he may be looking at her in his peripheral vision. She is cute, with soft blond hair falling like feathers around her delicate face, warm blue eyes, translucent skin.

"But what's she doing there?" Yunji says.

"What do you mean?" I say, puzzled. But then I see the Girlfriend of Curley walking by the table and stopping. And sitting. On the other side of Penny, animatedly trying to engage her in conversation. What is she doing, ruining Leo's moment? "Aghlumphhh," I can almost hear him say, his frustration noise.

"Oh I know what it is," says Oliver, stealing one of Zeus's kimbaps. "In study hall, of course where we're all supposed to be quiet, she was whining loudly to her friend about her parents thinking she can't get into a good college."

"Is she smart?" I ask.

"What do you think?" says Yunji. "You can almost see side-boob with that cut-out shirt."

"What you wear doesn't have anything to do with intelligence," I say gently. "She still could be smart."

"Trust me, she's not. She's never made honor roll. And look at those dumb braids."

Today she's wrapped them into two Mickey Mouse ears but at the sides of her head. It's a little bit Princess Leia in *Star Wars*, a little bit like an African style that I feel I've seen in some magazine, maybe one of Appa's *National Geographics*. But do I have to—ahem—reiterate to Yunji that hair, looks (size?)—has zero bearing on your intelligence, your heart?

But I want her to like me. I don't want to criticize her. "Maybe if she spent less time following Curley around and more time studying she could be smart," I say. It came out snarkier than I intended. On the other hand, the Girlfriend of Curley is still chattering away, having rudely inserted herself, full in Penny's face, forcing her to look at her, and turning away from Leo. Yes, I'm a little pissed at her.

Yunji regards me, like there's been some kind of test going on, and I've passed.

"Me-yow!" she says approvingly.

"Well, she's not good at academics or sports," says Oliver. "I think she's planning to establish a 'track record'—as she said—of 'service.' Of working with kids with disabilities as her 'talent.' I guess for the school her parents really want her to go to, they have a whole section in the application on volunteer work."

"Well, that's not so terrible," I say. "Maybe she'll learn something. Better than having your parents pay a bribe to get you in."

Yunji looks at me. "It doesn't bother you that she's just using Penny and maybe your brother and everyone else?"

I shrug. It's not like this hasn't happened before.

"People from Big Brother and other programs always come around for Leo," I tell her. "Some people are cool, but for at least fifty percent, he's a *project*. A merit badge." And then within ten minutes, they see how hard it is to work with him. He's not going to sit still while they read to him. He doesn't know turn-taking, so he can't be taught a game. If he doesn't interact, it's not a lot of fun. They can't go to a movie or be buddies or anything else Instapix worthy.

They rather quickly determine it's not rewarding enough for them and stop coming after giving it the old college try for a few weeks. Getting pinched or spit on is not the kind of stuff people like to see in posts.

"You know, once," I recount, "this guy must have thought this was some easy volunteer job and then saw it wasn't. I mean, I'm sure Leo was giving him a hard time of some sort, but the guy excused himself to the bathroom. We kept waiting for him to come back. Umma finally knocked on the door, worried something had happened. Well, something *had* happened. He'd left via the open window, who knows when.

"So far," I say. "Curley's girlfriend's interest seems harmless." It's good, I think. I saw a documentary once about these super-Christian moms who had a change of heart when it turned out their kids were gay or trans. They like literally had to choose, was their beloved church right, or was it right to just love their kids in whatever package they came in?

- - - - - - - - - - - -

After school, I go to the Mod to fetch Leo.

"Hey, LL Cool K," I say to Leo. "Hi, Ginger."

"His stuff's by the door," says Ginger, not even saying hi to *me*. "He had an up and down day, you'll see in the notes. He had regulation problems about thirty percent of the day." I know I should thank her for being so thoughtful, packing up his bag, but there's a burning in my gut as I watch her talk in front of Leo.

"Leo the Lion," I say, a bit pointedly. "How was your day?" Ginger doesn't notice my tone at all. She's bent over a book, scribbling—probably a bunch of end-of-day notes—like she's on death row and making a last-ditch bid for clemency. I can hear the *screek* of pen on page. Apparently, in our school district, there are way more special education students than there are aides, so people like Ginger, instead of just having one student they work with all day, have several, and they each need home notes.

"Honestly," Ginger mutters, "I don't remember any special-needs kids when I was growing up, except one kid with Down syndrome. Now half the boys have autism. And peanut allergies! Egg allergies. Gluten! Casein! Soy! Kids who'll die if they touch a pea. How are we supposed to keep up with that?" She's said it almost accusingly, as if my generation has opted for deliberately wonky immune systems just to mess her up.

Umma carefully packs Leo's lunch in a stainless lunch box, and repeatedly tells Ginger to be careful about Leo touching anyone else's food because he indeed has an egg allergy. I'm trying to imagine multiplying this by the X number of students and their parents that Ginger has. No wonder she's developed such a terse manner. Pick up, drop off, chop-chop-chop. I'm sure she wants to get home, too. But then, ironically, this makes *her* act out the same social deficits she's working to get Leonardo out of.

I want to sarcastically remind her to "Look: eyes, say goodbye, Ginger," but she doesn't even notice we're leaving.

- - - - - - - - - - - -

Yunji and Zeus are waiting for us, sitting side by side on the hood of Zeus's Kia, heels on the bumpers, like they're in some teen movie. Leo trots forward, does a kind of bouncy skip, and reaches them way ahead of me. There's actually something relaxing about watching him go ahead of me, to a safe space, for a change, rather than him following me, grazing my heels, head down, following only. I make a note to tell Umma I think this walking therapy is really helping.

"Hey there, Leo Kimster, what's up?" says Zeus. He lifts his hand for a high five, Leonardo complies, a little limply. His timing's off, but he makes up for it with an enthusiastic "Uhhhnnnhhhhhh!"

Everyone perks up around Zeus, who I see subtly shift his own timing and placement so their palms meet perfectly. I don't know what it is about Zeus that he's so good, but not in a do-goody kind of way. He'll come into a room and make sure to say hi to everyone. "Hey! How're you doing?" in such an enthusiastic, interested way, you just have to look back at him and smile, open up your heart to him.

I feel like if I did that, though, everyone would just look at me like, "Why's the fat girl being so friendly all of a sudden? What does she want?"

And if I said hi to a room and no one said hi back, I think Zeus would take it in stride, not blame himself. Me, I'd be devastated.

"Oh, wait, I forgot my chemistry notebook," says Yunji. "Ugh, I always do that on lab days! Be right back."

"Hi, everyone." It's Calvin. He's looking curiously at Leo, who has his head down and is quietly humming to himself and flicking one finger against another. He's happy in his own world right this minute, so I'm not going to drag him out, make him perform a "hello." Instead, I wave at Calvin.

Leonardo suddenly sits up straighter, looking around, like a deer trying to make out a scent in the air.

It smells like jasmine, actually. Like we're in the tropics, not in the burbs of Sunnyvale.

The scent is coming from the Girlfriend of Curley, who is walking in our direction.

"Hi, Zeus," she says. She appears to just be walking by. Probably to get a ride with Curley. You can't have a driver's license until eighteen in our state, but clearly that doesn't stop him, neither do the cops. I'm wondering if what Yunji was saying, about his family owning basically the whole town, is true. It must be, I'm thinking, or he has one of those hardship licenses where he needs to drive a tractor on a farm or something, and I'm pretty sure, living in the Gabilan Tower, that is not the case.

Leonardo suddenly falls into step behind her. He fails all his gross motor tests during an evaluation and yet he's fast and light as a cat at other times. I'm still sitting there before I realize this is happening.

"Oh!" she says, whipping her head around, which makes her loosened Kylie braids / Mickey Mouse ears swing open like a bead curtain.

Leo's jaw hangs loosely on its hinge, his face lights up. A snake charmer facing a jillion undulating snakes.

"Leo, Leo," I say. He's mesmerized. He's in heaven. Before I can stop him, he puts his hand out to try to catch a braid, same way he sometimes tries to catch sunbeams.

"Don't touch me!" she squeals.

At the exact wrong time, Curley enters the scene, a bag full of golf clubs slung on his shoulder. His one gloved hand in a fist as he runs over, the clubs clanking against each other in the leather.

"What the hell are you doing to my girlfriend!" he roars. "Get away, freak!"

"He grabbed my hair," she moans, hand to her scalp. Is she crying?

"He did not touch her!" I find myself yelling, even though I can not positively 1000 percent guarantee he didn't make fleeting contact with a braid. Or two.

Or maybe even, possibly, three. But he didn't *touch* her, like, not sexually.

"He has a condition," I say. Of course I feel bad talking about him in front of him, but in a panic, that's all I have.

"Get away from her, retard!" As if Curley would listen to me. Leo's starting his humming—the upset kind. He looks so confused.

Curley draws out a club from his bag like a sword from its scabbard.

- - - - - - - - - - - -

All I remember next is seeing Zeus in my peripheral vision. The squeaky-crack-voice of Curley's girlfriend screaming, like fabric ripping as Curley cocks the club.

Leo does what Leo does when he's confused: he bites. He lunges forward and manages a mouthful of Curley's fleece jacket. Curley is staring at his chest in horror as Leo opens wider for a bigger bite. Curley raises the club higher.

I rush toward Leo, managing to wedge myself between him and Curley. A noise like *thok!*, a pain in my shoulder, and I tumble into my brother.

I'm dimly aware that Zeus grabs Curley from behind by the collar of his vest.

Curley makes an "Ack!" noise and drops the club with a clatter on the sidewalk as Zeus pulls him out of range. I try to reach back to where my shoulder is numb. I'm practically on top of my brother and can smell a sweaty Leonardo smell—is he scared? Will he bite me? But he suddenly loses interest, plonks himself down, sitting cross-legged on the sidewalk, humming to himself, rocking, seemingly completely unaware, or uncaring, of what's just happened.

"Georgia! Are you all right?" Zeus is kneeling next to me, gingerly touching my shoulder. "Don't move, let me look at this." I'm so embarrassed I leap to my feet, but my legs bend, like those supports on the collapsible tents when they dismantle them. He smartly grabs my waist, to not put pressure on my shoulder, and sits me back on the sidewalk.

"Is Leonardo okay?" I ask through gritted teeth.

"He's fine, totally fine—but Curley just clobbered you with his golf club."

"What the fuck are you doing?" Yunji is screaming at Curley.

Curley is red as a firecracker. His short blond hair is standing up straight like it's steaming. He has his phone out. "I'm calling 911 because Special Ed Retard here tried to sexually assault my girlfriend."

"What?" I scramble to my feet and almost fall down again.

"Whoa there—" This time it's Calvin, catching me before I fall. His arm is so much thinner but just as strong. He turns to Curley. "You assaulted her With. A. Weapon—"

"Fat ugly bitch protecting her monster brother—"

"My brother has an intellectual disability!" I feel I am screaming but only a hoarse croak comes out. "He wasn't trying to assault anyone—he likes string!"

"Curley," Zeus says, his voice suddenly full of authority. "Are you for real? Calling the police on a disabled kid of color?"

"Did you see what that perv did to my girlfriend? She's crying. He's a menace. Put him in jail. In a home, I don't care." He stabs at his phone. I have a terrible vision of police coming, Leonardo not answering any of their commands like that time in the garden. Them trying to put handcuffs on him or something, Leonardo struggling, guns drawn—

"Oh my god, I can't believe something like this happened to me," Curley's girlfriend moans.

"Put it away." Calvin, who hasn't said a word this whole time, steps forward with his phone out. "I caught the whole thing on video. If anyone's getting booked for assault, it's you. You know how hard you hit Georgia?"

"Not going to look good on an Ivy League college application," Yunji adds.

"Shut up," says Curley, eyeing Calvin, Yunji, Leo, Zeus, and me in turn.

"Let's just move along now," says Zeus. Calmly. He has a kind of authority that makes everyone—from both sides—look to him. "Curley, don't call the police unless you're planning to get yourself arrested."

"Not likely," Curley smirks before turning to his girlfriend. "You okay, babe?"

She sniffles, nods. We watch the two of them drive away in his giant SUV.

"Georgia, do you need to go to the hospital?" Zeus touches my "good" arm. I see, or think I see, Yunji cut her eyes at him.

"It's just bruised," I say. There are some advantages to being a big girl. "I've broken bones before, I'm pretty sure I'm okay. He hit me in the meaty part of my shoulder."

"Did you really get that on video?" Zeus asks Calvin.

"Yes," Calvin says. "There's an app, Just-Us. It's to automatically start recording encounters with the police."

We're all quiet, thinking of why he might need that.

"I guess we should just go to hagwon," says Yunji. "We can get you some ibuprofen or something. You know, Curley has like ten relatives on the police force. Like I'm not even sure *with* the video that they wouldn't have stuck us all in some paddy wagon and arrested us. My parents would have a bird."

Zeus turns to Leo, who is still repping and rocking. "C'mon, Leo, bro, we've got some shrimp chips waiting for you back at the ranch."

"The ranch!" he cries happily.

Twenty

At hagwon, we all go in the back. I'm walking in hunched over, doing whatever the shoulder equivalent of limping is. I look like Quasimodo. An older, haggard-looking man, reminiscent of the man who was getting his hair cut when I was, passes us as he goes out. He gives us a funny look, but Yunji just nods at him.

"Oh, whoa," says Yunji in private, when I take off my T-shirt in the bathroom. "There's a huge lump like you have, well, a golf ball stuck under your skin."

"Zeus, you do tae kwon do, you should take a look at this," says Yunji when we're back out.

"Uhhhh—" I say.

"Okay. May I look at your back?" I nod. He gently pulls back the neckline of my T-shirt, shining a light from his phone.

"Ouch," he says. "That lump is a bone bruise. I used to get those in tae kwon do. They hurt like hell. It'll slowly get absorbed back into everything. Hey, we can still go to the police, you know."

"No," I say. "We got Curley to shut up about it, about Leo 'molesting' his girlfriend. That's all I want."

"Maybe Curley will behave, now that we've got him going all Arnold Palmer on you on video," Yunji says.

My thoughts exactly.

"You sure you're okay?" says Zeus, taking one more peek. I feel—I swear!—his breath on my neck.

"It's just bruising," I say.

"I've got some Advil," says Calvin, digging into his bag.

"Nah, nah, let's do this the Korean way," Zeus says. "Yunj, you got some ice, Salonpas, Tiger Balm?"

Yunji laughs. "How many *ahjussis* work or camp out here? They won't miss it if I took a dozen." In fact, the old man we'd seen earlier was heating up some instant cup ramen when we came in. Yunji finds him in another room, speaks to him in Korean, and he goes to the daybed and from underneath pulls out a worn duffle, hands over a tiny glass container of Tiger Balm, and what looks like individually wrapped sheet masks, but instead of a beautiful woman's face on them, they have a drawing of a man gripping his lower back, a red dot with pain waves radiating off it. Salonpas. Calvin runs next door to the Mozart Café for a grocery bag of ice.

"Cold goes first," Zeus says, and puts the bag of ice, wrapped in a towel, on my shoulder over my clothes. The cold and the pressure make a strange, crawly sensation, and I try not to yelp. In a few seconds, it starts to numb.

After ten minutes, Zeus removes the ice and Yunji sits on me like she's riding a horse. I can hear the crinkles of the package as she opens it. I can feel my T-shirt being lifted. My first panicky thought is I don't want them to see or even feel my muffin top overflowing the waist of my jeans. Then I think, I am right now obsessing over back fat while this guy Curley won't stop harassing poor Leo.

While obsessing, I don't even feel her putting the Salonpas thing on—it looks like a huge, square Band-Aid. But then the numbness of the ice pack gives way to fire.

"Ow!" I rear up, suddenly alive.

"It's just capsaicin, the stuff in hot peppers," she says.

"It hurts," I complain.

"The hot brings the blood to it. You gotta just be a Hwarang warrior," says Zeus. "That's what you are."

I wish I weren't lying on my stomach and could see Zeus's face when he says this. What does he mean? And if I could see, I'd peek at Yunji's face, too—is she mad? Does she agree? Is Zeus flirting with me?

"Hot and cold, shocking it is the best thing," Zeus says. "You want to set off danger signals to your body so it rushes all the blood and nutrients to heal it faster."

As I'm lying there like I'm suntanning indoors, I'm watching the hagwon from a different perspective, like how the trees and their leaves look so different when, instead of standing parallel to the tree trunks, you lie on your back, cradled by the roots, and look up, and the most mundane scene ever is completely transformed.

The older Korean man combs his hair (a strangely fashionable cut on a weathered face), puts his duffel back under the daybed, and walks out. I hear more than see the back door shut. Calvin is in his isolation seat, studying. Oliver is too, but he's playing a video game—he does this surreptitiously in school, too. I suspect he lives more online than he does in real life. The twins are having a Korean lesson with Yunji holding a white board where she's drawing Korean characters, erasing them, starting again.

Zeus is sharing a bag of shrimp chips with Leo, explaining the foil inside the bag, same way he did with us, as if Leonardo understands. And maybe he does. I can hear the squeaky sound of their crunching, like Styrofoam being crushed in hand.

The other day, Zeus came in wearing a whole sheet of the foil like a cape. It had a pattern with a picture of a teacup and it said "GLEEN TEA GLEEN TEA GLEEN TEA GLEEN TEA," repeated like a quilt.

"You can see why this one got rejected," he quipped. "But this stuff is so strong, and light, I can't bear to throw it away. It'll get stuck in a landfill where it's not going to biodegrade, because it's metal—it'll drift to an ocean and strangle some fish, or a sea turtle will eat it thinking it's sea lettuce."

Yunji teased him that he wasn't an ecowarrior, he was just a hoarder, and he parried that it's an immigrant thing, that his grandparents made a whole house out of crushed cans during the war. Nothing should ever be wasted. Especially this kind of foil, because it's extra thick for lining wholesale sacks of coffee and tea.

Earlier, when Mrs. Dongbong brought in some snacks, she grilled Zeus. Maybe to avoid asking about the ice packs. "How are your parents? How is Moksanim liking being back in Korea?"

"They're great," he said.

"You didn't want to go back with them?"

"No, ma'am," he said. "I like Korea—a lot. It's just not my place. Besides my parents and grandparents, of course, who I miss, all the people I love are here."

Yunji blushed.

"But your uncle," she pressed, "how is it living with him?"

"It's all right. Jungnam Uncle does his best, really. He's had a hard life."

"Aren't you afraid to live with him, after what he did to the kyae?"

"Well, I—"

"Mom, no need to give him the third degree."

Zeus shot Yunji a grateful smile.

- - - - - - - - - - - -

By the time Umma arrives, I'm repaired enough that I can get into the car without her noticing anything is amiss. When I'm twisting around to get Leo's seatbelt on and my face is pointed away, I let myself wince.

"That was really nice of Yunji to have you bring Leonardo to the hagwon."

"It was," I agree, and turn. "Wasn't it, Leo?"

"Nnnnnnah!" he says.

- - - - - - - - - - - -

The next day at lunch, Leo and Penny are sitting together again.

The hagwon crew is going to sneak out tonight and go to a Japanese karaoke place in Herbert Hills. It's an expensive restaurant that serves things in endless courses, catering to rich white people. The bar has a karaoke space. No one knows them, so everyone just thinks they are employees. They always make sure to go when they have enough money to tip generously. Apparently, when the crew does this, they also drink. Yunji looks much older than sixteen, and she also has a fake ID. I can't help imagining what it would be like, being in a dark, moody place, sitting close to Zeus.

"So is it hard living with Leo? Do you ever wish he were normal?" Yunji asks, almost as if part of my skull has turned transparent and she is reading something in my mind.

"Yunj," says Zeus. "What kind of question is that?"

Normally, I hate that question—and the person who asks it. But I also have a Leonardo rule: whoever is authentically nice to Leo, especially in times of stress, gets my undying loyalty. Like the hippy guy at the farmers' market who was always flirting with me, eating this unspicy vegetable slop they sold as "kimchi" with his hands (ugh!), sucking it from his fingers a little too vigorously while looking into my eyes. Gavin was his name. Well, once, Umma and I were out with Leonardo and he started in with his barks, grabbing at a lady's string bag. She looked frightened, then disgusted.

"You shouldn't bring someone like that out in public," she scolded Umma.

A couple of shoppers nearby seemed to agree. It was getting hard to hear over Leo's barks and yips.

"Hey, lady, please don't buy from here anymore," the hippy guy said. I looked. He was addressing her. She looked surprised, outraged, like he was talking to the wrong person.

Like he should be telling that to Umma.

"I mean it," he said. "This guy is my friend, and he's awesome. You want him to stay home? *You* stay home."

The woman huffed and went away. The man asked Umma if it was okay to give Leonardo an organic apple. She said yes.

Gavin the hippy man did not stop flirting and doing that weird kimchi-eating thing. I still hated him for that, but his kindness to

Leonardo overrode it all. Umma seemed to feel the same way. We bought most of our produce there and not at the other stands, until one day there was a new guy at the stand and no one knew where Gavin had gone.

- - - - - - - - - - - -

Even though I don't know how much of a friend the prickly Yunji and I will be, she's on Leo's side, so I am on hers.

"Honestly?" I say. "This is just my life. He's my brother. Yeah, it's limiting. But also, who wouldn't want their brother to be in their life?" I pause.

"You don't have other siblings, right?"

"Nope. Just Leo and me. I think it's more difficult for my parents," I say. "My mother hoped at some point when we were older that she could go back to work, but she's basically quit everything for Leo."

I'm thinking of how, should Leo do something magnificent—get a girlfriend, a job, learn how to read—not a whole lot, in terms of his care, would change.

Unless he suddenly became neurotypical, i.e. "normal," and without seizures, which I honestly think won't/can't happen. I try to imagine a normal walking talking Leo, with his same disordered teeth—that's almost weirder.

"I don't want to get married and definitely don't want kids," Yunji declares. "It's always harder for the woman. Like, do you think my mom dreamed her whole life of being a receptionist at a haircutting place? She was a music major in college! And for me to have to think about her sacrifice for 'the family'—for the kids, which means kid, which means me—every minute of the day?"

"I think our parents want us to be happy, whatever that is," I say.

"But I bet that's what *their* parents told them when they were kids. So?"

So? I don't know what to say.

"Are you saying having kids is a *trap*?" says Zeus.

"I might be," Yunji says. "Like an evolutionary thing."

"That makes sense, like propagation of the species," says Oliver.

"Like, I read somewhere that's why, evolutionarily, babies are cute—otherwise who would want to spend so much energy taking care of something that only cries and poops?"

"You know, kids grow out of that," Zeus points out. "They're not like that forever."

And that's how it normally works. When I was middle school age, Leo would have been old enough to babysit me. That was the plan if Leo had been a normal, everyday human. I wonder if he had been, maybe Umma and Appa would have had even *more* kids.

What happens, I wonder, when you have a story in your head? And a nice story. Umma and Appa were going to work hard to establish a happy family. Appa was going to make up for the loneliness of his childhood by having a ton of kids so they wouldn't ever have to be lonely like he was.

But what happens when your actual story doesn't match with your noble intention? I'm thinking of Appa's occasional bursts of shouting at Leo. I can't even remember—a single time—what he was shouting. But his voice was so loud and angry, it made me feel like shrinking away.

I think about, too, how, if we're just hanging around and Appa catches sight of me, he'll smile, almost like a reflex. It's cute. But he never does for Leo. He always has a slightly disappointed, exasperated look on his face, even if Leonardo isn't doing anything wrong. The tips of his lips curve down, his jaw hinge pokes out: a lump of tension. I heard Umma whisper to him once, "Can't you at least act pleased to see your own son?"

"When he shows me how smart he is, I will," he said back, in a voice I hadn't heard before. It reminded me of the inside of a cave.

"Don't be too hard on your father," Umma said later. "He feels like he can't let himself be happy until he knows Leonardo will be okay."

"But why doesn't he think Leo's okay now?"

"You know what I mean."

"But that's not fair to Leo."

"I know."

We shuffle out as the warning bell rings.

"I'll come pick you up," Zeus says to Yunji, leaning down to talk intimately in her ear.

And I feel a genuine pang.

- - - - - - - - - - - -

The next day, Curley's girlfriend's hair is out of the Kylie braids, back to just hair. It looks way better that way, I don't know why she bothers; from sitting with Shauntae one morning while she was getting her hair braided, I was surprised and dismayed it took *hours*. First, we chatted and laughed. Then it still wasn't done by lunch, so we ordered in. Shauntae gracefully and delicately ate her sandwich as the lady continued to braid. We chatted more. I got sleepy. To stay up we watched videos on my phone. At one point, we both fell asleep and the braider yelled at her because her head was lolling all around. It was also not cheap.

Shauntae said her hair was too curly to do much else, other than cut it close or straighten it. She was on the track team and liked that she could just tie the rest of it back, not soak her scalp in chemicals.

I wonder if the Kylie braids took as long to take out as to put in. What a production.

"*Anyong yay dull ah!*" Zeus joins us with his regular tray of kimbap. I'm thinking, a little jealously, how he buys them at the Arirang Market and then picks Yunji up and they come to school. I wonder if they had a good time last night at karaoke.

He's missed a patch of beard on his chin and his stubble looks adorable, but I won't tell him that, of course. It's unusually warm today and he's wearing a tank top and I notice—can't help it—he has almost no body hair, it's like he's sleek as a bone.

Quit staring! I remind myself. I also refrain from glancing at Yunji to see if she's seeing me stare at him.

"*E go bow jar,*" he says, flipping a colorful wallet onto the table in the middle of us.

"Nice," says Calvin. "Did you get it at Fair Trade Caravan?"

"Nah," he says with pride. "I *made* that sucker."

"What do you mean you made it?

"By the hand of Zeus. I used to be an origami nut when I was like twelve."

"What's it made out of, paper?"

"It's made out of Tyvek coated with aluminum," Zeus says. I reach to touch it. It's lighter than paper. I flip it over.

GLEEN TEA

GLEEN TEA

GLEEN TEA

"You made it out of the bag!" I say.

"Yep." He's beaming. "This stuff folds a lot like paper and holds its shape—but the aluminum makes it tough and durable, almost impossible to tear, like paper would."

Calvin is opening it, peering in. "This looks professional. Like you could really use it as a wallet—it's sewn on the ends"

Zeus beams. "Yep. I came up with a design, then came in early, sweet-talked Ms. Camilla, and she let me use the home ec machine to sew it up before school started."

"That's a manly hobby," Yunji says.

"Running an industrial machine to stitch metal—yep. I'm a man, it's manly." Zeus proudly opens the wallet. There's some slips of pastel paper inside: play money. Yunji said his family is poor, but "he hides it well."

"Dude," says Oliver, folding it up and slipping it in the back pocket of his jeans. "*Taebak*! You should sell these on Getsy!"

"You say that about everything I make from the Mylar, like that Tin Man costume—that took me ten hours. So I'd have to sell it for two hundred bucks to make a profit off my time."

"Yeah, that was amazing, even though we didn't win." Apparently for CA's Talent Night last year, Zeus had made Tin Man costumes for the hagwon crew and they did a synchronized K-pop dance to a song called "Follow the Yellow Road," by an Asian American group, playing on the word "yellow," as in "Asian," and words like "No chinks in these bricks!" They lost to Curley and his crew doing some kind of gangster rap in something that sounded dangerously like blackface.

"We were freaking *robbed*," says Yunji.

"The living Tetris game was pretty good, too, I had to admit," Oliver adds. He tells me that a bunch of kids from our math class, including a few from the Asian "nerd" table across the way, put together a Tetris game that used remote controllers to do a light sequence that the actual people, using the choir risers to stand on, used as cues to move. "That one," he says, "was by far the most imaginative, original, time-consuming thing. It was amazing. But of course you have student judges—they didn't even place in the top three."

"Hey, but back to the Zeus wallet, the Zwallet," says Calvin. "It looks fairly simple to make."

"Way fewer folds than a crane," he confirms. "And cheap, if not free, raw materials. I really started doing these crafts because I can't stand wasting all that Mylar," he says.

A pause. Zeus is suddenly frowning. Hard.

"Hey, Georgia, let me ask you this: can Leonardo fold things?"

"Ha!" I say. "Actually, one thing Leonardo is really good at is paper crafts." When he was in middle school, often nothing would calm him down except to be given a stack of paper to fold or cut up. The teachers quickly learned from each other that if they parked him facing the corner and gave him his stack of paper and scissors, he could be occupied for the whole forty minutes, folding, creasing, cutting, creating confetti. Not good pedagogical practice, of course, but it did keep him calm.

I'm looking over at him now. He's eating his lunch, rather neatly, I must say. He is doing better, I know it. He's sitting next to Penny again and looks so pleased, I find myself smiling.

I notice, then, that Zeus is looking over there, too, and that his expression mirrors mine. He glances back at me, still smiling, and nods at me. My heart not only bursts but it takes off wildly, like those catapulted bombs in Angry Birds that when you tap them on their trajectory, they explode and fly even *higher*.

But I am quite certain Yunji likes Zeus. And I am nothing if not a loyal friend, thinking of how she came to our rescue against Curley, even despite the trouble he could make for her family. I am careful not to look at her, because that would acknowledge, I think, how close—romantically or not—I am feeling to Zeus. And she knew him first. So I don't look at either of them, but I can feel the air is alive around us.

Twenty-One

On Saturday I'm up at my usual time, 5:00 a.m. Shauntae used to make fun of me for being such a nerd, keeping to such a schedule even on weekends. But for me, this is the only time I can claim as truly mine. Day, of course, is for school. Much of the night is Leonardo walking (or tantrumming) around, the rustles of Umma and Appa getting up to check him for SUDS.

Leonardo usually falls in an exhaustion-sleep by 5:00 a.m. This means a nice hour or so to myself, quiet, dark house, as if I am the only person in the world. The world, then, can be anything.

By six, the house rustles and heaves again. We are often roused by Leo's inhale-barking. Appa, even though he was at work late last night (full moon, when accidents abound, patients at the ER so numerous they get piled up like cordwood, lots of X-rays and things needed), is showered and shaved and dressed. He is always prepared for the world, outward facing. For him, ablutions are like prayer, like power.

Today, he's in a button-down shirt and pants that Umma has pressed so nicely the pleat in the front is sharp as a knife. He's going in to work—Saturday, Sunday is meaningless to him, as cancers and broken bones keep coming every day. Umma and I eat breakfast (me, cereal; her, rice she reheats by pouring hot water on it, adding a drop each of soy sauce and sesame oil). I'm off to Saturday hagwon, which they also call the *hangul hakyo*, because it's mostly set up for Korean lessons. I'm bringing Leo. But also just noticing we haven't heard him lumbering around. It's 8:30.

Umma and I glance at each other. We're thinking the same thing. SUDS.

"I'll go check on Mr. Sleepyhead," I say, as breezily as possible.

Leo's closed door suddenly looks like the door to the basement in every teen horror movie. At night it can be like walking into a room seeded with trip-wire mines. If he's actually asleep and we accidentally wake him, he can start attacking, the pupils of his eyes flat and dislike, unaware that he's being violent to real people, not just in his dream. When I'm home with Umma alone, I go in with a giant green therapy ball held in front of me like a giant belly in case Leonardo charges at me. Once, he did, with such force he bounced off the ball. At least the shock of that woke him up enough that he just sullenly stood by as I changed the sheets; the skunky smell of urine was what had drawn us in.

His door doesn't squeak as I open it; Appa keeps the hinges sprayed with WD-40. Leo's form is a lump on the bed, like a berm of earth, not quite distinguishable as him in the murky light behind the closed curtains.

I peer over him so I can see his face. His eyes are closed in a way that doesn't look natural: Instead of the top lid closed over the whole eye, the bottom lid seems to extend upward to meet the top. Like a frog's eyes. Or, like he's dead.

Even in the gloom, I can see a map of blood vessels in his lids, so pale and translucent, for they are never exposed to the sun.

Underneath, his eye twitches.

My knees almost buckle with relief. He's just sleeping extra heavily. There's a slight smell of urine—it's been too long, some nighttime urine has probably leaked. But for once, maybe he's gotten some good sleep. I back out of the room. Sleep is good for the brain. A relatively good day. Sheets can be washed, Leo can be, too.

Umma's looking up at me happily, expectantly, because I have returned, smiling. "Sleeping like a baby," I say. "Um, though he might have wet the bed, just a little."

"Let him sleep—teenagers need their rest," Umma says. She looks visibly relaxed, and I can't help but wonder if it's also because Appa's not here. If he were, he might yell at Leo, "What kind of teenager wets the bed? Are you a teenager or are you a little baby going *wah . . . wah . . . ?*"

- - - - - - - - - - - -

"Hey, what's up, my bro?" says Zeus to Leo at hagwon. Leonardo beams.

"My bro?" he echoes. Zeus has brought stacks of the GLEEN TEA Mylar bags. On the big table, on a bed of newspapers, he slices them with a huge X-Acto knife braced on a ruler, then runs what looks like a tiny pizza cutter down it.

"Fancy sewing stuff you've got there," says Yunji.

"This is a pattern marker," he says, smiling. "Yep, same thing if I were making a dress."

"Dress," says Leo.

"Hey Leo, do you like origami?"

"Excuse me," says Yunji. "Not origami. Can I remind you this is hangul hakkyo: it's *jong-i jeobgi.*"

"Gami," says Leo. "Jub-gee."

Calvin leans over and informs me, "*Jong-i jeobgi* just means *origami*—the word for *paper*, plus *folding.*"

"Yes, *jupda* is *to fold*," says Oliver, who, despite all his surfer-dude clothes and wild hair, is really smart. "That's the infinitive. When you add the *gi* to a verb it creates the gerund."

"Someone is a model hangul hakyo student," Yunji says.

"I like language," Oliver says. "If you understand the underlying structure first, it's a lot easier to learn." He's actually jockeying to become the editor of the school paper—he'd be the first Asian American editor of the *Cambridge Academy Bugler* in its history. Everyone says he's a great writer, and that he even writes poetry.

Zeus takes out a Sharpie and, with the ruler, marks the corners and the fold lines, exactly like an origami—jong-i jeobgi, sorry—pattern. He writes down 1, 2, 3, 4, 5, circling each number. He does it two more times. Then he traces all the lines on a piece of paper, making extra thick lines. He makes a stack of templates.

"Wanna do it together?" he says to Leo.

"Uhh!" says Leo, which sounds an awful lot like a yes. Calvin and I sit down with them and take the other two templates. Yunji exhibits a kind of hauteur like we're doing a kiddie craft project. She declines to accept one of the models but still hangs around as Calvin, Oliver, and I watch Zeus expectantly (and I have to say I love having an excuse to look at him).

With strong, sure hands, Zeus shows us how to fold, and how to use a fingernail to get a good crease. He gently puts his hand over Leo's and draws his fingers down the crease. This is Leo's fun, I'm thinking. It's almost like repping on Angry Birds. Zeus is extra patient. Leonardo doesn't understand the sequence, but he does get the folds. He is, in fact, the first one done with his.

"Yunj, doesn't your mom have a sewing machine? Can I use it?"

Yunji looks slightly panicked.

"Zeus the god of gods is not going to turn into a girl if he shows us how to sew," Calvin says, rather perceptively.

"Hey! What would be wrong if I did?"

"Nothing. I'd just want you to make me a dress, too," calls Oliver, from the beanbag chair.

"You guys are weird," Yunji grumbles. But she goes into a supply closet and returns with a sewing machine. It's tiny, like half the size of a normal sewing machine, and has a Finnish name and is already threaded, not with a spool but with a giant cone of thread. It looks like something you'd use in a factory.

"My mom sews and fixes the capes for Bomb sometimes," she explains.

"Oooh," says Zeus. "It already has a divided presser foot."

He shows us how to run stitches on three sides—zip, zip, zip!—while keeping our fingers away from the racing needle. I keep waiting for the tissue-thin Mylar to rip, but it doesn't. The needle goes up and down, in and out, puncturing the foil, each stitch regular and true.

"Here, I need to adjust the tension," he says, leaning over. "Excuse my arm." He smells so clean, like sage, like fir trees, like ocean spray. Ugh, maybe I should write a poem about it. "See how the stitches are looser at the bottom?" he shows me my piece. The top looks great, the bottom is a bit of a tangled, loose mess. "We need to adjust to make sure the tension on the top matches that on the bottom. So when we do it right"—He runs a line of stitches—"it looks the same on both sides, all the work of the stitches locking is done in between the layers where you can't see."

He shows me the perfect line of stitching.

"I had no idea that's how sewing machines worked."

My stitches, even tension adjusted, zigzag too much and are unusable. Unlike fabric, we can't pull the stitches out and try again, because (I tried) the Mylar will rip. Oliver makes a passable wallet, Calvin, too—and all with Leo's folding.

Then the Korean teacher, a middle-aged man who teaches at City University, arrives. "*Anyonghaseo,*" he says.

"Anyonghaseo," we all say back. I'm equally excited to learn Korean. I'd assumed Calvin was going to go back to studying, but there he is, learning Korean with us. Since I don't know anything, he, Zeus, Yunji, and Oliver all sound like experts. It's so tantalizing that they can all do something I hope I can do in the future.

- - - - - - - - - - - - -

I'm waiting for Umma to pick me up. And Calvin. Saves Dr. Charlie time. Saves the planet.

I glance at Leonardo to make sure he's okay.

He and Calvin are holding hands.

When Leonardo likes people, he likes to hold their hands. Sometimes, though, he can start holding on too tightly, and if the other person panics and tries to pull away, that paradoxically makes him hold on even more tightly—like one of those Chinese finger traps—which can lead to a scary spiral. He did it to Ginger the other day and she complained to me. "He could have broken my fingers, you know." As if he did it on purpose! As if I were his mom or something and was supposed to do something about it (as if Umma should be to blame).

But it makes me happy that (1) he likes Calvin, (2) if he's holding Calvin's hand he probably won't run off, (3) that I have a friend who'll hold Leo's hand.

A Korean auntie walks of out Bomb, her new perm poodle-curly. She stops to blatantly stare at Calvin and Leo, muttering something that sounds like *omo* or *homo*, and it suddenly comes into focus that Leo, my brother, forever a kid to me, is almost a man. In a parallel universe, he would be driving *me* home.

"Wait, what the heck is she doing here?" Calvin says. I assume he's talking about the auntie, but he's looking in the opposite direction. I follow his eyes. It's Curley's girlfriend with a fluffy little dog with a wheat-colored tail. Despite the municipal signs that say All Dogs Require Leashes, her dog is loose. She's "walking" while texting on her phone. She bulldozes a passerby with her inattention.

"Hurt you," Leonardo says, stiffening. I shove Leo, and Calvin—because Calvin is attached to him—back into Bomb Haircuts. "He's scared of dogs."

The girlfriend sees me and stops.

"Hi, Georgie, funny seeing you here."

"Georgia," I say. "And funny seeing *you* here."

"Why? The dog groomer is here. Curley's family owns this whole thing, you know. So what are you doing at Pecan Plaza?"

As if she can't see this is almost all Korean and I'm Korean. "Waiting for my mom. I go to hagwon here." If she's always hanging out here, maybe she's picked up some Korean.

"Hagwon?"

"It's like study hall."

She pauses, then laughs. "Oh my god, how nerdy, I mean, you get out of school and just do study hall all weekend?"

"It's more like Fight Club," I say.

"Haha, you're funny. Anyway, I've got to get Betty to her hair appointment."

"See you."

And with that, she walks down to the store at the end, Paws and Claws Pet Grooming, and disappears.

I open the hagwon door.

"Coast is clear, Leo. No dogs."

"No dogs," he says, but more like an imperative.

"You're safe," I say.

"You're safe?"

"Leo, we won't let anyone hurt you," says Calvin.

"Hurt you!" says Leo. You can almost see his anxiety climbing, like the mercury in a thermometer.

"You want to sing a song?" asks Calvin. "Let's sing 'Swing Low, Sweet Chariot.'"

As they sing (and where is Umma?), I see Calvin unobtrusively unlatch his hand from Leo's. He flexes his fingers a few times, then takes up his hand again. I wonder if Leonardo unconsciously crushed Calvin's hand when he saw the dog. Of course, I don't want to say anything in front of Leo. So instead I try to beam my appreciation at him. Calvin catches my eye for a second and smiles.

When we get home, I check Leo's fingernails first thing. It's Umma's job to clip them, but sometimes with her list of ten thousand things, she forgets. Then if Leonardo squeezes your hand, sometimes he digs his nails in too—you'll have a row of four (five if he also digs his thumb into the web of your hand) red crescent moons. Once, he even broke the skin of my hand.

I text Calvin.

OMG I'm so sorry about that.

About what?

About Leonardo squishing your hand.
He does that when he gets scared.

. . .

I'm fine

He is a gentle person underneath all that. He
doesn't like dogs, huh?

I think it's the thing he's most scared
about in the world.

He's smart. I don't like dogs, either.

How about cats?

. . .

I like cats. They don't bother to impress you.

He sends me a row of emoji cats, the last one of a cat with hearts
for eyes.

Is it possible to have crushes on two boys at once?

Twenty-Two

At lunch, Calvin and I are discussing irrational numbers when we both look up and see Curley's girlfriend heading to our table—again. It's kind of been no secret she has the hots for Zeus; she's openly mooning at him in the halls. Not an irrational choice. And I kind of like that the stereotype of Asian guys as less masculine or datable or whatever is completely disproved in Zeus. He has at least three girls who have crushes on him.

Curley's girlfriend is here without her Mermettes. She's wearing a low V-cut shirt that displays her cleavage. Cleavage is against the law at Cambridge Academy, but I know she's worn this shirt before without any problem. Ironically, a few weeks ago I was stopped and issued a warning ticket. It was super hot out and I was wearing a dress. It wasn't low at all. It's more because I have such big boobs, when I wear a bra that keeps my boobs off my stomach, my cleavage basically goes up to my neck. I kind of laughed it off when the hall monitor gave me the ticket. Also, how can that be some *male* person's *job* to look at girls' cleavage?

Curley's girlfriend, in the meantime, positions her cleavage at the back of Zeus's head. When he abruptly turns, looking for the wall clock, he almost bumps into it. He turns back fast.

"So, hey, Georgia—" she says.

"Me?"

She smirks. "Is there anyone else named Georgia at this table?"

"Okay."

"I wanted to talk to you. I volunteer at Service Dogs International, and I think Leonardo should get a dog."

"*What*?" I can hear Calvin cracking up behind me. So hard the bench is shaking.

"A dog is the last thing Leonardo needs," I explain to her.

"No, kids like him *love* dogs. They calm them down. It's medically proven."

I shrug. "Maybe so but Leonardo gets scared out his mind by dogs."

"You just need to expose him more. He might have a phobia, but he could get over it."

I can't help laughing, joining Calvin.

She frowns. "I don't see what's so funny."

"We saw you the other day at Pecan Plaza, with a dog, a really little one. Leonardo got scared."

"Ah, Betty. She's a foster for Service Dogs. I can only foster one during the school year."

"How long have you been doing this?" I ask.

"Two years." She flips her hair, revved up, seemingly glad for an audience. "It kind of drives my parents nuts; they don't get why I'd foster a dog and not get to keep it. But they don't start the service dog training until they're almost a year old. And a lot of them don't make the cut as service dogs."

"What if they bite people?" asks Oliver.

"Well, that, and other things." She glances over at Zeus, who's eating a sandwich today: white bread, Spam, kimchi. He gets up to go to the hydration station; the disappointment in her face is palpable. "Some of them can be too cute, I mean too friendly, or not have a good attention span, things like that.

"What happens to them if they flunk out?" I ask.

"Oh, they get adopted. But I'm proud to say every one of the dogs I've fostered has gone on to be a registered service dog or an emotional support animal."

Ah, I'm thinking, that's why that dog we saw looked so small. A puppy of sorts.

"So I thought I could maybe like come to your house some time and bring Betty? She's really well trained. And maybe then Leonard could see how cool dogs are."

"Take my word for it. Leo's so scared of dogs, he's practically allergic."

"Did he have a bad experience? He must have! Humans are hard-wired to love dogs, and vice versa."

"He's always been scared. So we keep him away from dogs. Like, you aren't going to force a kid who's scared of heights onto a roller coaster."

"Well—" She stands up taller, hands on hips (also, Zeus is returning from the hydration station). "That's exactly what I'm saying, he needs ex-po-sure."

This is going nowhere. Plus, I want to eat my lunch—we have five minutes left.

"Thanks," I say. "Why don't you get me some materials about your organization—later?"

Her face lights up. She whips out her phone. "Great! I'll email you our website. And get you some brochures."

"Oh geez," says Calvin, watching her leave. "Georgia, she's going to get you killed by a golf club."

"Calvin, you don't have any gang buddies to protect her?" Yunji says, laughing. "From the hood?"

"Not funny, Yunji—" I snap, before I am even conscious I've said it. An itchy silence descends on the whole table. But there, I've said it.

Now, I'm worried I said the wrong thing. Like, Georgia Buzzkill, soon to be sitting at her own table again, especially after Yunji's been so nice to me. In fact, I owe my whole social life to her.

Also, was I being patronizing to Calvin? Calling him out for being Black? I can't look at either of them.

"I suppose I could round up my friends from Great Books," Calvin says, evenly. "Or maybe even the math team. But I don't think it's about Georgia. She's just a conduit to Zeus—*he's* the one who needs to be careful around Curley, methinks."

Zeus says, oddly serious, "Girls with boyfriends are definitely not my type."

"What is your type?" Yunji wants to know. "All guys seem to like blond hair and big boobs. It's like something that comes with the Y chromosome."

"I have a type," is all Zeus will say, looking straight ahead, not looking at her and winking, as he should. Yunji frowns.

"That girl comes up with the dumbest excuses to talk to you," she says, a bit sullenly.

"That's true," Calvin agrees. "She's trying to sell an iceberg to the *Titanic*."

I glance over at Leo's table. He is there with Penny, Jack, and the aides. And Curley's girlfriend is there, too, now chatting animatedly with Penny. Sure Curley's girlfriend is vapid. Sure she's probably doing this to establish a track record of volunteer work to put on her college applications. But maybe, just maybe, I'm wondering, she really, actually is sincere? Penny is gazing at the ceiling, genuinely laughing. Why shouldn't a popular girl take an interest in her?

And even, let's say, if the Girlfriend of Curley has the most selfish ulterior motives—if she even accidentally becomes more empathetic, I don't think I'd care. Let her be a phony if that ultimately makes her a better person.

- - - - - - - - - - - -

The other day, Leo needed his meds, so I brought them to the Mod during my study hall. They had been having an occupational therapy group doing potato stamps. Leo was the only one who didn't successfully dip the cut-up potato in the paint and press it on the paper.

He put his fingers in the paint. Tried to lick his fingers before Ginger could clean them. Grabbed the potato and mushed it on the side of the table. Threw the remaining piece of potato at Ginger. All the while Penny was methodically stamping and then decorating a beautiful card.

Of course, none of that says anything about Leo's actual intelligence—maybe he's bored! Maybe an almost-eighteen-year-old doesn't want to be doing potato stamps, something I did in first grade. But Umma and Appa just fret over the bad school reports. And I can see why they worry. Penny seems miles ahead of Leo, like I could see her later having a job or something. Leo doesn't have to conform to anything. But in order to work, everyone has to conform somewhat.

I have been imagining forward, about how things are going to be in college—studying, new friends, hopefully no Curley types. In my schoolbag, in fact, I have my "invitation to apply," plucked out of the mail before anyone saw it. Appa would flip out if he saw which college it was. They are even offering an all-expenses-paid visit. Next year is when we will all start applying. Miss Wick, my college advisor, said that if I really like a school, I should do "early decision" because my odds will be better. It's almost a hack, that schools like to fill their classes with committed students early, as it increases their yield, takes more of the unpredictability out of the "game." They certainly didn't seem to have all these "hacks" at City High.

I show the letter to Calvin.

He whistles through his teeth. "Wow! That's amazing, Georgia. Like, seriously."

"But how would they even know about me?"

"I bet you had great PSAT scores." I did.

But later, this made me realize I bet he also got such a letter. He's just too modest to turn the conversation to himself. He probably got five letters like this. There's no way he didn't.

I like this school because it's not a banker factory like some of the other good schools. And, it's in a city.

The obvious problem is its location.

Appa keeps saying when the time comes, I need to make my choice and not think about Leonardo at all.

How can I not think about him? It's like asking me not to breathe. I can agree to not think about it. But I will still do it.

I remember one sibling group, where this girl, Cara, talked about how destructive her disabled brother was, how the whole family lived like there were trip wires stretched all over the house—and they inevitably went off—boom!

Boom! Boom! And when they finally, reluctantly sent him to a residential school, at first, the quiet that followed was so strange it was almost anxiety-producing. But then it just became peaceful, normal, predictable. They could hear things like their neighbor's leaf blowers again—or each other's voices. They went out to get ice cream, like a normal family, for the first time, well, ever. That first weekend without him, they went to bed on a Friday and got up Sunday, that's how sleep-deprived they were.

I keep in touch with this girl, usually a text here and there. She's in college and seems happy. I don't see any pictures of her brother on socials though. Not a single one. Not like she posted many before (his face was always beat-up from hitting himself), but I can't help wondering, is *he* happy? Or is he just out of sight and out of mind for the rest of the world? Is someone thinking about him? Or is he just being parked somewhere to save the rest of the family? Isn't his life worth saving, too?

It's like that philosophical train wreck question.

You are a train engineer. A train is speeding toward a crowd of people. There's one guy standing off to the side. If you pull a switch, the train will divert, kill that one guy, but save the crowd.

Does saving more people make it worth sacrificing the one?

Who gets to be in the crowd? Who is the one guy?

This wouldn't be the first time someone suggested we shouldn't waste our lives on a futile cause like Leo, like moths hurling themselves at a light.

It was Appa I overhead once saying, "We can't let Leonardo bring Georgia down, too." He even called it a "meaningless sacrifice." Living in a city apartment, paper-thin walls, they thought they were speaking privately, but I heard every word.

Cara from the sibling group did admit that her brother's "home" was stinky, like urine. He had bruises the staff said were from falling off the monkey bars. He didn't have the grip to pull himself up on monkey bars. But worse, in her book, he had mismatched socks on, one black, one white.

"It's like they couldn't even be bothered to put matching socks on, like who cares? To them, he's just a retard who's out of it and hits himself and just needs to have his feet covered."

"You shouldn't use that word," the counselor leading the session said.

"*I* shouldn't use that word when people might be hitting him? What person would automatically assume someone doesn't care that their socks match!"

I think that would have been the detail that haunted me the most, too—even more than the bruises.

Leonardo has huge feet. They are a rhomboidal shape, widest at the toes, like a frog's. His toes are also big and long, not curved together but spaced out with huge gaps between them, like slats in a fence. It makes getting his socks on like hooding a moving, struggling cat, especially with his colony of toes wiggling. I have a way of gathering up one of his men's XL gym socks, stretching the mouth wide, and basically lassoing the top part, then rolling the sock down quickly. He will not hold his foot out for me to do this, it can take ten to fifteen minutes sometimes, and it's the worst if we're already rushed.

But he had matching, clean socks on his feet. This is a mandate. My commitment. The heel must be in the right place: on the heel. It's like he knows I love him because I'll spend all day getting those socks on his damn weird-shaped feet. Perhaps even more importantly, however, it says to the outside world, this boy is loved. I count on the monkey-see-monkey-do aspect of humanity.

It's a fact that I can't sock his feet from across the country. Would I instead spend all day worrying about Leo?

I'm afraid to look at the brochures, to learn anything more about this college in case I'll like it too much. I decline to tell my parents about the offer of a free visit for the same reason.

- - - - - - - - - - - -

It's my turn to go to the hydration station. It's so near to the jock table, though. Generally, I try to make sure I'm hydrated before lunch. But

I'm parched. I eye Curley to make sure he is safely occupied before I venture out.

The Curley table holds quite a crowd. A dozen athletes from various teams, Curley's girlfriend. She says something I can't hear. Curley tilts his whole torso back and laughs. He's wearing his usual varsity golf fleece, unzipped so you can see under it a T-shirt with a silhouette of an automatic weapon that says "Come and Get Em." It makes me wonder what the school would do if Calvin wore something like that. City High didn't have a dress code, or one I ever saw enforced. Cambridge Academy forbids shorts (even with the weird eighty-degree days of October), "provocative" clothes for girls (cheerleading outfit exempted), no male nipples (Zeus is playing with fire with his tank tops), open-toed shoes (Zeus again), and "clothes with slogans that are overly political or hateful," and of course the cleavage patrol.

I'm filling my bottle when I hear, "God, as if you'd know."

Curley is speaking to his beloved. "You can't even change a tire on a car! Hey, guys, she didn't even know you have to loosen the lug nuts *before* you jack it up—hah!" He looks for approbation, which he gets in the form of guffaws and snickers. Her face turns red and she looks angry and sad at the same time. "But that's why I'm trying to learn," she mutters.

"Women!" He rolls his eyes. He's not done. I don't think he'll ever be.

Curley's girlfriend is so pretty. She reminds me of those perfect blond girls with the light eyes and the luminous skin, not like mine with the yellowish cast that seems to gather light rather than have it bounce off, radiant and pearly. But alone among the guys, in their shiny green golf shirts, the shoes with the spikes on them, she looks a little forlorn, an exotic bird in a zoo. Something bred for its looks alone, something bred to be gawked at and nothing more, until it gets too old and will be discarded.

Twenty-Three

On Saturday, Calvin and I are chattering about our Great Books this week. Calvin's parents are dropping us off early because Dr. Charlie is going on a business trip and they will drop us off on the way to the airport. Dr. Charlie (the driver in the family) pulls up to the front, but Bomb Haircuts is closed; it doesn't open until noon on Saturdays.

"Someone will come as soon as we ring the bell," Calvin assured them. His mom kisses him out her open window. We wave until we see them turn onto the street. Then we go around to the back. The extension's door is already cracked open in welcome. The rest of Pecan Plaza is puzzling. Across the way, a semi—Lee's Quality Asian Food & Produce!—is unloading; we hear the hum of its refrigeration. Mr. Lee, the dry cleaner owner, is directing a young employee (his son?) who is loading up a van with racks of clothes sheathed in plastic. We wave to him and walk into the hagwon to the surprise of a dude *sleeping* in one of the day beds.

He's snoring away, limbs overflowing from the narrow bed. I've never seen someone sleep with such abandon. There is a well-traveled extra-large wheelie bag at the foot of the bed. It's shiny with dirt, the top zipper is open. There's a bunch of plastic grocery bags sticking out of it. The sight is so unexpected, we forget to lower our voices. He bolts up, sees us, says something like, "Aye, sheesh." The first thing I notice is that he only has one hand. He gets up stiffly and walks to the back door, grabbing a grubby coat on the way and plastering a hat on his head with his one hand, coming back, as an afterthought, for the wheelie bag, which has a bum wheel that skitters over the floor as if reluctant to leave with him.

"*Me an ham knee da*," apologizes Calvin. Yunji pops in, yawning, her phoenix-hair slightly unkempt.

"Um, who was that?" Calvin asks.

"That was Bae," says Yunji.

"Your *bae*?" He looks at her.

"Not like that kind of Bae. Bae is his name."

"Ah, like *bae*, the word for pear."

"Exactly."

"So he's not just some random guy who wandered in and took a nap on that daybed."

"There are a lot of new immigrants working at Pecan Plaza. My parents let them crash, even overnight sometimes. Like, Bae just needs a few days to get settled. I don't know what his story is, but he'll be moving on pretty soon."

"Good-u mow-uh-ning," says Oliver, in an exaggerated Korean accent, also coming through the back door. "Who da ahjussi?"

"That's Bae," repeats Yunji.

"Where do you guys live?" Calvin asks.

Yunji pauses, looking at us appraisingly. "You really want to know? Our secret? So don't put that in the paper, cub reporter Oliver."

Suddenly, it hits me: "Do you live here?"

She nods. "Upstairs. It's not zoned for residential use, but that's just stupid."

I agree. "In the city, people live above their businesses all the time."

"Exactly. This makes it so much easier for my parents to get to work, to take care of me when I was little. And now they can help out other immigrants. And not just Koreans, we've had Mexicans and Colombians stay here—they work at Koryo and Arirang."

"Like, Zeus is probably eating Mexican kimbap," says Oliver. "Mr.

Oh has them doing all the prepared food. He's not great with the labor practices—I think he paid them like five bucks an hour. They went on strike last year!"

"See what I'm saying, about Oliver, cub reporter?" She rubs her temples. "I actually think Oliver hanging around, asking them all these questions, like 'Is Mr. Oh paying you under the table?' 'Do you know what the minimum wage is?' actually gave them the idea to strike."

"I did not encourage them to strike," Oliver corrects. "That's not what journalists do. But my questions may have made them think about their collective situation a little better."

"You never wonder why that kimbap you and Zeus buy every day is only two bucks a roll? Or that we have to lie about where we live in order to live here?"

"Where do you technically live?" I ask. "For school registration purposes."

"Herbert Hills." She pauses and looks around. "Might as well have a fancy fake address. You know, when Zeus's uncle was having his troubles, Zeus stayed here, too."

Ah. I'm wondering, was *that* why they were so close?

"After Zeus's uncle ran off with the kyae, he left Zeus all alone. Like how is a high school kid going to pay rent on an apartment? So Appa had Zeus working here cleaning up. Then his uncle came back and now those two live together—for now."

That napping guy. I try to picture him as Zeus. No wonder Zeus didn't exactly get to concentrate on school that year.

"So obviously no one can know we live here. Curley's dad would have us all evicted."

"They don't already have any clue you're here?" Oliver says.

"They don't. The *noraebang* is open all night, so is the café, so there are always lights on in Pecan Plaza. We have blackout shades on all the windows upstairs. My dad is extra paranoid so he installed an industrial hood on our stove so that it vents out the roof and toward the restaurant; no one's going to smell our dinner at Bomb Haircuts."

Zeus comes into hagwon with a big grin on his face. "Yunj," he says.

"I was just chatting with your umma. She said we can use the sewing machine as much as we want as long as we buy the thread and keep it oiled and stuff."

"You sewing yourself an apron or something?"

"No!" he hoots. "These!" He presents a small stack of wallets. "Leonardo folded so many I didn't have time to get to them all."

GLEEN TEA GLEEN TEA

GLEEN TEA GLEEN TEA

We study to the whir of the Finnish sewing machine.

Zeus presents us with a stack of wallets. The last bit of Mylar was only half printed with GLEEN TEA, and cut off, it makes its own cool, unreadable language.

Oliver is already transferring his money into one. "Dude, you really should sell these—I'm serious. At least like at the Christmas gift fair or something. Earn snack money for hagwon."

"What should we call 'em?" Zeus asks, after stuffing a handful of his usual shrimp chips into his mouth.

"Dude! You spit on me!" Oliver yelps, play pushing him away.

Calvin flexes a finished wallet. "Flexible but strong. I love these. How about Leo's Bendables?"

"That's a good name," says Oliver. "Like I said, you should sell them."

"That's exactly what I'm thinking," says Zeus. "They're so easy to make, we could sell them at school and stuff, maybe get the bookstore or like the stationery store here to put them by the register. So we need a catchy name with *Leo* in it. Also so we can have a hashtag. So let's think of a good one and stick with it."

"Leo's Flexibles."

"Leo the Lion."

"Leo's Lucky Rabbit Wallets," I say.

"We could start an Instapix for him and at him on social," says Oliver.

"Maybe celebrities will fight over the right to carry one to the Oscars."

"I'll write the copy," says Oliver.

"I'll do the numbers, to make sure it's profitable, supply and demand," says Calvin. "Unless you want to do it, Georgia."

"We can do it together."

"Hey!" says Zeus. "Is that a yes, Georgia? Can we do this as a project—not *for* Leo, but with Leo? You know how the little middle school kids are always coming by with their lousy candy that people buy anyway because they need to be nice? Well, we're going to have a beautiful product they can use, that has a story."

"And is eco-friendly," adds Calvin. "Upcycling. Taking stuff out of the waste stream. All the stuff young people our age are into. Oliver, write that down."

"Roger!"

"Man," says Zeus, patting my shoulder. "I'm so glad you guys moved here. I haven't felt so jazzed in ages."

"You just like having an excuse not to study," says Yunji. She's smiling, but I can tell she's a little annoyed. I think if I were the big person on campus and some new kid came along and I helped her get her bearings and had her join everything and then she took everything over, including her boyfriend, I'd be mad, too.

Of course, that's not what's going on. I am not going to steal Zeus, would never do that to a friend (but: do I wish I *could*?). And what's she so threatened about? She's definitely the alpha of all the Asian kids at school, while the most interesting thing about me is my brother.

"Here's this week's leftovers, check it out." Zeus hands me a stack of raw Mylar. Our fingertips touch, and I almost feel like I've been shocked and pull my hands away. I can't help but steal a glance at him. His cheeks are red. Not pink, but Hawaiian Punch red, like the way Appa's whole face gets when he drinks alcohol.

To hide, I pretend to examine the Mylar. "This is really pretty—" Peachy colors, with a curved design of . . . rabbits. "Oh my god," I say.

"You okay?" His eyes are big. Cheeks still red.

"Leo's favorite, favorite animals in the world are rabbits."

Zeus grins. "Well, we are in luck then. Some non-Asian placed a huge order for Lunar New Year but it's Year of the Pig this year, dummy!"

"Didn't you say 'Leo's Lucky Rabbit Wallets' back there?" says Calvin. I nod.

I smooth down the Mylar, which shimmers on its foil side. This whole stack probably has fifty sheets, from which we can cut the material for a dozen wallets per sheet. He hands me the template and ruler. "Bring it home and see what he thinks."

- - - - - - - - - - - -

While we're waiting outside for Umma to pick us up, Calvin says to me, "He likes you, you know."

"Who?" I feign disinterest.

"You like him, too," he says. "Zeus."

"Zeus?" I laugh, unbelievingly. "He's practically married to Yunji."

In fact, Yunji did once confide to me that she did, one day, see herself going to college, getting an MBA, and taking over Bomb Haircuts, maybe making it into a chain, for Korean shopping centers everywhere. And with Zeus. "He's so good at doing all the practical stuff. And wouldn't he be a perfect hair model?"

"I like him—who doesn't? But I don't *like* like him," I say, out loud, to convince myself. He loves Leonardo as much as I do. And so I shall avoid having some delusional dream where we marry and take care of Leonardo together, forever. It's too tempting.

"Good," says Calvin with a bit of a slick smile. "So maybe there's still hope for me."

I don't know what to do with this except pretend he's kidding. And maybe he is. I bump him with my shoulder. He bumps me back. Umma shows up, then, waving out the van's window. There's Leonardo in the back.

Twenty-Four

We start selling Leo's Lucky Rabbit Wallets at school. Oliver writes the copy that we hand out with each wallet. He sat down and interviewed me—and Leo—for his story. He brought it to the school paper, and they liked it so much, they had him write a longer article, and they published it. Occasionally I can hear people saying hi to Leo, not just Curley's girlfriend. He doesn't always respond. Actually, he rarely does. But I love hearing, "Hey, it's Leo!" When Leo comes to hagwon with us, he eats all the snacks. Oliver or Zeus or Calvin take him to the bathroom as if it's no big deal. Because he's taken so often, he's never had an accident at hagwon. I'm proud of this. He loves the beanbag chair, and sometimes he just plays on his NAD the whole time. But sometimes he folds. And folds and folds and folds.

Good thing, because there's a run on the wallets. The *Cambridge Academy Bugler* is online, so we even started getting email orders, from all over the country: Nebraska, Minnesota, California, Massachusetts.

"These are so light a first-class stamp works," Calvin declares. "If you really get serious, there's bulk mail. But I think for now what we need to do is set up a website or something. Sell them directly, cut out the intermediary."

"You sound very businessy, Calvin," I say.

"Yeah. I just like it. My parents don't have business as their top choice of careers, like, we already have enough of that in society."

"But you're good at it," I say. "And if you like it, well maybe the 'good for society' part will come later."

"What do *you* want to be?"

"A doctor." Then I pause. "Actually, I don't know. Medicine is something I might want to *do*. But honestly, I don't know what I want to—"

"Hey, you know," Curley's girlfriend says, sashaying up to our table. "About those wallets." But of course: there's an open space next to Zeus, well, maybe half an open space. To our astonishment, she jimmies herself in there, one leg in, one leg out. Facing Zeus, her back rudely to Yunji. While we're staring at her, open-mouthed, she tosses her hair in a semicircle that Yunji makes a big show of spitting out.

"Hello, can we help you?" says Yunji. She's glaring at the space where Curley's girlfriend's back is, right in front of her face, like a closed elevator door. Zeus, for his part, is tilted back on an axis so severe he's practically in Oliver's lap. I curl forward a bit, feeling the phantom golf club hit my shoulder, as I always do in these moments, my heart beating out of control. Their whole group already thinks we're a bunch of Asian nerds, so why can't she just leave us alone?

Yunji continues to glare at her back. "Does Curley know you're here? Is he going to attack us with a golf club again? Threaten to call the police?"

She smirks. "I don't answer to Curley."

Yunji's snort is audible.

"I wanted to talk to you about the wallet."

"Do you want one?" says Calvin. "They're three dollars—quite the bargain for something so durable and light. Get them before they become exclusive and the price goes up."

"I don't need one, but—"

"Buy one as a present," interrupts Yunji. "Or a donation. They're like Girl Scout cookies."

"Yunj, let's at least hear what she has to say." I surprise myself sometimes.

Yunji's eyes roll, she turns away in a queenly posture.

But I persist. "Go ahead—"

"Well, you see," she says, excitedly torquing around to look at me, "I've done some research on disability and the law. What's neat is that if you have a documented disability, you can get a break on small business laws and regulations."

"We're not running a sweatshop," says Zeus. She seems happy to have an excuse to turn back to look at him. "We all work on these after school and on Saturdays. Leo and all of us.

"But see, if you had a story to these, you could sell them maybe on Getsy, with a much bigger markup. Like selling the story, not volume. Maybe even establish a 501(C)(3) for tax exemption—that would improve your revenue even more."

I stare. Is it bad of me that I'd assumed "tax exemption" to be outside of her sphere of makeup and things like that? And didn't someone else suggest Getsy and it seemed smart?

"You could charge like fifty dollars for a real Leonardo Wallet—"

"Leo's Lucky Rabbit Wallet," I correct her.

"—made by Leonardo himself. Make a website. Like, what a great Christmas or graduation gift."

For a ditz, she actually seems to have some thoughtful ideas, I am thinking. Zeus is scratching his head. Calvin has this look on his face that he gets when we're doing a story problem, like he's seeing a blackboard in his head, following along, but isn't sure what the solution is ultimately going to be. Yunji is frowning.

"How much of the raw material can you keep getting from your uncle, Zeus?" I ask.

"Oh god, as much as we need, forever," he says. "I think I mentioned we have stacks and stacks in the closet because I just couldn't throw them away. A lot of them have really pretty color printing on them. And they misprint something maybe once a week. There's so many ways this can happen, sometimes it's just a misalignment with the machines."

I have a sudden vision of some celebrity bragging about her Leo's Lucky Rabbit wallet. And it's for a good cause! Captioning it with #LeosLuckyRabbits, posing it with whatever gooey coffee drink or outdoor scene or whatever she's taking a picture of. They are flat and light as a feather, as Calvin pointed out; we can just shove them in normal envelopes along with the story Oliver wrote for the same cost as mailing a letter.

What if, I am thinking, this became a business that could sustain Leonardo long-term? Like, his finger-repping could be put to good use!

"Girls like that piss me off so much," says Yunji, after Curley's girlfriend has gone away. "Her super-rich parents will bribe her way into college. She's just using Leonardo for some scheme she has, you know."

"You just said her parents will bribe her way into college," I laugh. "Then what use does she have for Leo?"

"You know what I mean. She doesn't consort with people like us, or Leo, unless she is directly getting something out of it."

"Maybe she realizes she needs a hobby beyond Curley," Calvin posits. I have been noticing that Calvin is indeed quiet, but when he speaks up, it's usually to say something kind—and profound. I get that feeling in my stomach, like the world's gentlest gut-punch. We both happen to glance at each other at the same time, then look down.

Great. I am just crushing on every boy in my orbit. Not a good look.

"I have an idea," Yunji says. "Let's make Leo's Lucky Rabbit Wallets into our service project."

"What's that?" I ask.

"For hagwon, we do a service project every year. One year we cleaned up trash by the highway. Another year we made kimbap to bring to the Korean senior center—"

"Ha, we never heard the end of it from those halmonis about what blasphemy it is to use avocado in the recipe," says Zeus. "We did it because it was expensive!"

"I think it's a great idea," says Calvin. "I need more service for my application anyway."

"I don't know," I say. "I mean, like making Leonardo into a *cause*."

"We're not saying—" says Yunji.

"He's a person, not a cause," I snap. Something inside me snaps, too. Maybe this is why I can't get close to people. Sooner or later, no matter how great they are, they will say one of the poisonous phrases.

I could never do what you do.

I just don't have the patience.
You are the world's most amazing sister.

I am not an amazing sister. I am a sister. "And he's my brother, he's not a charity case."

"I'm not saying that at all," Yunji says. But I think she can tell my ears are closed. I don't want to listen to her. People will eventually show you who they are, I am thinking. I grab my stuff and march off to one of the unoccupied cafeteria tables, the exact one where I started that first day, it turns out. I'm like a salmon or something. Everyone knows I'm mad, and I'm glad of it.

- - - - - - - - - - - -

When we're waiting for our ride (Umma's turn), Calvin doesn't say anything to me. But he hands me a banana oyoo, my favorite. And I take it. I drink it, a little angrily, though. Its sweetness fills my mouth, and my stomach. I'm a little less grumpy.

"*An young ha say yo sun-seng-nim,*" Calvin says when Umma picks us up. She laughs, as always, charmed. He's said it before, and Umma said he is saying hello and respectfully calling her "teacher" or "doctor," instead of auntie, which is also appropriate, but Umma appreciates this choice of formality, which is almost always just given to men. I can see why she likes that. Calvin is so smart, I secretly wonder if he'll eventually be the best Korean speaker in hagwon. Calvin said his parents want him to be a doctor, but he's interested in diplomacy, or maybe political science. "Or," he's mused, "maybe I just like saying *poli-sci.*"

When we drop Calvin off, he doesn't say anything, but pats me on the shoulder. It makes me realize how much I had wanted someone to reach out. Not necessarily run after me and apologize profusely—that would be me being manipulative. Calvin's also not apologizing, I note. But the ensuing surge of anger doesn't wash over my entire brain, as it did at lunch. Calvin is so interesting, the way he sits with things, doesn't have an immediate rejoinder that would make a person seem "smart" or "witty."

"I even got put in a slow learner's class when I was in elementary school," he told me once. "Because I didn't run around chattering like all the kids—also I'm the one Black kid, and I'm not running my mouth off. Must have autism!"

"So what happened?"

"My mom made me have a formal evaluation—like not the school psychologist but at the Child Development Center in the state capitol. Like, thousands of dollars."

"So unfair!"

"Yeah, so then after all the different evals showed I was not only not behind, but *ahead* in most things, my mom formally submitted all this to the school *and* under the disability law charged *them* for the evals."

I blink in admiration. I do blink a lot (is that a rep?) But it made me wonder if law is a profession that could be worthwhile and also personally helpful. For me and Leo. Education law. Disability law.

I take a Calvin-like moment to ponder. Maybe I'm legitimately mad. But maybe, also, Calvin didn't *do* anything he needs to apologize for. I'm just mad that he didn't speak up. But is that a story I made up in my head, about how he feels about Leo being used as a project? Calvin in particular seems to treat words as something precious, not something you can just push out for free with air rushing through the epiglottis. I should keep in mind he doesn't say stuff just because he is expected to. We live in an impatient culture, and people expect you to text back right away—and to say something, practically anything. No one likes the awkward silence. But what if you don't know, exactly, what you want to say? I could learn from that. Where I always feel there's this "right" thing I'm supposed to say, and it won't be okay until I say it, even if I don't feel it. Do I want to run my life as a script?

"Bye," is all I can muster, but I think/hope he knows me well enough to take this as a peace offering back.

- - - - - - - - - - - -

I've been helping Umma put Leonardo to bed. Appa is at the hospital. It somehow got too late to read to him, so we each go in to kiss him on his forehead.

Earlier, someone rang the doorbell, someone collecting for this or that charity. Leonardo had just gone to the bathroom and was walking around naked. The woman was shocked and for a second I thought she was going to start shrieking, but Umma just quickly gave her a donation and eased her out. After she shut the door, we both leaned on it like we were keeping monsters out, looked at each other, and started laughing. And laughed some more. We laughed until our stomachs hurt.

"I feel like I just ran a mile," Umma gasped. "Feels good."

We've calmed down now.

Leonardo is old enough to vote, to be drafted, but he is the most innocent being we know. He never lies, doesn't covet things, doesn't care about pants. Why can't there be prizes and accolades just for him being the best Leonardo he can be?

"I love you so much, Leo," I say in the darkness. I kiss him on top of his head, where his hair is so thick, it feels like kissing a hedge. "Nnnnnnuna," he says, sleepily. I feel a huge wave of love engulf me, it's almost too much.

Back in the kitchen, I whisper, "You heard that, Umma? It's getting clearer. He really is saying 'Nuna!'"

Umma smiles at me. "He always knows who you are. When you were both little, when he was hurt or upset, he ran to you, not us. The doctors said that was the only developmentally normal behavior he did, turning to someone for comfort."

"He did?"

"He did," she confirms. "But, you know, I want to talk to you about that."

"About?"

"It's wonderful he is trying to say 'nuna.' It's possible his brain is developing a little more as he's gotten older. But I don't know if he'll ever be able to live on his own."

"He doesn't have to," I say. "He just has to be Leo."

"Yes, but you have to have a life. Listen, Georgia, I don't think he's going to get better, so we need to face that."

Sometimes, I don't know which I dislike more, Umma's pessimism or Appa's disinterest coupled with his idea Leonardo will just "snap out of it" someday—Appa the uber rationalist said that in his dreams, Leonardo talks all the time. Does he think that's going to make it come true?

"There are things we have to deal with now that he's older."

"Like what?"

"Like guardianship. If something happens to your appa and me."

I gulp. I always hate thinking of this. That one or both of my parents could die.

Don't die! is all I can think.

"Halmoni and Haraboji are his backup guardians, as they have been for you, too," Umma says. "But after you turn eighteen, you don't need a guardian. But Leonardo will."

"Of course," I say. "That'll be me."

I can hear my English teacher, or Oliver the editor, scolding in my ear about the nominative case. "Of course it's going to be, er, *I* as guardian—" That sounds weird. "For Leo."

She shakes her head. "We have already put aside some money and a life insurance policy in a special-needs trust and appointed a law firm to disburse the trust."

"What does that even mean?"

"That if something happens to Appa and me and Haraboji and Halmoni—none of us are going to live forever—then the law firm will take over to manage the funds for Leo's care."

"Leo's care?" I am almost shouting. "What, like he's a pet? A plant?" Umma's eyes film over. I didn't say that right. But I'm starting to panic.

"What does that mean? I'm right here!"

Umma sits back. "Georgia-yah," she says. "You have been the best sister to Leo—"

"Best sister—I'm his *sister*!"

"You are his sister. You are also someone with her own life," Umma goes on, a little shakily.

I'm starting to cry and I don't know why. I guess it's because I think this discussion is heading to a place I don't want it to go.

"We, Appa and I, think, well, and this is partly because of us, you have ended up with so much responsibility for Leo. We want you to have less, so you can concentrate on studying."

"Umma, I'm going to a hagwon after school—Korean study hall."

"I didn't finish: we want you to think about having your own life. People grow up and leave home. Not just you, but also Leo. I went to a seminar recently to learn more about adults with disabilities. They don't like being treated like little kids all their lives. They want to be as independent as possible, too."

"Sure, I get that," I say. "Of course. But are you saying you want me to spend less time with Leo? Because I don't want to do that. I *like* being with him."

The other Saturday, we went to Founders Park ("Where the women are handsome and the men all look like Mark Twain"—Calvin). There is a secret clearing if you worm your way between some hedges, and we made our way to find it again. I brought water (Leonardo doesn't sweat like normal people, so he has to be hydrated) and then we just sat on the fallen log that makes a perfect bench. There had been a slight breeze, the loamy smell of earth. Leonardo was also uncommonly still, peaceful.

As we sat there, what looked like two round, fluffy pom-poms came into our line of sight.

Baby rabbits. I couldn't believe how small they were. I couldn't help scanning the sky for hawks, in the tall grass for itinerant cats. These little things were smaller than mice. Certainly smaller than the rats we had in the city.

I was surprised Leonardo didn't jump up and down in surprise and scare them away. "Rabbits," I whispered. "Lucky rabbits."

"Lucky rabbits!" he yelled, and sent them scurrying. They had been so tiny, maybe he hadn't recognized them as rabbits. He once found a pine cone out in the woods and pressed "strawberry" repeatedly on his NAD. It wasn't snack time, I assumed he was merely randomly repping, but then I noticed the picture of the strawberry was taken from above, and the way the tiny seeds spiraled down the fruit, there was indeed a pine cone shape to it.

"Wow, it looks like a pine cone—the shape!" I said. Leo stopped repping right then. Was that coincidence? Or did he stop—phew—because his dummy nuna finally "got" what he was so laboriously trying to say?

I remember Calvin telling me how patterns in nature—like seeds, pine cones—can be mapped using mathematical equations. Like, things in nature look symmetric, but they aren't one to one, like how things like leaves are the same shape but they just get tinier and tinier. There's math for that! "These equations are part of something called 'chaos theory,' and they're super complicated. But they map how like, if you look at the center of a sunflower, they're not just packed with seeds like at a factory, they have small seeds that radiate out and become larger ones." I think of how in strawberries, the seeds seem evenly spaced, but actually, they get closer together as you get near the bottom. It's orderly *and* beautiful *and* a bit wild—not chaotic, I'd said to him.

"Well, you use the same math, if you can believe it, for weather systems. If you graph them, the data points look totally random. But if you run them through the equations and then graph them, they make the coolest patterns. It's 'chaotic' because it's for nonlinear things that are effectively impossible to predict or control, like turbulence, weather, our brain states, and so on. Like, the Euclidean geometry we learned in middle school is just lines and angles, as opposed to fractal mathematics, which captures the infinite."

How do we even know then what the chaos of Leo's mind might express if only we knew the right equation (also, only Calvin can make *geometry* sound so exciting)? This isn't like Appa's dreams where Leo talks. I have less of an idea of what would need to happen to get Leo talking in real words and sentences versus the idea of Leo just thinking so differently that we can't understand him and that the NAD is an imperfect thing and no one wants to bother to *try* to find another way. See, I've been with him for so long, I can kind of gather some of these breadcrumbs in the woods. To everyone else, I'm just some kid, what do I know?

But I know my brother. I think he has so much more to say to the world. But so few people want to take the time to listen.

The bunnies came back. I couldn't believe it. The little fluffs had wide-open, exclamatory eyes. They came out hesitantly, ready to bolt, but they were much closer to us than they were before. Like Leonardo was just another gentle being they knew wouldn't hurt them. Then, when Leonardo and I didn't move, by happenstance or design, they became used to us, started to pull up bits of grass and chew. Their tiny little jaws looked like the world's smallest threshing machines. It was hard not to laugh. But for Leo's sake, I stayed still. He eventually pulled his head up and said, "Rabbits," quietly. The bunnies kept eating. The whanging buzz of cicadas made me feel sleepy. I didn't see when they finally hopped away.

When Leonardo stood up when it was time to go home, I saw a stain on his crotch. Probably from all the water we drank. Appa, had he been here, would certainly have been upset.

Umma would have been neutral to slightly exasperated, depending on how her day was.

I didn't overly care. These were light cotton pants, elastic-waisted, almost like surgical scrubs. They'd dry as we walked. When we got home, I'd put him in the shower, get him a snack, get him ready for the therapist.

Honestly, I could see doing this for the rest of my life.

Whether or not I had a boyfriend or a husband or kids or pets or whatever.

The room would be made for Leonardo first.

- - - - - - - - - - - -

"What I'm saying," Umma continues. "Is that Appa and I have come up with a plan. You can be as much in his life as you want, but we're going to get a court-appointed guardian, a neutral person, to handle his affairs if we can't."

"Don't you think I should do it?" I practically yelp. "Family shouldn't do it?"

"No," she says, sadly. "You and Leo are both my children, and we are making these decisions as best we can."

"I can take care of him better than anyone can."

She smiles at me. "I know. None of this is set in stone. It can change."

But when I read more on the internet about guardianship, I'm shocked at how final it is. Whoever is the guardian has all the say over the person's decisions, where they live, how they live, their medical stuff, their finances.

And, it's irrevocable once the court case is done. I need to prove to Umma and Appa that I will do this. That I will go to college, pursue a profession, and Leo will live with me, or near me, always.

Twenty-Five

Today's hagwon is sparse. The twins are at a doctor's appointment. Calvin is getting his braces tightened. It's so busy in Bomb Haircuts the Dong-bangs, however, haven't even checked on us once. No one's even cracked a book. We're all bored. We're teenagers. That's our privilege. I look at my *1000 SAT Words* hatefully before putting it in front of me, like a prop.

Yunji brings out the fruit and some honey-butter potato chips. She frowns at Zeus, who's jiggling his leg, tapping on it with a pencil. "You've got ants in your pants."

"Call the exterminator," he drawls, his eyes half-closed.

"We should do something," I say.

"Like what?"

"Why don't we go out? We could go to CostCut and get some supplies."

Yunji counters, "We have all the Mylar. My mom doesn't mind us using her machine."

"Yeah, but we also need to replace he thread. Oh, and mailing supplies," Zeus says. "We can get all that in bulk at the CostCut. I love CostCut."

"Leo does, too," I say. "It's his Grand Canyon and Disneyland all in one."

"I'll bet," Zeus says. "There's so much to see."

— — — — — — — — — —

On the way to the CostCut, we debate the nuances of what to call the enterprise.

"It should have Leo's name in it, don't you think?" says Oliver.

Yunji turns around from the front seat. "What's wrong with Leo's Lucky Rabbit Wallets?"

"Yeah. But that is kind of a long string of words to just keep in your brain. Leonardo's Amazing Wallets?"

"That's just as long!" She oozes down into the seat with a *pfffft!* Puts her bare feet (she also had black polish on her toenails) on the dashboard.

"Or, Leo's Luckies?" Oliver tries.

"But then we don't know what 'it' is," says Yunji.

"Plus it's a brand of cigarettes," Zeus laughs. "Oliver, you are *so* innocent!"

Even though Zeus is the PK, Yunji told me that Oliver's parents—both engineers—are the "churchiest." In fact, they make him wear his shirts buttoned up all the way to the last one.

"Makes me look like I'm in special ed—" he said, until he saw me glaring at him. "Oops, I'm so sorry, Georgia."

"Don't say sorry to *me*."

"Sorry, Leo, bro, that was really uncool of me. I won't do it again."

"I do know this for sure," I say. "Nothing with dogs."

As we ponder, Zeus starts going on excitedly about starting a nonprofit business entity for Leo. Like a real business.

"Don't tell me you got an actual idea from that bubble-headed cheerleader," Yunji moans.

"We already have such low overhead," he says, practically with glee. "Tax exemption. Why not? It's kind of brilliant. More to go back to Leo."

— — — — — — — — — —

Inside the store, Yunji throws a supersize bag of Twix into the cart. Zeus takes it out.

"This is a business expense, Yunj, we can't have extraneous stuff in it."

"We're using *my* family's Costcut card for your scheme. Who's the one who's going to be in trouble?"

"I am saying that having candy on the receipt with the other mailing supplies may be confusing. Not like buying the Twix is illegal."

"I'm also saying, hey my family pays for the membership, so shouldn't you not be telling me what to do?"

"Aren't I, like, family?"

Yunji pauses, as if pondering what, exactly, these words mean.

"Not yet," she says, finally.

"Yunj, you know what I mean. But I'm serious about this business— we can't have Twix on the receipt—"

Trailing the two of them, bickering like an old married couple, I have a pang, seeing a future that wasn't going to happen: my can-be-too-long Saturdays taken up by Zeus and me on a shopping trip, Leo along with us. No Yunji, just us. It's a small and petty and *ridiculous* disappoint-ment, but it's also making me wonder, what if this, our next generation, could be like this? Not like I have to be married to Zeus (but I can feel a blush just thinking this), but that we could always be here for Leo, an assembled extended family . . . helping him to run his business, helping him to live his life? With all of us?

Zeus grabs a stack of small padded envelopes, mailing labels, tissue paper.

"I think each unit should be wrapped nicely before being put in the envelope," he says. "Maybe even in a small box, if that doesn't cut into the profit margin too much."

"Each 'unit,' 'margin,'" Yunji mocks. "You sound like a CEO."

"Maybe I *will* be the CEO of Leonardo Kim Enterprises," he says. "Georgia will be the vice president."

"Isn't that sexist?" I say.

"*Leonardo* is going to be president, obvi," he says. "You could be chief financial officer. I'll be chief operating officer." And I realize I don't know anything about business. "Or house physician."

My phone pings. It's Calvin saying he's still in the orthodontist's waiting room and is working on the website. Did we want it to be called Leonardo's Lucky Rabbit Wallets or Leo's Lucky Rabbit Wallets?

> We don't know—yet

I write him back.

> Not sure if the emphasis should be on
> Leonardo or the wallets. Input welcome!

No hurry. I can put a "mask" on it and deal
with the name later.

We pass the flower section. There's a bunny planter peeking out behind a potted fern, almost like we're outside at the park again. I'm thinking of how Leo's walking therapy gains have plateaued (but Umma still has faith). At night he sleeps stiff as a board on his back, arms to the sides, like Frankenstein, his legs rigid as a toy soldier. He doesn't curl up or even fling an arm to the side, or manspread. I wish he would. During the day, he still has long periods where walks on his toes, like he's wearing invisible high heels. If he does this too much, he'll have to have another operation where they make cuts into his Achilles tendon to stretch it out. It sounds so barbaric. It is. At night, if she isn't too exhausted, Umma sits with him and pushes his toes upward, trying to counteract the contraction. Leonardo hit her once when she did it. I wonder if it hurts and he can't tell us.

Yunji finds some cute thank-you notes—with bunnies on them.

Zeus finds some decorative silver thread. "This is the stuff they use in the factory," he says. "Sometimes there's decorative stitching on the bags. Gold would be too tonal, I think."

"Thank you, Betsey Ross," Yunji says. "For schooling us with all your sewing knowledge."

"Do you have a *problem* with that?" His voice is gentle, but he's not smiling.

Yunji stops. She looks a little stunned. No one talks back to her, our hagwon captain. It's just not done.

"Problem with what?"

"With my sewing?"

"Look, it's just so, like, feminine."

"And the problem is?"

"There is no problem."

"Good. 'Cause I think every guy and girl should know how to sew and change a tire—can you change a tire?"

"Of course I can change a tire," she says, petulantly. "You saw me."

"Well, I don't have a problem with it, so if there's a problem with my sewing, I don't think it's me. It must be with you."

I can't help wondering: Where were they out in a car together? Date? Concert maybe? Did they get a flat and she changed the tire?

I see him touch the small of her back for just a second. A mollifying gesture. To whom, though, I don't know.

- - - - - - - - - - - -

By the time we get back to the hagwon, it's time to go home. I've started having Umma come get me in the back. If the back is good enough for Calvin, it's good enough for me. And I kind of like it. All the business and bustle is in the front. In the evening it's quiet, almost eerily so, in the back.

- - - - - - - - - - - -

Right now, it's dark and still. I can see, barely, the loading dock of the Arirang Market. It sticks out like a real dock, like on a lake. There must be a person standing on the end, quietly like me; all I see is the small glowing end of a cigarette, the tiniest red beacon, the sigh of a puff, of nicotine entering someone's bloodstream.

This back alley is the heart and the guts of retail. The front is just the lipstick. I try not to think about how the Mozart Café has rats streaming in and out of their dumpsters. Or how the clothes store takes old clothes and instead of donating or something they put them in the dumpster and pour bleach on them.

"Well, duh," Yunji told me, as I watched once, aghast. "If people knew they could get free clothes on Wednesday nights in the dumpster, who'd ever bother to buy clothes? Or the pastries at Mozart? And: it would be *people* and not rats pawing through those dumpsters. I guarantee you, Martha's Madras downtown does the same thing—a hundred-dollar pink sweater just to wrap around your shoulder becomes a rag when the season's over. They both cost like two dollars to make in some sweatshop in China."

This back place calms Leo as well. It's hard not to notice he does better where there are fewer people, fewer inputs. That's extremely human, however. I read a study somewhere that said when people are alone and their pet comes in, their blood pressure stays the same, or even falls as they pet it. But if a *human*—even a beloved human, basically no matter who it is—comes in, then their blood pressure rises noticeably. Being with people is inherently stimulating. And for me, when I'm alone, I'm no longer seeing myself through others' reactions. I forget what I look like—my bigness—when other people aren't around. Then I'm just a set of eyes looking into the world. I shouldn't use other people as a mirror, but that's how it happens. So difficult if the other people aren't sympathetic. My heart's full of holes and weak spots that people just push their finger through, like through rotten fruit. I wonder if this is what Leo feels. I wish I could ask him. Does he mind the stares, the whispers? Appa's exasperated looks? When Appa gets mad, Leo often acts *even worse*, which to me proves Leo doesn't know what's going on and isn't being intentional. Because if he could control himself, shouldn't he act *better* to prove to him he can?

On the other hand, what if no one believed in you, ever? And you just gave up hope? I could see feeling, what's the use? Like when I'm sick I'm grumpy and even though I try to be nice, want to be nice, I can't be. Maybe if we give Leo hope for something, things can change.

"Hey, Georgia."

Zeus steps out of the shadows. End of the hagwon day, he'd been sweeping up, and opened the back to shake out his broom. He's briefly backlit by the open door, but then he comes out, shuts it behind him, and we're in the dark again.

"Hey," I say.

"Hey, Leo, bro—"

"Leo bro." Leo is finger-repping, so I reach over and gently pull his hands down. Zeus puts the broom handle under his armpit and fishes in his jeans pocket and then hands Leo something that flashes briefly in the light like a fish's belly. A strip of Mylar. Green on one side, foil on the other. Leo starts stroking it dreamily, reverently, repetitively, which makes me wonder, how is his repping any different than when people twirl their hair, or other tics that some find adorable?

While I'm pondering all this, Zeus finishes shaking out his broom, I assume he is going to go back in, but then he comes to stand by me. The two of us stand there, side by side, looking out into the dark. I see, or think I see, Zeus's profile next to mine. We could be on the shore of a beautiful lake, on a seashore. Standing on the edge of the world somewhere. It's always like that when I'm around Zeus. He's casually leaning on the broom, his arms flexing out of his tank top. There's two millimeters of space between both of our upper arms and I want so badly to traverse this space.

"Georgia—" he says, more like a whisper.

I hear an approaching car (truck? tank?) and step back.

Umma drives up.

I almost want to laugh (or cry) at her inadvertent bad timing, I've never known the van's engine to be loud, but it sounds to me like a jet engine.

"See ya, Georgia. Leo," Zeus says.

He puts his hand out for a high five that Leo happily gives him. Then he faces me, leaving his hand up, looking at me rakishly.

"Don't leave me hanging, Georgia peach," he says. His palms are warm and dry—and callused.

"He seems like a nice boy," Umma says as we drive.

- - - - - - - - - - - -

When we get home, my phone pings. Zeus. He's never texted me before. I didn't know he knew my number. I wonder if he got it from Yunji.

Some suggestions? Lucky Rabbit, Leo's Lucky
Rabbits. We have SO much old rabbit foil btw.

I'm holding the phone in my hand, and it's warm. Is the phone itself warm, or is this part of my full-body blush. I'm texting with the mythological Zeus.

. . .

. . .

I keep watching the dots. Waiting for what's next. It's a thrill. It's a crush. It's impossible. I'm thinking of the asymptotic functions we are learning in calculus, where it goes right up to the line, closer, closer, closer—but never touches. This is what we are.

It will run out, someday. The thrill, the crush. Everything does.

I can't wait for something that can't happen. I shut my phone off and slip it into my bag. Leo is still repping on the foil.

Twenty-Six

Sometimes, life just comes at you without waiting to see if you're ready.

Zeus wants to get dinner. Like, now. On a school night. Too many things are happening at once.

"I don't think my mom will let me go out," I say, practically as a breather. Today, he walked me to my locker, waited for me to get my books so we could walk to his car together.

Together.

Like boyfriend and girlfriend.

Yunji was already there, at the car. Her eyebrow shot up like a Mexican jumping bean. "So that's where you were," she says.

Zeus didn't answer.

Finally, I just said, out of Yunji's earshot, "Aren't you guys dating?"

"What?" he said. "Where did you get that idea?"

"I don't know," I blurted. "I mean, the way she looks at you—"

"I love her," he said. "As a friend. And yes, I am at Bomb Haircuts all the time, I have become part of their family. But I don't feel anything for her, you know, that way."

The problem is, I can't, however, reassure myself that I am now officially free to proceed. One of Yunji's signature moves is pretending to claw her eyes out while moaning "guys are soooooo dumb!" Now, I'm wondering if this is ninety percent directed at Zeus. I make a mental note to text Calvin later for a temperature check by a neutral observer.

But Umma, overhearing me talking to Zeus, asks if it's one of my friends from hagwon, and I tell her yes.

"Who?"

I tell her it's Zeus.

"If he'll drive you, you should go," she says. She doesn't seem to think it strange Zeus already has a license.

"You've worked so hard this week, Georgia, there's no harm in going out for a bit. In fact, if you could get your own supper, that would make it easier for me to get Leonardo to bed, fewer distractions for him."

Really, what else can I do?

- - - - - - - - - - - - -

Zeus picks me up.

I have a momentary flash, wondering if my "friend from hagwon" were Calvin, if Umma or Appa would have had a different reaction. Well, Calvin *is* a different person. And it's Zeus who's waving to me sunnily from the window of his janky Kia.

We go to Sunnyvale's Big Chief diner, an old-timey diner in posh Herbert Hills. We are led to a corner booth, expansive view of the parking lot. But as we sit longer I notice that beyond the parking lot you can also get glimpses of the river in the dark as the light from the moon silvers off it. It's so strange being out on a weeknight, not with my parents. But Zeus already has so much adult responsibility, it seems, he carries himself like an adult. He orders coffee, for instance, and drinks it. "It's been sitting on the burner all day and it's like syrup—the way I like it, actually," he laughs. He proffers the smooth china cup to me, but I demur.

The Big Chief Diner has a blinking red neon Indian head in profile. Full headdress, war paint, that strikes me as not so cool. But I wonder if it's been here forever, authentically old school, as in old-school racist. Where keeping it, defending it, shows you're somehow "better" than racism. I used to feel that way too about changing the names of some of the streets around us in the city. Shauntae even participated in some of the signature drives, and I'd say, but it's *always been* Calhoun Street. Like we can still keep calling it that, calling it the street name but not the racist person."

"This street name is honoring a racist person," she'd explain. "Just keeping it is racist."

Calvin said it's only in wealthy white areas where people still use Native American imagery in a nonironic way: the cigar store Indian, the red-painted mascot, summer camps named after Geronimo.

I'm thinking now, what would it be like if they cast Zeus's handsome profile into neon, called the diner the Korean. How alienating that would feel. Like white people get to be individuals and have streets named after them. But people in certain groups are forever stuck in their groups, which kind of makes them not people. I don't even know how old Sunnyvale itself is—I think it was established in 1996, recent enough they should know there are easy ways to find a better name. The Star Diner. The Jukebox Diner. Whatever. There's only one diner in town, not like people won't be able to find it.

The menu is basically greasy and white, as in white food: potatoes, rice, garlic bread, tapioca pudding, round-the-clock pancakes. When I ask for some hot sauce, the indifferent waitress brings me a crusty bottle of Tabasco. I'm a little surprised we don't go to Pecan Plaza, and I tell him that.

"Two young people eating together in the eyes of nosy Koreans is a bad idea."

"Why?"

"You clearly did not grow up in a Korean community."

"You're right," I say. "Lots of other minorities, but not other Koreans, or even a lot of other Asians."

"Yunji and I *used* to date," he tells me abruptly. "Hagwon is awkward-won."

I am not sure how I'm supposed to respond to this. Make a joke? Be the friend with a shoulder to lean on? All that my inner self is doing is back-flips—fixating all my cognitive bandwidth on the "used to date." "Used to." Okay. But also "date." They *dated*!

All to the detriment of my conversational bandwidth. I say something scintillating like, "Duh" and "Um" and "Really?" Trying to stay nice and neutral.

I'm not interested in Zeus. I'm not interested in Zeus. I'mnotinterestedinZeus. I'mnotinterestedinZeus.

Then I just blurt, "Oh! Like, when did you break up?" I want to kick myself. Only marginally better than being Captain Obvious and changing the subject.

"Last year." He is unfazed. I, on the other hand, am nervously picking the red crust off the Tabasco bottle, realizing that's gross, wiping my hands on a napkin.

"But can I tell you something, Georg?"

"You can tell me anything." I want to sound like a friend, a really really good friend, one you can tell things to, without worrying about romantic interest muddling it. I want to be a clear and true friend. Like loyal to my friend Yunji without whom I wouldn't even *know* this guy. Yunji was my key to hagwon. And how nice she and her family have always been to Leo. In the city, people seem better about helping out, like we're all crammed together and know we will all need help in the future. Here, people don't want to "get involved." High fences. "Privacy." We live in a freaking gated community. The Dongbangs have no reason to, but have helped us out in so many ways.

I try to show the calm, engaged earnestness in my eyes. I am a true friend to *both* of them.

"We were just high school kids, obviously. You know her. She's an amazing person. I kind of fell in love with her family, too. But, see, as it went on, I felt like with her I was supposed to not just be me, Zeus Pak, but also be *this world* for her. Be this whole world and be whatever person with all the traits she and her parents idealize. That's a lot to ask a dude who's just beginning to figure out himself."

I don't want to say anything that sounds judging of Yunji, so I don't say anything.

"Most couples break up over stuff like intimacy. We broke up over me not going to college. Of wanting to learn a trade. I mean, *her* dad didn't go to college."

"The sewing," I say, lightly.

"Yeah, like Koreans can be super judgmental and there are some people—especially the church people—who are all mooshi-hey and look down on her dad. Like, he's a businessman, and, well, *hair*. She wants me to be strong and masculine and there for her, golfing buddy for her dad, all that. I'm just a kid."

He pauses. "See, I've supported myself. I *get* the man, all respect." He makes the *Hunger Games* three-finger salute. "He and her mom figured out, even in this hostile town, how to support themselves. Including making the hagwon."

I think of the twins, Chandi and Pandi, with the constantly harassed executive mom. Yunji's mom charges her a lot for hagwon, but the lady is still delighted because it's way cheaper than any daycare or after-school program and certainly way cheaper than having a nanny—and everything times two. It's like you can make something where everyone wins but it might not look super prestigious or whatever. It's more like you just have to have the creativity and courage to just *do*.

"Did you really flunk last year?" The words come out before I can stop them.

"If you call being held back flunking, then yes. That year my uncle was hiding from everyone, dodging ICE and then of course the other angry Koreans. He didn't want me to open the door; we pretended no one was home. I just couldn't go to school. Then when he disappeared, he didn't exactly leave me with anything to pay the rent with. Or for food."

"Were you scared?"

"Yeah, of course. I was worried about what was going on with my uncle but I also knew my parents would have immediately made me go to Korea. So . . . I didn't tell them. I was on my own. Doing illegal odd jobs and stuff like doing errands for these middle-aged Korean uncles and their underground gambling den. Making just enough to eat and live, as we say in Korean. That is, until Yunji's folks took me in, gave me what I like to call a work-study job. And man, her mom is such a good cook. I thought I was in heaven."

"Are you mad about being held back? Because it was mostly because of being absent?"

"Oh, not at all. I *was* absent. Those are the rules. I do okay academically, but honestly, I prefer to be doing stuff with my hands. How about you? You seem to like school."

"I do like school." I pause. I carry the letter, like a talisman, with me. Hidden in a file called "cat photos." Not that my parents would ever snoop. But . . .

"I hope I'm not coming off as a jerk, this isn't a humble-brag," I say, showing the letter. "It's my dream college."

He reads it thoughtfully, his forehead squinched. What nice bushy eyebrows he has.

"This is *amazing*, Georgia. Have you shown this to your parents? They'll be so proud."

"That's the thing," I say. "I can't show them. *Because* they'll be so happy."

"Yeah, like getting into an amazing school would be kind of nice."

"Do you know how expensive it's going to be to fly there—and back? Probably I'd be home maybe once or twice a year, summers. Because my father is a doctor, I can't get financial aid."

"But what this is really about: you're afraid to leave Leo?"

"Well, I don't think I'd put it that I am *afraid* to leave him."

"How would you put it?"

"I don't *want* to leave him. To be away for six months at a time. I can just as easily go to State, which has a good premed program."

"Yeah, but why wouldn't you want to give yourself the best shot at life?"

"You sound like my parents. They keep saying I need to have a 'life'—like life is out there, separate from Leo. Leo *is* my life."

"Well, let me be the devil's advocate. If Leo were um, like other kids—" I can tell he's struggling not to say "normal."

"Like other neurotypical people," I say, gently.

"Yeah, if he were neurotypical, you wouldn't be making these consider-ations. You've worked hard, you'd go to the best place that would have you."

"But that would be the same for *him*. He'd be choosing whatever he wanted to do. But Leo doesn't get to choose anything in his life. There's so little we know he likes—food, bunnies, *me*. My dad is literally bugging me to spend less time with him. Like maybe if I got used to it, I'd realize it's more fun without him. I don't think so. Do you think, I don't know, going on *dates* or to football games or living in a dorm is going to be more important than my family?"

"But college—it's just four years."

"Some days I think that's really short. Like high school's gone pretty fast. Other days, I think, how can I spend *four years* away from him?" I ponder my hot chocolate for a minute.

"Okay," I correct myself. "Maybe I *am* a little afraid. Of people not understanding Leo if I'm away. I mean, even though he's my parents' child, they both sometimes only see his outsides. Me, I've been speak-ing Leo ever since I was born."

He blows the steam of his coffee, sips it with his hands cupped around the china. "Can I ask another question?"

"Depends on the question, I guess." Then I relent. He looks so serious. "Go for it."

"Do you think Leo will have a normal lifespan?"

"I don't know. I mean, Leo has some aspects of some things and some of others. He has epilepsy, but I recently realized that's just the word they use when people have more than one seizure in x amount of time."

"But he gets medicine for that, right?"

"He does. But it doesn't always work. And the medicines have weird side effects—like his teeth and jaw being deformed, that's one hundred percent from the medicine. Umma made them stop even though that medicine worked okay, but she thought if that happened even more, Leo would have trouble eating. As it is he has trouble chewing." Some-times, when he chokes, it's so scary to watch.

And then I explain to him about SUDS, the danger of nighttime seizures. I'm consciously trying to stay calm, like a doctor would, but as I stare at my mug, it blurs. "We all sleep with our doors open. Sometimes when he is about to seize, right before, he'll start slapping himself. Or he'll fall out of bed. Not always, but we can hear him and go help."

"So you're planning to stay up all night, probably forever?"

"Look, I haven't thought this all the way through. But yeah, I like being close to him, for if he needs me. And back to your question, no one knows, but it just seems like his lifespan might be short, really short. So why wouldn't I want to spend all the time I can with him?"

"So you're molding your life around an event that may or may not happen."

"I don't think I'd put it *that* way." I'm annoyed now. "No one knows what may happen. A meteor could crash through the diner window." I think of how when I was maybe nine or ten, Umma and Appa had the "what if something happens" talk with me. Appa had said, "You never know, your umma and I could get in a car accident on the way home from dinner tonight."

And I got so haunted by that, that whenever they were both out of my sight, I couldn't stop thinking about a grisly scene of them being dead, me an orphan, lost. Soon, with my waking up screaming in the night, my nail chewing, Appa backpedaled, saying, "Georgia, I was really just using that as an example. It's very unlikely we'd die. People my age have a ninety percent chance of living to the next year."

That made me feel a little better.

Then, just as I relaxed a little—

Aunt Clara was in a car accident. Technically, a guy in a pickup hit her when he was swerving around another stopped car—that was stopped *because Clara was in the crosswalk.*

"Yes, *may happen* are the key words. Like, if something happened to him while I was away, I don't think I could forgive myself."

"Do you ever think about what your life would or could be like without Leo?" he says suddenly. "I'm not saying this in a bad way, I'm saying it more like a thought exercise. Like, I'm always thinking about what life would be like if my parents never came here from Korea, and I didn't have to choose whether to follow them when they went back.

What would it be like to have one single identity, a unified history. Skip the confusion over who we are—Korean? American? Being just a Korean guy growing up in Korea, as natural as can be. Get it?"

"I do."

"A thought exercise. Who are you, Georgia Kim?"

Frankly, I'd never thought about this. Dared to think about this. Like it would somehow be a betrayal of Leo.

What would it be like? I'd be an only child.

Or what if I had a neurotypical sibling. A sister maybe. Would we fight all the time? Be close? Be competitive? Have a boring, quiet life, with pressure to get into a good school the only conflict. And blithely go on our way not knowing at all how things could be?

I wouldn't miss him if I never knew him. I would just go to college. The best one I could. The one I wanted to go to. I'd be dancing with glee right now, pasting that letter on my face, posting it on the socials. Then, with nervousness and anticipation, I'd pack up and *go*. I'd come home maybe twice a year. After, I'd try to find myself, like everyone else does. Find what I'm good at. Backpack around the world. Do some kind of art. Fall in love. Get married. Have kids. Or not.

"Zeus, I'd probably go to that college."

Zeus is silent. He looks over at me. Then he looks at a thread he'd pulled out of the hem of his tank top. He's playing with it, not unlike the way Leonardo would twiddle a piece of beloved stim-string.

"Look. I'm going to work with my uncle. I'm not leaving Sunny-vale anytime soon."

"And that's apropos of—"

"What does *apropos* mean?"

"Well, how does that relate to what you just asked me?"

"Ah. It means you should do what you think you are meant to do."

"I don't understand."

"Because, I'll be there for Leo—I promise."

"Promise what? What does that mean?" I blurt, a little more harshly than I should.

"I know, it's stupid. I don't know 'what' exactly. I'm just saying that

while you're in college, I could be there for him. I want to get his wallet
business going. I mean, first, it kills me to waste all that misprinted
Mylar. Second, I'm very entrepreneurial, where my family comes from
in Korea, it's in my blood. Third, I like Leo. I want to be a friend to him.
I'm not saying it like in a I-feel-so-sorry-for-him way. He's in there. And
to tell the truth, I think he knows on some level that because I'm a guy
and as big and strong as he is, well, that makes him feel more secure
and relaxed. Like, I can deal when he loses it. I'll always be gentle. But
I can stop him from hurting others, or himself." He daintily pokes a
french fry into a lake of ketchup. "Like, I feel like I could be good at
this, being Leo's friend."

"You're nuts," I say, but I can't help smiling. "And this is all so far
away still. I have to go on the college tour, then decide to apply, take
my SATs, do well on them, then apply next year, then get in before any
of this becomes relevant."

"Yeah, but wouldn't it make sense for me to start getting to know
Leonardo sooner, like now?"

"You're serious about this."

"Never been more."

My brain is lighting up like a pinball machine.

"Would you be willing," I ask, "to take a crisis intervention class?
Where you can learn how to de-escalate and also how to stay safe. Like,
most people don't even realize if someone comes after you, just step to
the side. Or if they are biting you, you should not pull away—your
skin will tear. And if you do need to intervene, like if you're in a public
place, or he's hurting himself, there's ways to make sure you don't hurt
him even accidentally."

"I didn't know stuff like that exists. Of course I'd take a class," he
says. "Just tell me when."

"Wow," I say. "You really *are* serious."

"I am." He frowns. "Georgia, why wouldn't I be?"

He excuses himself to go wash his hands.

Apparently, the North Korean government is based on a concept
called Juche, self-reliance. Like being so powerful you never ever need

help from anyone. That's kind of how we are, the Kim family. Not that we are powerful, but we keep this all to ourselves.

Outsiders couldn't do this. They wouldn't understand. And, really, we don't want to let them in. It's easier to do everything, keep the chaos inside our house, the way Appa made sure in this new house we had double-paned soundproof windows and central air, so if we need to, we can keep the windows closed year-round. But have we ever thought about how closing ourselves off keeps Leo's world so small? And ours too? That maybe by letting the people in, there's unpredictability, sure, but also joy?

Instead, we're just living in a wax museum, taking it day by day. As much as our family has been avoiding thinking about adulthood for Leo, I have started to. Partly because I am thinking of my own adulthood. And the sweet-faced Leonardo. What will he look like as an *adult* adult. Unshaven, huge. Those teeth that are like pegs, mismatched headstones in a cemetery. Two rows like a shark, or even a Halloween monster.

Another thing he has problems with is his hygiene. He doesn't understand the need, and because of his sensory issues, he doesn't like to be touched. He's had weeks where his teeth grew mossy; he had a rank but sweet odor, like when you wash clothes but forget to put in the detergent. That was when he was a kid. Everyone knows adults smell more. Someone has to soap up and scrub Leo, because he won't do it on his own. Right now it's Umma or me because Appa's never home. Now that he's older, a man, it's weird. And sometimes he starts fighting with you in the shower, and there's a danger of everyone falling down. Would Zeus come over if Umma needed that kind of help?

That's help he could give that I couldn't. But it's a dream, a fantasy. He'd need to be paid. How else would he make a living? But what if he could be paid? Wouldn't I rather have Zeus doing that than some anonymous orderly who's just doing his job?

He comes back from the washroom, orders another coffee. "Diner coffee is actually the worst," he admits. "But it does the trick."

"Won't it keep you up?"

"That's the trick. My uncle's on the wagon, but he needs someone to talk to when he gets home from his factory shift or he'll just turn to the bottle. The bottle's where everything started, so I try to chat with him when he gets home. If I drink this now, it'll kick in by the time I get home, but wear off when it's time for bed."

"Very smart," I say.

He drops me off at my house. The inside of his car is cozy. Worn, but neat. Safe feeling, somehow. I'm noticing how weird it is that even with the curtains down, you can kind of see into our house, like right into it. It was the same in the city, but there it was anonymous. Like, you just thought of the people you saw as on stage, the people seeing you were people you'd never see again. Right now, I can make out the form of Umma sitting at the kitchen table. Leo must be asleep.

"I'm really glad you moved here," Zeus says. I'm noticing there's a hole in the dashboard, where a radio would normally be.

"Thanks," I say. There's another squarish hole, like a missing tooth. Where a clock would probably be. This car is so basic.

"It's been the same Koreans here for forever. Nice to have someone new."

"So you just like me because I break up the monotony."

My mouth is open because I am talking. Next thing I know, I'm kissing Zeus. Or he is kissing me. We are like two planets gravitationally on a collision course with each other. I can feel the calluses on his hands, which are pressing on my back. He smells so clean, like pine needles. Even in the dim light of the car, the surfable wave of his hair gleams.

I run into the house just as my phone pings. It's a return of the blowing-heart emoji, the emoji-typo that started this whole thing. I slap my forehead. But laugh. This is not what I expected. I screenshot it to save it forever. Maybe I'll look back on this and realize I was utterly nuts. This is not what I wanted, what I set out to want. Yunji is still my friend. But let me be more like Zeus, so present for the today, the now, and enjoy this. So corny, but I think this is my first love.

I go to bed, drifting off with a smile.

- - - - - - - - - - - -

Suddenly I'm awake. I hear the sound of my parents' voices, arguing.

"I can't do this anymore," Umma says, quietly crying.

"You're his mother," Appa scolds.

When Umma and Appa are whisper-fighting, they don't realize how much I can hear. Perhaps it's that specific register; the buzzing of their voices is transmitted through the wall with great clarity. I pull my covers over my head. I can still hear them.

"I cook his meals from scratch, drive him to all his doctors' appointments, do the home therapies. There's also the mental load."

Scoffing noise from Appa.

"Who's the name of his new teacher?" she asks.

"That's easy. Mrs. Scott."

"Mrs. Scott was his teacher *last* year."

"I can't believe you're even considering it. He has two more years of school to go."

"That's just it, I want to do this before it's too late."

"Look, I know how much you do. I've told you before, we should hire more help. You need to take more time for yourself, so you don't burn out."

"This isn't for me, it's for Georgia."

"Georgia? She's doing just fine!"

"No, that's the problem. She's a good kid. No trouble. So we ignore her."

"We don't ignore her."

"The point is, Georgia needs a house that's quiet so she can study, without all the craziness and, frankly, danger—Leonardo tried to stab me with a fork the other day."

I force myself to poke my head out from the covers. They were thinking of sending Leonardo away because of me? And it's *Umma* who wants to, now?

I wanted to jump out and yell, "Don't use me as an excuse. You know I want Leonardo home. Don't you remember the news story about the Ivar School?"

- - - - - - - - - - - -

So it's with this that I go from thinking of Leonardo's Lucky Rabbit Wallets as a pie-in-the-sky idea to getting serious about it. Calvin has agreed to do the website. Yunji's mom is fine with us using the sewing machine and also using the hagwon space as a maker-space even after hours and on weekends.

We've gone with the name Lucky Leo's. We'll explain about the rabbits as long as that Mylar supply lasts, then move on to lucky something else.

At home when Leo's in the mood to stim (always), he and I fold dozens of wallets. I clip them together with a clothespin and bring them to school, then to hagwon, where we sew them up. The Dongbangs sell a few in Bomb Haircuts and ask us for more—it's so exciting.

"I know this sounds crazy," Yunji says. "But my parents are coming up on the kyae, and they said they want to give me a chunk—thirty percent. For Lucky Leo's."

I'm feeling delirious now.

Twenty-Seven

Leo's with us today at hagwon because Umma says she has an appointment. She doesn't say what it is, though. I worry she's going to a divorce lawyer or something.

"Maybe she and your dad are secretly meeting for marital counseling," Calvin suggests. He's the only one who knows about the conversation about Leonardo and the home. And how those two disagree. At one point, Umma fairly shouted, "If Leo leaves this home, I will, too!"

I've never heard her threaten something like that before, and it scared me. "So that would be good," he says, encouragingly. "There might be good stuff going on in the background that you don't know about."

"Not with Leo." I shake my head. "I can't think of a time that was ever true."

Calvin doesn't say anything more. It's like, instead of just blabbing platitudes to fill the space, he lets the space sit, empty. So that my feelings can fill it. I feel awful but calm. Like I realize that even if I feel bad, my feelings aren't necessarily right or wrong. They're feelings. Including the feelings I have, well, for him. He's reached out to hold my hand, like a friend, and I let him. On top of this all, I'm worried I might be promiscuous.

Sitting side by side, I'm suddenly aware that my ample torso is actually bigger than his. He's slim and reedy and, especially when you include my breasts, I'm a big girl. But there's something attractive about his washboard slimness, too. I like him. I might *like* like him. His mom has made him wear blue-light blocking Urkel glasses, and they are adorably nerdy on him.

Zeus enters right at the moment, his flip-flops clapping on the floor. He literally puts on the brakes, stares at the space where our hands are meeting. I hadn't been conscious of it, exactly.

"Oh, didn't mean to interrupt," he says.

I yank my hand away.

"You're not interrupting," I say. But that sounds somehow stupid. Plus the yanking away of the hand. I'm a jerk. Is Calvin going to take it racially? I look helplessly at him. But he, as always, is without judgment. He's just so kind. Like he's somehow skipped all the mean high school stages and is mature inside, even though he's still sweetly teenage Calvin on the outside.

"Let's get the line going," says Zeus gruffly. I feel a little bad, but about what?

I'm not "with" him, or Calvin. I have commitments to neither. I have to say it's a little bit of a thrill. At City High, Shauntae had a pack of admirers shadowing her wherever she went. No one ever looked at me, the Asian fat girl. I like being a little unpredictable, even just to myself, for once.

Leonardo is already folding away: one, two, three, four, five. He is a good mimic, and right now he's got his reps on. Yunji holds the sheet for him as he runs his fingertips down it.

"Press hard," she reminds him. She follows up with a metal origami blade that sets the crease. She can be a little abrupt with him, a humorless supervisor. At first, that annoyed me—was she scared of Leo? Repulsed by him? But now I'm seeing that she's treating him with the same brusqueness that she does Chandi and Pandi. She's not being patronizing, fake-cheerful, treating him, or them, like babies. I can't help thinking of Ginger, with a bit of a burn, how she wanted to make a "social story song" for Leonardo set to the tune of "Itsy Bitsy Spider."

"He's developmentally delayed, but he's not two years old!" I want to scream.

If Leonardo has any awareness, and I know he does, flipping the utility table would be an appropriate and clever bit of communication, I think. Except that Ginger might be too dense to pick up on it.

Leonardo right now is concentrating, occasionally frustrated. He has little beads of sweat on his forehead and not just because his body has trouble regulating temperature.

He's working.

- - - - - - - - - - - -

Lucky Leo's is open for business! I kind of want to kiss Calvin—and Zeus—and Yunji. And Mrs. Dongbang for bringing us snacks and letting me bring Leo. Mr. Dongbang for taking a few minutes, when it was quiet, to have Leonardo sit in the barber chair to "practice" getting a haircut.

Mr. Dongbang especially focuses on the tickly places by his ears. He sat so well, one day Mr. Dongbang gave him an actual haircut, after hours when the place was empty. Leonardo made that weird rooster-lunge with his head once but sat for the rest of it. Mr. Dongbang gave him a classic Bomb haircut, longer on top to take advantage of Leo's copiously thick and wavy hair, sculpted tight on the sides. He handed Leonardo a hand mirror, and Leo, instead of looking at it, immediately began repping on the mirror's smooth surface. But I could see his smile. He was proud of himself. No more home haircuts with Umma randomly sawing at his hair or Appa with that horrible and ineffective contraption, the Flowbee.

"You hair look nice," says Mr. Bae. When he has extra time, he sits with us and folds, too. He is shaven and clean, and there's no sign of the ganky suitcase.

Here are all these people, zero of whom have any expertise with Leo's special needs. They've done tons more than any doctor has ever done for him. Maybe I can just marry the whole hagwon crew.

"Psych!" says Calvin, peering into his laptop. "We've got five orders through the website. And not people we know. Holy moly, one of the orders is from Canada!"

"Lucky Leo's, international sensation!" says Zeus, and I'm relieved because I can feel everything is all right between him and Calvin. Lucky Leo's, bringing peace to the world.

"We need to get these out right away," Calvin says. "Be professional."

Zeus is already ransacking our supply shelf. "Yunj—where did the address labels go?"

Yunji hits her forehead. "Oh my god, I forgot. Umma needed some name tags for some church conference thing. She needed a lot of them. I let her take those and was going to go to CostCut Saturday and get more. I forgot. Sorry."

I can understand why she forgot: we took the SAT practice test last Saturday. She and Calvin and I. Afterward, we were so intellectually sucked dry, we didn't even say goodbye to each other. I didn't know what they did, but I went home, ate, then passed out. When I woke up, it was still strangely light out—it was the next day. But it was as if my whole body had stopped, whatever food I'd stuffed in my stomach was still there, heavy and sore. I wanted to sleep more, but my eyes wouldn't shut. Rising from the bed felt like rising from quicksand.

And though everyone from our table was sitting in their seat in the test room, Zeus wasn't there. I saw Yunji looking around. Presumably for him.

He could still take the ACTs. Or go to community college.

That would not be acceptable to the Dongbangs, or to her, I'd wager.

But I'm wondering how Appa and Umma would feel if I were dating a guy who didn't have a college degree or just went to a community college. I already kind of know how they would react. And it would not be good.

I wonder if Yunji, of all people, her dad being a hairdresser and business owner, can get that not everyone is meant to go to Harvard. That people have blue-collar jobs, even people as devastatingly handsome as Zeus.

Back to my own situation, a brain teaser: Which would my parents object to more, no-college Zeus? Or Calvin?

When Appa was working in the city, there would always be racial tensions. People would call him names. But when he said things about

"Black people," I'd be quick to correct him. "Those are stereotypes, Appa."

"You don't see what I see, Georgia," he'd say. And he's right.

"But it's still a stereotype, what you're saying." Sometimes there's nothing more frustrating than being a kid.

There'd also been a period when Black, Korean, and Caribbean store owners, all crammed into one neighborhood, would have a clash. The Koreans always accused the Black kids of stealing. Sometimes they did. The Caribbean people, too. Weirdly, even though they were Black, they sided mostly with the Koreans, as immigrants. Umma and Appa always sided with Koreans.

"CostCut run!" declares Zeus.

"We can't all fit in your clunker," Yunji points out.

"I'll stay back and keep Leonardo company," I say.

"No way," says Zeus. "Leonardo has to pick out his own stuff!"

It's time for Yunji to tutor Chandi and Pandi anyway, so the rest of us pile into the car. Of course I'm scared Leonardo will have a tantrum, not unknown to happen, while we're packed like Vienna sausages.

"Leonardo do," he says, when I try to help him with his seatbelt. "Leonardo do, Leonardo do." He is showing off. He stabs the buckle with the other end. Normally I do it for him, but now as I venture to help him guide it in, he twists away.

"Leonardo do Leonardo do Leonardo DO!"

The slot that the metal tongue goes into, something we all use without thinking, suddenly seems impossibly small. Being crammed in here, it's hard for me to see what's going on. Leonardo is starting to stim on it, getting increasingly agitated. HOW DOES ANYONE EVER GET THAT SLIM METAL PIECE INTO THAT THIN LITTLE OPENING?

"Leonardo DO!" he screams.

Just as it seems we are about to tip over into full-blown tantrum, we hear a click, and the belt is secured. Zeus starts the car as if we haven't been holding our breaths for the last three minutes.

- - - - - - - - - - - -

We all know CostCut is Leo's happy place. He actually skips a little ahead of me, and Calvin and Zeus can't help laughing. "He's a happy guy," says Zeus, and for now, I agree.

Once we are in, safe in the store, we all relax a bit. "Remember, Leo, follow the rabbits if you get lost," I remind him, although he's not going to be out of my sight for a second. Calvin has never been in a CostCut before, and his impulse is to ride the giant shopping cart like a scooter, but Zeus stops him.

"Dude, this is a business outing. Let's act accordingly."

Calvin nods. Soon we are walking around not like a bunch of spirited high school kids but like a mom and dad. We're all Mom and Dad, and there's Leo, gently plodding along behind. I walk half turned to monitor him in case he tries to touch someone. Heaven forbid he try to grab someone's locs or something, a tassel on a hat.

Calvin returns with a case of address labels. "This should last us for a while."

"You know what else we need, is some kind of tissue paper, both for padding and also to make it decorative," says Zeus.

We head to the craft area. Tissue paper. Tape. A backup ginormous spool of thread plus sewing machine oil because we used all of Mrs. Dongbang's. We find some decorative mailing envelopes that are both cute and incredibly cheap. They are in blue, which I always thought was Leo's favorite color.

"We have to show Calvin the sample row on the way out," I say.

Zeus agrees. "We did miss snack time."

"The special thing about CostCut is the full-sized samples," I explain. "If you're clever, you can corral a whole meal plus dessert and coffee."

Calvin rubs his hands together in anticipation.

"Chicken teriyaki!" Calvin cries, pointing like a sailor who's just spotted land after months at sea. Leonardo is behind him, sniffing curiously. It smells delicious. Leo darts past him toward the sample table.

"Oh wait, is that—" Zeus begins.

Curley and his girlfriend are also at the sample stand, which is front of the refrigerated deli meat section, with so many types of sliced, plastic-wrapped meat it looks like a meat bingo card. She is standing in front of the table with a portable grill on it, an impaled piece of chicken in her hand. But she's not eating it, she's shoving it toward her huge purse—through which a dog's nose is protruding.

I start running toward Leonardo at the same time as the little curly haired dog jumps out of her purse and lands right on the sample stand. "Betty!" she screams, as the dog's paws scramble on the table and then he lands at her—and Leo's—feet.

"Hurt you!" Leo screams, and his arms are flailing, fists flying. The dog is barking and yowling and doing figure eights around the table legs as Curley and his girlfriend try to get him. As I grab Leo around his waist, we knock into Curley and his girlfriend, and somehow all of us go down. Curley's jacket opens and there's a flash of what looks like an old scroll, with a screaming eagle on an American flag.

The first thing I see as I untangle us is Curley reaching into his jacket. The sepia-colored scroll is the design of the Constitution.

We the Peop is all that fits on it. The holster.

The holster.

Of a gun.

All words become noise. Time stretches like taffy. All I can think or say to myself—or is someone else saying it?—is:

A gun!

A gun!

Which is black.

All black. Doesn't look at all different from the starter pistol from track meets. It's a little bit smaller than you'd think. It has ridges on the side that remind me of the gills on a shark. I think all this in about 0.3 seconds while my mouth does its thing:

"Don't shoot!" I scream.

"Curley, no!"

I hear a kind of echo.

Zeus picks us both up off the floor, sets us on our feet. I am behind Leo. "The rabbits, let's go to the rabbits," I whisper as calmly as I can, both palms on my brother's back, I am pushing as hard as I can.

We are all running when the gun goes off. And then again. And again.

My ears are ringing. But it's the eye I'm drawn to. It's in Leo's neck and it's open and crying red tears that slowly ooze downward. This eye is looking back at me. Looking back at me unblinkingly, going, "Why?" and "Why didn't you protect me?"

Nuna, keep me safe.

The eye is open, even though everything else about my brother is still. I hear a scream coming from somewhere. But then that, too, is drowned out by a sharp sound, like a whip cracked by my ear.

Twenty-Eight

SUNNYVALE—Shots were fired in self-defense inside a Cost-Cut discount store during an argument Friday evening, killing a man, sparking a stampede of terrified shoppers.

The shooter, whose identity has not been released because he is a minor, said he was at the sample counter with his high school classmate when they were attacked violently and without provocation. Several injuries including the victim were reported.

Shoppers and employees described terror and chaos as the shots rang out.

Will Lungo, 45, of Herbert Hills, said he and his wife were shopping for food for a birthday party when they heard gunshots.

"I kept hearing shots . . . one . . . two . . . three . . . ten. An employee came and helped us out through the emergency exit."

The victim and his companion, also a minor, suffered injuries and were taken to Sunnyvale Hospital, where they were released later in the day.

To: <classlist> Cambridge Academy:
From: Principal Gerard
Subj: Zeus Pak and Georgia/Leonardo Kim.

It is with great sadness we report that after an accident
at the CostCut on Highway 6, a member of our community, Leonardo Kim (Special Ed Mod) has passed away.
Georgia Kim (junior) and Zeus Pak (junior) are at Sunnyvale Hospital, and we are all praying for their speedy
return. For students who want someone to talk to, counselors will be standing by.

To: \<classlist\> Cambridge Academy:
From: Principal Gerard
Subj: Update

Funeral services for Leonardo Kim will be held at the Korean First Methodist Church & Institute of Sunnyvale on Saturday at noon.

A school-wide memorial, prayer session, and tree planting will occur on the green on Monday. For students who want someone to talk to, counselors will be standing by.

Questions Linger after Shooting Incident at CostCut

THE SUNNYVALE INDEPENDENT

By Miles Gordon

A Cambridge Academy High Student whose name is being withheld as a minor was involved in an altercation with three other classmates, Leonardo Kim, Zeus Pak, Georgia Kim. Eyewitness accounts vary. One of the perpetrators was known to have a documented history of violence. He died on the scene. Four people, including the shooter, were hospitalized.

"It was so fast," said Will Lungo, who had been in front of the refrigerator case when the shooting started. "But the guy involved was a big guy, very intimidating. I wouldn't want to be fighting with him."

"But who starts shooting inside a CostCut?" countered his wife, Mary. "There are little kids in here, all those employees, the sample lady—he should have just called 911 and not taken the law into his own hands."

CostCut, in compliance with federal law, allows guns on the premises.

Current 2019 law states that unless expressly forbidden via clear signage, guns are allowed in all public areas, retail spaces, recreational and entertainment spaces, schools, and houses of worship, with local, state, and federal government offices the only exemption.

This case draws similar questions to the Yellow Rose of Texas Church shooting where a gunman armed with an assault rifle was subdued after churchgoers employed their own weapons but also accidentally harmed several bystanders, including killing a five-year-old girl.

Local Sunnyvale police are investigating. So far, no charges have been filed.

Dear Dr. Kim,

It is with great sadness that I read of your son's violent demise. I cannot imagine how devastating. All of us at the Harvard University Institute for Human Genome Development and Eradication of Neuropathological Disease via Nanotechnology express our condolences.

I hope as a fellow scientist you'll forgive the brashness of this request: we would like to have permission to autopsy Leonardo Daewoo Kim's brain to help us further our essential research into neurodiversity. Time is, of course, of the essence. We would send a team over at our own expense. You wouldn't have to worry about a thing. And given that the brain is one of the pieces of soft tissue that are conventionally removed during embalming, it should not affect at all any viewing or burial plans you have.

Because of the timeliness of this request, I will be following up with a phone call and consent forms are attached to this email.

OPINION

THE CAMBRIDGE ACADEMY BUGLER

By Oliver Lee

Our friend Leonardo was murdered. His sister, Georgia Kim, and Zeus Pak were gravely injured, shot by another classmate, Mark Curley, as they shopped at CostCut for a school project. No charges have been filed against Curley even though he shot three unarmed people at close range and in the back. Mark Curley claimed he feared for his life under the state's Stand Your Ground law.

I was there.

First: I didn't see what happened, I'd just gotten a phone call and was looking at my phone, while Leo, as we call him, went with Georgia to the sample table.

That's how fast it happened—gunshots and three people on the ground in the time it took me to look down and try to figure out who was calling.

My friend's blood is on my hands—literally.

The police made me leave the scene and even took my phone. All the photos were erased when I got it back.

Don't you think it's a little funny that the CostCut, which is so famous for its surveillance camera that there's a whole channel of memes and video clips:

Creatures of CostCut.com

Grifters of CostCut.com (when people stage fall to try to sue)

Wild Children of CostCut

CostCut Fails

Hundreds of thousands of videos.

And yet no videos could be found in the Herbert Hills-Sunnyvale CostCut on that particular day solely at the meat counter where the sample table was set up?

I have contacted every major media outlet to talk about how every person in this shooting knew each other. It was classmate killing classmates, more like Parkland, Columbine, (there's a whole Wikipedia entry on this, divided by centuries, if you care to look: https://en.wikipedia.org/wiki/List_of_school_shootings_in_the_United_States). But remember how the new media wanted to talk to everyone after Parkland, and all the high school students (rightly) became celebrities and gun control advocates? But how quickly it went back to Stand Your Ground and Good Guy with a Gun, and then police in schools giving parents DNA test kits in case their kids get their faces blasted off by a classmate with a powerful gun.

The threat was not the teen with special needs, or his sister or his friend who rushed to help him. *The problem is idiots with guns.* Don't you think Leonardo Kim feared for his life? Leonardo could not always control his movements and had a neurological disorder that made it difficult for him to communicate and for others to communicate with him. Sometimes, he had meltdowns, which is part of his disorder, he had an extreme phobia to dogs (which are not allowed in CostCut—see the signage below). He did not deserve to be executed, especially by someone who continues to refuse to take responsibility and walks free. The police have failed to bring charges. CostCut claims that their surveillance cameras, scattered throughout the store, were not operational, just at the deli meat section, at that time.

But they won't allow an independent investigation of this. Local police say they have verified this verbally, and that's enough.

I want to know how unusual is it for CostCut to leave a camera broken for months—and is this against company policy?

We, the friends of Leo, demand that the police open an investigation into the case. Without video evidence, it's impossible to say what actually occurred. But as a group, we declare it was unlikely an unprovoked and savage attack as the shooter has described. And there was a history of Mark Curley verbally assaulting Leo Kim with ableist slurs. We are going to write to all the newspapers and take to social media. #JusticeForLeo-GeorgiaZeus #disabilityRights. Please share.

#ReleaseTheVideos #ReleaseTheVideos #ReleaseTheVideos

CostCut Shooting

THE WASHINGTON POST

SUNNYVALE - A shooting of an emotionally disturbed man and his two accomplices after he assaulted an armed shopper has drawn criticism of the local police for, as the gun control and disability activists groups claim, "failing to fully investigate a crime, including illegal gun ownership by a minor." Sunnyvale Police say they have completed a long and thorough investigation and "unequivocally believe this shooting was justified," said Coleen Q. Restra, Communications Officer of the Sunnyvale Police Department.

The victim was knocked unconscious for a full minute, and when he regained consciousness, he was fighting for his life and that of his companion, who he bravely defended.

"I can't believe something like this happened here," said Rose Anderson, a longtime resident of Sunnyvale. "This is something that belongs in the city. We're good people here, who care about one another, churchgoers. We are actually lucky there weren't more deaths caused by the rampaging mentally ill man who came from the city."

The suburb of Sunnyvale has also had an increasing Asian population, including many people who have moved from the city. It is unclear if this was a gang-related altercation aimed at terrorizing white residents of this normally peaceful suburb.

NATIONAL

THE NEW YORK TIMES

Are School Shootings Now Occurring outside the Halls?

A high school student shot and killed a classmate along with severely injuring two others—at a CostCut deli counter, where the shooter also injured (not fatally) several shoppers.

"I don't care how you classify it," said Megan Rainy, an ER physician and public health professor who is one of the only academics in the nation who has received the go-ahead from the NIH, along with her research partner Sarah Temple, PhD, to study the medical and psychiatric effects of gun violence. "Not only is there a young man dead because of guns, the survivors and bystanders are affected with long-lasting, sometimes debilitating trauma. This is one of our country's most urgent public health issues."

SAMIZDAT.STACK.KEEPME.XYZ

by Oliver Lee

At Cambridge Academy, there is one cafeteria table where the students have been wearing black armbands for months now. It's not a militant sign, even still, the principal is considering forbidding this kind of "incitement" against an "innocent" member of our community." The students insist that in Korea, this is a ritual sign of mourning, that they have been marked, to show themselves as part of the community that has been affected.

"When someone dies, too often we just carry the hurt on the inside," said Yunji Park Dongbang, a junior. "This way, other people know we hurt. For we wear it on the outside."

"Unnecessarily provocative," said Principal Gerard. "Unnecessarily endangering a member of our community. Terrorism by another name."

Gerard also canceled a tree planting as well as an article the *Cambridge Academy Bugler* was about to run, about how a group calling itself (and I am a member) #JusticeForLeoGeorgiaZeus #JusticeForTheHagwonCrew is pushing for another investigation, a possible civil suit, more media investigation, also to see if racism was involved. The group did organize several protests. One was at the CostCut where Leo Kim died. We were all arrested by the police and now have police records. I will be waiting to see if this affects our future college applications.

As with this, and everything, we don't know where this goes next, but thank you for subscribing to the KeepMe newsletter. If this newsletter needs to go down, check your Semaphore or C-kret app. We aren't going to stop until there has been #JusticeForLeoGeorgiaZeus

NATIONAL

The shooting of a mentally unstable man who killed a child in a CostCut six months ago made national news and reignited a debate over the rights of the mentally ill and cognitively disabled, including their rights to be out in public where they may harm or injure or even kill someone.

Correction: An earlier version of this story reported the victim had been attacked and killed by a mentally unstable man. The victim, whose name is being kept anonymous for privacy reasons, was not killed but suffered injuries and was hospitalized briefly after the attack.

POLICE REPORT

From the time the shove occurred to the victim
discharging his gun:
5 seconds.
The attacker was killed on the scene. Necessary
Collateral Damage: 1; Nonfatal injury: 2
Forensic ballistics report: eight "cop killer" bullets
were discharged, matching firearm on the scene.
Nonfatal wound in the neck, c-3,
Fatal wound in the back t-7, through heart, exiting
through the sternum.
The angle suggests a trajectory of at least 10 feet.

FOR INTERNAL DISTRIBUTION ONLY

Epilogue

"Yunji, I got it."

"Zeus, let me at least support your arm."

"Yunj, I *got* it. This is embarrassing."

"Why should it be embarrassing? You just got out of the hospital."

They both glance at me, and I don't know how to take their gaze. The bullet that grazed my temple and knocked me out then went into Leo's chest from the back, exploded into shrapnel, and killed him. It literally shredded his heart. I only had to be in the hospital overnight. The doctors said I'm "fine." I don't even have a scar. See?

But of course I'm not.

- - - - - - - - - - - -

"Well, well," says Curley, who is walking to the hydration station, his glance sweeping over Zeus's withered leg. "Not such a tough guy, are we?"

One of Curley's bullets shattered the bones in Zeus's shin, creating bone fragments that acted like shrapnel inside his own body. The bones can never be reconstructed back to their original strength, left scarring in the muscle. It's an unusual sight to see a high school student using a walker. He drags his foot, has to check it hourly. If it turns blue, or black, amputation has not been ruled out. The pain, Yunji told me privately, is almost unbearable, and she's worried about the handfuls of pills he takes. Instead of hagwon after school, Zeus has to go to physical therapy, which, if you can believe it, is even more painful. But Zeus doesn't have medical insurance like the rest of us who are on our parents' plans. Zeus's parents enjoy universal healthcare—but in Korea. Zeus is stuck with Medicare or Medicaid or whatever program the government will allow him to use. That's why he never misses a torture session because he has no idea when the government will just say, "That's it, you have all the therapy you need." And about our mental therapy needs? The school brought in counselors for a week. A *week*. The week we were all still in the hospital.

"FUCK YOU CURLEY!" Yunji screams at his back.

"What's their problem?" the girlfriend laughs, her sweet, trilling voice filling the cafeteria. Her shoulder bag is moving on its own, like a bag of beating hearts. Inside is her little dog, whom she has been feeding scraps of seasoned taco meat, his favorite. In taking the meat he nips her fingers with his tiny needle teeth, which she endures until she gets mad. She pinches him so hard on his tiny black jaw he yelps, a helpless, muffled mew. "I mean, tragedy about the disabled guy, yeah, but god do they have to keep carrying on like this? It's been weeks!"

"He tried to sexually assault you, babe." Curley takes her elbow. A little too strongly, a little too possessively for her taste, but he is her knight in shining armor. He protected her, in front of everyone, has been on the national news. His parents are so proud. The NRA gave him a special award, which the school will be displaying in its trophy case until Curley graduates and takes the gun-shaped plaque with him. When they have a family together, they will put this on the wall next to a giant picture of their wedding. They will be the Curleys then. He will protect them. He will stand his ground.

Like royalty, they leave the cafeteria, ready to face their bright, shining futures in a world so safe, nothing can possibly go wrong.

Acknowledgments

My last YA novel came out around twenty-five years ago, and I never dreamed I'd be writing another one. In 2020 editor Daniel Ehrenhaft brought back my first YA novel, *Finding My Voice*, which rekindled my love for the genre, and I couldn't be happier that he edited this one as well and deserves a lot of credit for taking on this book that deals with so many hot-button subjects—thank you for taking a chance on it and making it so much better. Thank you to the Blackstone team, Ananda Finwall for your excellent eye and copyediting.

Auntie Grace Talusan, who happened to be visiting when *Of Mice and Men* was on Jason's reading list and she took over and read (and kept reading, at his behest!) his daily bedtime reading session.

Cecilia "Bachi" Guevara, Safa Setzer, Kobe Lee Whitfield, everyone at the Atlas School, especially Amanda Friedman for the love and care of my son Jason which also makes it possible to write.

Of course, thank you to my family—especially Karl, who was there for my first young adult novel more than thirty years ago and now for my newest. And thank you to Jason for being my inspiration in all things, always. You are magnificent, and I love you.